Murder Marks
the Page

Books by Karen Rose Smith

Published by Kensington Publishing Corp.

Murder Marks
the Page

Karen Rose Smith

KENSINGTON PUBLISHING CORP.
www.kensingtonbooks.com

KENSINGTON BOOKS are published by

Kensington Publishing Corp.
119 West 40th Street
New York, NY 10018

All Kensington titles, imprints, and distributed lines are available at special quantity discounts for bulk purchases for sales promotion, premiums, fund-raising, educational, or institutional use. Special book excerpts or customized printings can also be created to fit specific needs. For details, write or phone the office of the Kensington Special Sales Manager: Attn. Special Sales Department. Kensington Publishing Corp., 119 West 40th Street, New York, NY 10018. Phone: 1-800-221-2647.

KENSINGTON and the KENSINGTON COZIES teapot logo Reg. US Pat. & TM Off.

ISBN: 978-1-4967-4703-7
First Kensington Hardcover Edition: April 2024

Library of Congress Card Catalog Number: 2023949926
ISBN: 978-1-4967-4705-1 (ebook)

10 9 8 7 6 5 4 3 2 1

Printed in the United States of America

To my husband and son, who have taken this thirty-five-year writing adventure with me. I love you both to the moon and back.

ACKNOWLEDGMENTS

Thanks to Officer Greg Berry, my professional law enforcement consultant, who always provides the answers to my questions and as much information as I need.

Chapter One

Jazzi Swanson's fishtail braid slid across her back as she managed to steady a mini-paddleboard hanging on wall pegs. She was giving it a last pat into place above bookshelf cubicles when the bell sounded and the front door of Tomes & Tea opened and closed. From her perch, Jazzi glanced over her shoulder.

Theo Carstead was striding toward her. She suspected he was going to ask her a question she didn't want to answer.

At age twenty-five, Jazzi could count at least ten reasons why she didn't date . . . or want to. The last time Theo had come into the store, he'd started to approach her but she'd been called away by a customer. Maybe he'd simply wanted to buy a particular book. But if she listened to her woman's intuition, as well as interpreted correctly that twinkle in his eyes . . .

She brushed her Cleopatra bangs aside as he closed the space between them.

Theo blasted her with his thousand-watt smile and tilted his head in a way that made his cleft chin even cockier. "Need help up there?"

She stayed put even though pressing her shins against the ladder rung was uncomfortable. "Nope. I got it."

"How about help getting down?" Theo's brown hair hung long to his neck. It was thick enough that when he brushed his hair over his brow to the side, it stayed put. He was amazingly attractive.

She studied his outstretched hand and stepped down under her own power. Then she faced him. "Can I help you with finding something to read . . . or maybe iced or hot tea?"

"It's May, Jazzi. Who drinks hot tea in May?"

Everyone who came into the store knew her name. "Tea lovers," she answered lightly. She closed the ladder and carefully propped it against the sea-glass-colored cubicles that were lit by neon green and blue LED lights.

"No book. No tea." His gaze ran over her royal-blue tank top and white wraparound skort with blue polka dots. "I just stopped in to see if you'd like to have dinner with me tonight. Any restaurant you'd like."

Wow, *that* was an offer. In the lake resort of Belltower Landing there were scads of restaurants to choose from, some with entrées that would cost more than her monthly food budget. Although she *could* possibly be attracted to Theo, she suspected he was only in town for the summer. She wasn't in the market for a summer romance . . . or any romance.

Dawn Fernsby, Jazzi's partner in Tomes & Tea, had finished with a customer at the tea bar and crossed to Theo. "Jazzi and I have a business dinner after closing. She's not free tonight."

Theo narrowed his gaze at the two of them. "A business dinner? I suppose partners need to do that now and then. Or you could postpone your dinner and I could expand your horizons."

Belltower Landing might attract thousands of tourists during its summer season, but it was still basically a small town. Residents with less than six degrees of separation knew everyone who lived here year round. Most kept track of the tourists and summer renters. Theo Carstead had brought his deejay business to the resort town for the summer and had already played parties for a few of Belltower Landing's wealthiest and well-known residents.

Keeping her tone calm and gentle, she met his gaze. "As Dawn said, I'm busy tonight." She hoped she was telling the truth. They hadn't planned a dinner. After all, they lived together in an apartment upstairs. But maybe something had come up that Jazzi wasn't aware of.

He gave them both prolonged stares. "I'll try again another time."

Theo was wearing olive cargo shorts and a dark brown tee. As he left, Dawn tore her gaze from his lean but fit back. "It's a shame he knows he's a babe magnet," she mused.

Jazzi took hold of the ladder, ready to return it to the storeroom. "I was ready to tell Theo *no.*"

Dawn's short brown hair was streaked with blond. Bangs emanated from a high side part and she had a habit of brushing them away from her green eyes. "I just gave you a little more breathing room. Maybe you'll want to reconsider," she said as she helped Jazzi with the ladder.

They passed Erica Garcia at a stand-alone bookshelf. Erica was in her late forties and loved books as much as Jazzi and Dawn. She'd been clerking for them since Tomes & Tea opened three years ago. She'd taken Jazzi and Dawn under her motherly wing and often offered them advice.

Jazzi and Dawn carried the ladder between round tables with metal and enamel chairs in various colors. They kept the shop bright and cheery during all four seasons in New York State.

As they passed through the doorway into the storeroom, Dawn assured Jazzi, "I wasn't simply giving you an out for tonight. We do have to have a serious discussion and it *is* business. How about dinner at The Wild Kangaroo after closing?"

The Wild Kangaroo was an upscale pub that was one of

Jazzi's favorite places to eat. It was run by Oliver Patel, a thirty-something with a killer Australian accent. If Dawn's discussion about Tomes & Tea was a serious one, Jazzi would prefer to have the discussion at The Wild Kangaroo.

As Jazzi and Dawn walked past the town green with its three-story-high bell tower, its large clock facing the shops along Lakeview Boulevard, Jazzi felt the breeze coming off the surface of Lake Harding. The town and surrounding community of Belltower Landing spread around a lake with a perimeter of about thirty miles. Verdant grass had just been mowed at the edge of the green along the shore, its scent growing stronger in the damp dusk settling around the town. The police station, firehouse, and steepled stone church spread in the opposite direction from where Jazzi and Dawn walked. They were heading toward the marina and dock but wouldn't be going that far. Jazzi often wondered why the philanthropist Phineas J. Harding, who built the community for the purpose of recreation and a harmonious life, didn't name the resort after himself rather than the bell tower.

The bell in the tower chimed eight times as she and Dawn passed art galleries, a wine store, a leather shop, and a variety of other businesses to approach the strikingly red door of The Wild Kangaroo. After Jazzi pulled open the door, the usual sounds from the pub spilled out—chatter, laughter, the clink of glasses and serving trays.

Oliver Patel himself welcomed them into the pub with a smile. Even though the pub was always off-the-charts busy, he treated each customer as if they were special. That probably had to do with his success with the pub. Oliver was tall, at least six foot two, and was distinctly interesting. Short wavy blond hair, longish on the top with a side part, blue-blue eyes, a scruffy beard-stubbled jaw that was sharp and determined, coaxed Jazzi to study his face anytime she came in.

He motioned to a table in the corner that had just been vacated. "It will be cleaned off in two shakes of a kangaroo's tail," he said in that accent Jazzi loved.

The Wild Kangaroo was distinctive, just like its owner. The brick serving-bar fronted dark wooden shelves that held all the bottles and bar implements. Silver barstools stood in front of the bar. The silver theme held with the metal chairs at the solid black round tables while gray and black triangle squares decorated the border around the shelves. A large wooden kangaroo hung in the center behind the bar with smaller versions on each wall. The smaller versions were surrounded with framed photos of Australia. The large blackboard listed the day's specials, which today included barbecued snags, curry pie, crab sticks, fish and chips, and pavlova. The round high table in the corner would be adequate for any discussion Jazzi and Dawn had to have, also offering a bit of privacy.

They settled in at the table and a waitress dressed in black shorts and a black top with a kangaroo logo printed on the pocket came to take their drink orders. Dawn ordered a draft beer while Jazzi ordered lemonade. After the table had been cleaned and the waitress brought their drinks, Jazzi took a swallow of her lemonade and studied Dawn.

Jazzi's journey to becoming an adult had taken a few twists and turns that she hadn't expected. But Dawn Fernsby had been a gift. They'd met in college when they'd both attended a group for adoptees. They'd later become roommates, bonding over the emotional road adoptees traveled. Although Jazzi had searched for her birth mother when she was in high school and found her, Dawn hadn't taken that step. She was still considering it.

Instead of jumping into a discussion about the bookstore, Dawn said, "Tell me again why you don't want to date Theo. He throws the best parties and has all kinds of fun connections, including people in the entertainment industry. Besides that, he's good to look at, and he's intelligent enough to have a decent conversation with."

Jazzi laughed. "Are those my three requirements?"

"I don't know what your requirements are."

"I know Theo might be a fun date," Jazzi admitted. "If *you* want to date him, you're welcome."

Dawn shook her head. "He wants to date *you*. That's evident whenever he comes into Tomes and eyes you. Sometime you're going to have to get over that breakup you had in college."

Jazzi thought about it. As a sophomore in college, she had transferred to her boyfriend's college at the University of Delaware, fully intending to continue her Bachelor of Science degree in human services. But after she transferred, she and Mark broke up instead of growing closer. That had been a huge disappointment. He'd been her first serious relationship.

"I'm over it. But I changed my life for Mark. I was happy where I was, but I thought we were serious. He kept bugging me to transfer to be with him. So I did, and you saw what happened. I won't ever change my life for a man again."

"I think finding out about your birth dad has something to do with you keeping up your guard."

Jazzi had decided to search for her birth father around the time she'd met Dawn. Dawn had supported her in her search but . . . Jazzi had discovered her birth dad had died during his service in Afghanistan. That knowledge along with her breakup had thrown her into a tailspin. "Probably so."

All of it had just made her feel . . . protective of her heart. Although she loved her family in Willow Creek, Pennsylvania, she'd often come home with Dawn to this town that was quirky and different. She'd learned how to paddleboard, kayak, and enjoy afternoons on Dawn's parents' pontoon boat. Since Dawn's parents owned an outfitters shop, Jazzi and Dawn had both worked in the shop during their sophomore and junior summers. Her senior year, Jazzi had decided she didn't want to pursue a master's and a PhD degree in human services. She'd wanted to be done with school.

Around that time, her grandparents had sold their decades-established nursery business in Willow Creek and decided to bestow on her and her sister a monetary gift to help them establish their lives. Jazzi had decided to open the bookstore in Belltower Landing and convinced Dawn to opt into the project with her savings too. Jazzi and Dawn were serious about adulting and wanted to establish their own lives around the bookstore and tea bar.

"What you're saying is that I don't want to attach to a man because he'll just leave." In her more self-reflective moments, Jazzi believed that was probably true.

"Something like that. And you're aware enough of it to know it, so you might have to fight against it." Dawn was staring at Jazzi through her brushed-over bangs, and Jazzi had to smile.

"Maybe I do. So tell me what's going on."

"Let's wait until dinner comes," Dawn said with a sigh, as if she wasn't in a hurry to talk about whatever it was.

The waitress came over and took their orders. Soon, over barbecued snags served with mashed potatoes and grilled onions, they were ready to talk.

After a last forkful, Dawn wiped her fingers on her napkin and leaned back in her chair. "I don't want you to freak out."

"I don't ever freak out."

Dawn leaned forward again, moved her fork to the side then back into place. Evidently whatever she wanted to say was difficult.

Jazzi braced herself as best she could, not knowing what was coming.

"My parents want me to sell my share of Tomes and Tea."

Jazzi felt her mouth drop open, and she swallowed hard, trying not to let her mind spin into disaster thoughts.

"My dad examined our profit and loss statements," Dawn went on.

"Those statements showed profits before the tourist season even started," Jazzi pointed out.

"Maybe so. This summer could equal last summer, or be better or worse. Of course, we don't know. But the bookstore is barely paying a living wage for you and me. We're hardly even pulling in enough to pay Erica and temporary help."

Jazzi and Dawn lived in the apartment above the bookstore and tea bar for a reason. Neither of them was extravagant, and they budgeted monthly for food and utilities.

"Maybe I should talk to your parents," Jazzi offered.

"That won't do any good."

"They blame me for you wanting to search for your birth parents, don't they?" Aware of that fact, Jazzi didn't know how to breach the distance between her and Dawn's parents.

"No, they don't blame you. They know I was attending the adoptees group in college before I even met you. But they do think if I find my birth parents, I'll pull away from them."

"I still think they believe I'm leading you down the wrong path. I would never convince you to do something you don't want to do."

"I know that. Jazzi, I'll be honest. I don't want to find someone to buy me out. That means we need to do anything we can to bring in more income, especially over the quieter months."

Jazzi's supper felt like a rock in her stomach. "I know one thing that would help. We need to up our social media presence. We need the attention of a few bookstore influencers that would not only help us, but draw people to Belltower Landing. We need ideas on how to do that."

"Yes, we do, and I know how to get them," Dawn offered.

"You know someone with connections?"

Shaking her head, Dawn answered, "No. But I know a group of people we can rely on—our book club. We're meeting tomorrow night and I think we should bring this up. Our core members want to keep Tomes and Tea thriving. What do you think?"

"I think it's a start."

Jazzi's personal style was eclectic. Tonight she'd braided her Rapunzel-length black hair into a part fishtail braid and part Dutch braid hanging to one side. When she'd turned twenty-one, she'd gotten a butterfly tattoo behind her right ear. Rebellion? A chance to assert her adult power? Something fanciful that for the most part was her own secret adornment? She had attached lapis pierced earrings to accompany her overall denim shorts and white crop top. She wore sandals all summer for practicality's sake, whether she was working in the bookshop or slipping them off for a water sport.

As she and Dawn pushed three round tables together in Tomes & Tea and circled chairs around those, Jazzi saw her partner had changed into an orange and green flowered sundress with swingy gold triangle earrings.

"Did you dress tonight to impress Derek?" Jazzi asked.

Derek Stewart, one of their book club regulars, flipped houses for a living.

"I only dress to impress myself." Dawn winked as she slipped another chair into the circle.

As Jazzi brewed peach tea and set up the tea bar for cups of hot tea or iced, the members of their club began trickling in. Unlike some book clubs that discussed one novel at a session, these readers brought in whatever their latest read was to talk about. They exchanged book selection ideas that way, sometimes settling on one tome to delve into. This way tourists could participate in their group too.

Fifteen minutes later Dawn had served elderberry muffins from the Dockside Bakery, their supplier for baked goods, and taken a seat beside Derek. As the group stopped chatting and sipped tea, Dawn sat up straighter and brushed her hair away from her eyes.

She surprised even Jazzi when she asked, "Does anyone want to buy out my interest in Tomes and Tea?"

She was met with shocked silence until everyone started speaking at once. *Why? How? What do you mean? You're not closing, are you?*

The voices were all smashed together until Dawn raised her hand to quiet them. "I don't want to sell," Dawn assured them, "and Jazzi doesn't want to close the shop. But here is our problem." She laid it out plainly, as she had to Jazzi.

Fingering the yellow wrap on the end of her braid, Jazzi waited for comments. Could they expect their friends to have any answers?

Parker Olsen was the first to speak. That didn't surprise Jazzi. He was a software applications developer and tech guru. He'd dabbled with coding since he was ten. From what Dawn had told her, during his college years, he'd created a video game that had gone viral. Its popularity had padded his retirement account. At twenty-seven, and unlike many men his age, he was clean-shaven, his medium brown hair short. His jaw was square and his eyes cocoa brown. He and Jazzi had been friends since she'd worked at Dawn's parents' outfitter shop—Rods to Boards—during her college days.

"First of all," he said, "we have to track connections any of us have to promote Tomes and Tea. Influencers are a good way to go, but you also need to do more here."

"Like what?" Audrey Garcia asked. "Sorry, Mom couldn't come tonight."

Audrey, Erica's daughter, was a pet sitter and also filled in at Tomes & Tea when they were busy. Audrey's sparkling, almost black eyes drew in humans as well as pets. She had a warm customer-relations aura, like her mom.

Parker quickly said what he had in mind. "You could have a

virtual-reality event. I could set that up. That kind of experience fascinates people."

"Speaking of events," Derek contributed, "how about showcasing books about home improvement for a week? I can come in at specified times and answer questions about projects."

Jazzi's throat tightened as she considered her friendship with these people who were willing to give their time to help the bookstore. Addison Bianchi and Delaney Fabron gave each other a look as if they were exchanging some kind of information. They both had gone to high school with Dawn and had kept up their friendship over the years. Addison was a stay-at-home mom with a three-year-old daughter. Addison had long golden-blond hair and Disney-princess wide hazel eyes that made her everybody's sweetheart. Delaney, on the other hand, with her caramel-shaded wispy chin-length hair, dark at the roots, and false eyelashes seemed to be her exact opposite.

Delaney seemed to understand the message Addison was sending her. Delaney shrugged and her low-necked chartreuse blouse dipped lower. Since she worked for a public relations agency, she was used to presentations. "You have to think much bigger. Last year I had an account for a model who wrote about her runway experiences. I say engage her for a book signing. She has thousands of followers. If she posts about Tomes and Tea, that could get you plenty of exposure. I can look into it. Just say the word."

Kaylee Washington, property manager of the Belltower Landing Camping Lake Resort nodded vigorously. Her springy, dark brown wild curls nodded with her. With her light brown skin, full mouth and swingy gold hoop earrings, she was striking. She came to book club events religiously. She reminded them all, "Remember Belltower Landing is having a Welcome Summer event on the summer solstice. I overheard Theo Carstead saying he was contacting country star Evan Holloway to do a show at Belltower Landing for the event. The mayor is overjoyed. Just imagine if Evan Holloway visited Tomes and Tea and posted about it."

Everyone was nodding vigorously. Jazzi was excited about the suggestions, but also nervous. "I'm not sure what the best way is to make all of this happen."

"I could email Evan Holloway's PR staff, but I don't know if the message would ever get to him," Kaylee said.

The last member of their group tonight, Giselle Dubois, who owned a cleaning service for expensive lake-view houses, fluttered her heavily mascaraed eyelashes at Jazzi. "I know of a much better way." The expression on Giselle's heart-shaped face was mischievous.

"What's that?" Jazzi asked, her heart pounding a little too hard because maybe she suspected what was coming.

"Go on a date with Theo Carstead. We all know he hangs around Tomes for a reason. He might be able to help convince Evan Holloway to stop here."

Parker gave Giselle a look as if he didn't like that idea at all.

However, Kaylee, who always kept her eye on business, offered, "You want to save your partnership with Dawn, don't you?"

"Of course, I do," Jazzi answered quickly, but then picked up her cup and took a deep swallow of her tea. Was she willing to do almost anything to save Tomes & Tea?

Dawn threw Jazzi a hopeful smile. "We'll consider everything you've said. Delaney, if you could look into the runway model, that would be great."

Derek took another muffin, bit into it, swallowed, and laid it on his paper plate. "Before we delve into books we read," he said, rubbing his beard, "I want to warn you all about the robberies that have been happening in Belltower Landing."

"What robberies?" Giselle asked.

"One last week and one this week in the McMansions, over on the east end. But that doesn't mean they'll stop there."

"Why do you think there will be more?" Kaylee asked.

"One burglary could be random," Derek remarked with a flip of his hand. "But two probably means something more serious is going on. Those houses have alarm systems."

Jazzi hadn't heard anything about the robberies. Maybe the police were keeping them under wraps for some reason. On the other hand, news from the big houses, as some called them, sometimes didn't make the trip down to the main part of the town.

"Any store robberies?" she wanted to know.

"You would have heard about them if there were," Derek answered. "No flash mob robberies or anything like that. This seems to be quiet and the owners of the houses that were robbed don't want the news getting out."

"Maybe because they feel foolish. Maybe the failure of their alarm systems will send a bad message for the companies securing them," Parker suggested.

"I'm not sure. I just wanted to warn everybody," Derek said.

After a bit more chatter, Jazzi pushed back her chair. "I'll refill tea, then we can talk books."

She was thinking about everything that had been said when she headed for the tea bar with its glassed-in station for baked goods. A counter with a sink stretched behind it and floating shelves above it held teapots and mugs. They served tea in disposable cups with the Tomes & Tea logo, a stack of books with a teapot perched on top. Lighting for the tea bar glowed from a Sputnik linear chandelier with clear glass globes. It illuminated the area as Jazzi opened the refrigerator to pull out the pitcher of tea she'd prepared for refills.

To her surprise, Delaney followed her. "Anything I can help with?"

"Sure. After I refill the dish with muffins, you can take that and I'll get the tea."

Jazzi handed Delaney a plate. Delaney stared at it as if it held a few secrets.

"Thank you so much for your suggestion," Jazzi said. "If

you can convince the model to make an appearance at Tomes, Dawn and I will be forever grateful."

"I'll be glad to look into it." Now Delaney looked up at Jazzi. "There was something I wanted to ask you about."

"Go ahead."

"I have a friend who was adopted."

Jazzi's senses all prickled. This was a subject that was very dear to her. "How can I help?"

"I was hoping you'd ask that," Delaney responded with a small smile. "Brie needs someone to talk to her about being adopted and her feelings about her birth parents. Do you think you and Dawn could talk to her about what you've experienced? I know you're in touch with your birth mother and Dawn hasn't decided to contact her birth parents yet. But I know she's thought about it."

"I'd be glad to talk to your friend. I'm pretty sure Dawn will say yes too."

"Great. I'll ask Dawn later. Can I give Brie your number?"

"Absolutely. We'll set up a meeting." Jazzi placed more muffins on the dish.

Delaney picked it up. "I'll work extra hard on getting that runway model to say yes."

Jazzi knew that was important. But just as important was talking to Delaney's friend Brie.

Chapter Two

The cylinder pendant lights with Edison bulbs lit up the checkout desk at Tomes & Tea as Jazzi closed down the register the next day. Across the store at the tea bar, Dawn prepared a pitcher of raspberry iced tea in preparation for their meeting with Brie Frazier. Brie had texted with Jazzi last night and had seemed anxious for the meeting.

Jazzi had switched on the digital CLOSED sign on the door but she'd told Brie simply to knock. The knock sounded at exactly seven fifteen. Jazzi turned off the lights above the sales counter as Dawn hurried to open the door.

Jazzi had set up a table with a basket of corn muffins. The Dockside Bakery added a touch of smoked paprika to them, and they were perfect for a savory snack. Jazzi had come from a family who believed food and tea enhanced any conversation, especially the more serious ones.

At the entrance, Dawn and Brie's chatter preceded them inside. Jazzi studied Brie as she gracefully moved toward the table. Delaney had filled in Brie's background info. She was around thirty-five and worked for a nonprofit that brought disabled and disadvantaged children to Belltower Landing to learn to swim and boat. The first thing Jazzi noticed about Brie was her pale blue eyes. The second was the messy blond top-knot she'd arranged with chopsticks—at least that's what they resembled.

Jazzi thought about her own mid-back long hair, but dismissed the idea of arranging it like that. Today she'd pulled her hair away from her face and clasped it in a boat barrette. It kept her hair tamed, but added pizzazz—at least she hoped it did.

When Brie approached the table, Jazzi gave her a welcoming smile. "I'm Jazzi."

Brie nodded. "I've been in here before but you were busy. Delaney told me how you and Dawn opened the shop. Gutsy move."

Dawn brought the pitcher of tea to the table. "We did our homework with profit projections and surveys about book purchases in a resort town. We were lucky to find a storefront along Lakeview Boulevard."

"There wouldn't be a chance to rent or buy now," Jazzi said. "Prices have exploded. Anyway, that's not what you came to talk about. Let's sit."

As Jazzi poured tea into their paper cups, Dawn asked Brie, "How can we help you?"

Brie was tall and willowy with long arms and delicate hands. She was wearing a long-sleeved silky white blouse and jeans. She took a muffin from the basket, studied it, then broke it in two. "I've never talked with anyone who was adopted."

Jazzi exchanged a knowing look with Dawn. Dawn nodded to her, reading her mind.

Jazzi took a muffin herself while explaining, "Dawn and I met when we attended a group at college for people who had been adopted. I heard about it because I was majoring in human services."

"I saw a notice for the group on one of the college chat boards," Dawn added.

Jazzi further explained, "That adoption group helped both of us explore our feelings about our birth parents and settled questions in our minds about what we wanted . . . if searching for answers was best . . . or if we should simply let it alone."

Jazzi remembered the turmoil she'd been in after her breakup with her boyfriend, and how searching for her biological father had seemed to be the best thing to do. But answers didn't always bring peace.

Putting her hand to her glass of tea, Brie took a few swallows, then she admitted, "Up until now, I didn't feel any urge to find my biological parents. But I'm thirty-five, and my biological clock is ticking. Earlier this year—actually it was my New Year's resolution—I decided to actively start dating instead of working, paddleboarding, and living the single life. I want to meet the right guy and have kids. I work with kids every day, and I suddenly realized I want a few of my own. My thirty-fifth birthday seemed to have a lightning bolt attached to it, and that woke me up."

Dawn pushed her bangle bracelets up and down her arm. "Jazzi found her bio parents. I haven't yet. Do you want to find them to fill out your life story? Is that your reason?"

Brie swerved in her chair toward Dawn. "No, not just that. The medical background of my bio parents could be important to my health if I get pregnant. I do know my birth mom died when I was born. The facts could be important to me and any children I might have."

"That's a major consideration," Jazzi assured Brie. "Finding my birth mother answered questions about why she gave me up. It also gave me a sense of my roots. Even more important, I had a chance to have someone else in my life who I could love and who loved me. It wasn't easy at first, but I'm so glad I found her."

All three were quiet for a few moments.

"Have you begun searching?" Dawn asked Brie after she finished her muffin.

As Brie removed her phone from her jeans pocket and opened it, she surprised Jazzi. "I actually have my biological father's email address. We connected on the reunion website Bonds Forever. He now lives in Belltower Landing. I don't know when he settled here or if he knew all along my adoptive parents live here."

Jazzi had used that website when she was looking for her birth mother. But her birth mother hadn't registered on it. Jazzi saw the phone screen Brie had brought up with the email address—JCOV@belltowerlink.com.

Brie was staring at the address as if realizing it held the answers to all of her questions. Finally she slipped her phone back into her pocket. "Thank you so much for talking with me. I think I've made a decision. I'll email him tonight. But right now I have a date."

"I hope we helped," Jazzi said.

"You definitely did. After my date, I'll think about exactly what I want to say in my email. When I decided I wanted to find someone and get married, I started using a dating app."

"How's it going?" Dawn wanted to know, looking curious.

Brie grinned. "It's like constantly blind dating. You know a little from the guy's profile . . ." She added a caveat. "If he's honest."

"Where do you meet up?" Dawn asked.

Brie pushed back her chair and stood. "Tonight I'm meeting him at Vibes."

That restaurant was a popular and expensive one near the marina. "Good luck," Jazzi wished Brie, meaning it.

Finding the right person to love was an adventure. She'd witnessed both her own widowed mother and her great-aunt go through it. Nevertheless, she didn't believe she was ready for that adventure anytime soon.

After Brie had left, Dawn asked Jazzi, "Do you think we helped her?"

"We might have helped her sort some things in her mind. If she's ready to email her dad, I guess we did."

"But what if it doesn't go well?" Dawn asked.

Knowing her friend as she did, Jazzi realized that was Dawn's best reason for *not* trying to find her birth parents. What if it didn't go well? What if they didn't want her in their lives? What if her own parents wouldn't accept that new relationship?

Jazzi had gone through all that. Fortunately for her, her mom had supported her decision. Would Dawn's parents do the same? Jazzi wasn't so sure.

Straightening up the tea bar, Jazzi picked up one of the little brown bags with their logo on the front that held loose tea. They had a display next to the muffin case where people could pick up the bags and buy them. Jazzi had been thinking about that and thought they could do better at making the tea more profitable.

"Dawn, what do you think about a different packaging for our teas?"

Dawn crossed over to the tea display. "What's wrong with our packaging?"

"We want to increase sales, right?"

"That's our aim."

"I think different packaging could do it."

"Different packaging could increase the expense of selling the tea," Dawn reminded her.

"I know that. But the extra expense might be worth it, especially for tourist season."

"What are you thinking of?"

After staring at their logo, Jazzi set down the bag. "What if we sold tea in cute little boxes?"

"How would a box be different from the bags?"

"More colorful, cuter, something somebody would pick up

for a souvenir. What if we had a belfry box, a kayak box, a canoe box? Do you get my drift?"

"We wouldn't be just selling tea, we'd be selling a keepsake. Is that what you're saying?"

"Sure. Even kids might like those boxes after their parents use the tea. A parent might think about that. The belfry box especially would be a souvenir from Belltower Landing. In fact, maybe some other stores would pick it up and sell it in their stores too. Teas from Tomes and Tea sold in souvenir boxes." Jazzi was getting excited about the proposition.

"You know, don't you, that the box could be as expensive as the tea?"

"Maybe so. But think about selling them online too. We could offer them at our store website. We'd sell books and tea. We could even have boxes shaped like books. There's a packaging company down by the docks. They make the candy shop's boxes. I can make an appointment to discuss it with them. I don't want to lose you as a partner."

"I've been thinking about what we could do too," Dawn said. "How about taking on an investor?"

Jazzi shook her head. "That has to be a last resort. You and I know what we want. We work well together. We have the same ideas."

"Maybe that's the problem," Dawn offered. "But we'll see if Delaney comes through. And there is always that second option . . . you can date Theo."

She could be tempted. But would she consider dating Theo to save Tomes & Tea?

If Jazzi and Dawn's apartment followed any kind of design, it was probably bohemian Lakeview. Their couch, which was just long enough for one of them to stretch out on, was patterned in a fabric with a light blue background and little navy-blue triangles. They'd found it at a thrift store. The pillows on the couch were navy and white striped. The walls wrapping around the front windows were the palest, palest blue. They'd assembled art themselves. They'd found fabric by a well-known designer that was much too expensive to upholster with. It was an abstract of three sailboats on the horizon, with a magnificent sky of magenta tinged with gray. They'd attached the material around a canvas and had Derek frame it. It was striking over their couch. The wicker table underneath the canvas sported a lamp with a shade in striped navy and white like the pillows.

The living room wasn't big. There was another funky yellow fabric-covered chair that was sometimes hard to get out of. The rug on the floor had been another flea market purchase and the Native American designs on it were encased in large squares. The rug had embodied all the colors in their room, from bright yellow to pale tan to white and navy. They'd painted the few kitchen cabinets navy and the space had just enough room for a whitewashed table with shelves on the side and two low-backed whitewashed chairs. They'd refinished the top of the table in navy.

Jazzi and Dawn had been roommates during their junior and senior years at college, so they knew each other's likes and dislikes. Therefore, this apartment had been relatively easy. The two single-bedded rooms with the bathroom in between gave them privacy if not a whole lot of space. But they were okay with that. The building had a storage area in the basement that suited their sports needs. They stored their paddleboards there along with anything else they didn't have room for in the apartment.

Now with supper put away, a veggie omelet paired with those corn muffins, Dawn sat stretched out on the sofa streaming a movie.

Jazzi called to her, "I'm going to take the trash down."

They alternated chores and this was Jazzi's week on trash duty. She collected it from their rooms into a large black bag and tied the strings. The door from their kitchen opened onto a small landing. Stairs that hugged the wall of the building stretched down to the alley below. Another set of stairs led from a door in Jazzi's bedroom down to the storeroom of the bookstore.

As Jazzi stepped out onto the landing, she took a deep breath of the damp evening air. Setting down the trash bag, she turned toward the front of the building. She couldn't see the marina and the docks. As she stared straight ahead, she *could* see the smoky shadows of the lake. Blue-green during the day with sparkles on its surface, at night it took on a mysterious quality with shades of gray. She couldn't see the light from the top of the bell tower or the faint white glow from the lamp on the church's steeple. She *could* see dots of light straight ahead on the lakeshore. Flashlights maybe? Reflective headgear from joggers?

She really did love living here with a constant influx of tourists and interesting people as well as the residents who called Belltower Landing their home all through the year. It was an unusual mix but one that made life interesting. As she stood there, hands on the small deck's railing, she heard a sound but wasn't sure what it was or where it came from. It sounded like . . . a cat . . . a kitten.

Jazzi and her mom had found two kittens in their garden and had kept them. They'd grown into Jazzi's constant companions. She'd missed them when she'd gone to college.

Putting her hand through the red ties of the garbage bag, she pulled it along with her and raised it as she jogged down the stairs. The mewing became louder and more frequent.

Jazzi lifted the lid off the garbage can and dumped the bag inside, settling the lid firmly in place once more. Then she followed the plaintive sound to under the deck landing where a few empty cartons tumbled. The sound was pitiful and Jazzi moved the boxes to see what she would find, almost afraid to look.

A motion detector light under the deck went on as she moved around.

She spotted the tiny kitten who could fit in her hand.

"Where did you come from?" she asked softly, so as not to scare it.

The kitten looked up at her, ready to make a dash for anywhere but there. Before it could, Jazzi scooped it up and cuddled it into the crook of her arm. "No, you don't," she scolded. "You'll only get lost or find trouble."

The kitten looked up at her and meowed.

Jazzi guessed the little guy was about six weeks old. His basic coat of white fluffy fur as soft as cotton was patterned with dark gray designs from his ruff to his tail. His tail was shades of gray with a touch of brown. His face, white from his eyes to his chin, had black markings along his eyes that looked like eye liner. White streaked from his nose to the top of his head. What really got to her was the marking in the middle of his nose that looked like a heart.

Her heart melted. There was no question about what to do next. She was taking him up to the apartment with her. After running up the stairs, she let herself inside the apartment.

She said to Dawn, "I found something outside that I think we're going to want to keep."

Jazzi knew Dawn's family had rescued cats, so she'd definitely understand. Jazzi brought the little ball of fur over to Dawn and it meowed at her friend.

"My gosh!" Dawn took him from Jazzi's hands. "Is it a female?"

"Male, I think. Isn't he just too cute?"

"He's cute. But there are consequences to keeping him. Do you want a litter box in our laundry area?"

They used a stacked washer and dryer in a closet of sorts next to their bathroom. It didn't have a door. But Jazzi could deal with that if Dawn could.

"That's fine with me, but a litter box will have to be in the bathroom until we can get him checked out by a vet. Tonight we can set up a cardboard box with torn up newspaper inside."

Dawn was as enamored with the little guy as much as Jazzi. She cooed to him and stroked his markings. "What are we going to feed him? The pet store will be closed."

Considering their options, Jazzi made a suggestion. "The convenience store might have pet food. We can mince it up and mix it with water. I'll take my bike and ride over there."

"I'll fix a bed while you do," Dawn offered. "I'll leave a message on my parents' vet's answering machine and maybe we'll get an appointment with Tom Lee tomorrow."

"Sounds good," Jazzi decided, leaving her sandals by the kitchen door and changing into her sneakers that she kept there.

Jazzi's Mini Cooper sat in the detached garage out back along with Dawn's SUV. She didn't use it often, though, because she mostly rode her bike. That was more economical and good exercise. She'd started riding when she was a teen. The wind in her hair and motion of the wheels also helped her clear her head. She slid the wooden garage door to one side. She and Dawn had to take turns moving that door back and forth to drive their cars in and out. She definitely had more room on her side of the garage because of the size of the compact white car with a black top.

Quickly, she moved her bike away from the wall and wheeled it to the alley out back. Closing the door again, she headed to the convenience store on Black Rock Road. Steering away from the lake, she quickly covered the few blocks to the Stop & Go and propped her bike outside. The convenience store was open all night. Inside, it only took Jazzi a few minutes to find what she wanted. The store even had a small section with kitten canned food. That was perfect. She also picked up a pouch of dry food. She could mix that with water and crumble it if she needed to.

She'd paid and was on her way out when she recognized the woman who was approaching the entrance. "Hi, Brie. Imagine seeing *you* here."

"Same," Brie said. Her messy ponytail blew in the wind. "Last-minute snack?" she asked with a smile.

"No, I found a kitten and Dawn and I are going to keep him. We needed a few supplies."

"I'm just picking up milk and eggs. I'm glad I ran into you, though. How would you like to come over for a light supper tomorrow night? I emailed my bio dad and he invited me to his home on Friday evening. I have some questions about the first time I see him. You've gone through it with your birth mother. Maybe you could help me prepare?"

"I'd be glad to help you if I can. I think Dawn's busy tomorrow night—dining with her parents."

"That's fine. You're the one I really need to talk to. How's eight o'clock?"

"That sounds good," Jazzi agreed. "I'll see you then."

After Brie went inside the store, Jazzi dumped her bag into the rear basket on her bike. She didn't know if anything could prepare an adoptee for that first meeting. Brie would surely find that out.

Chapter Three

Jazzi's car was distinctive but not fancy. Her stepdad had helped her find the car, a 2015 Mini Cooper S four-door hatchback. It had moderate mileage for the year and would serve her well. Its white body, black top, and black interior had pleased her so far.

Jazzi drove east down a country road away from the lake and into the forest. She found the line of townhouses easily. Pine Tree Lane led to the small development. The units were set up in duplexes in a string of six. Each had a peaked roof and probably a cathedral ceiling. A large multi-paned window looked out over the front yard. Six steps led up to a little covered porch with a dark green door.

She parked in the driveway to the side of Brie's townhouse. As she did, she could see a detached garage in the back.

Brie opened the door before Jazzi ran up the stairs. "I'm so glad to see you. I'm getting more nervous by the minute."

Right away, as Jazzi stepped inside, she could smell the evidence of cooking.

"I'm making lemon pasta," Brie announced. "I hope you like it."

"I like *any* pasta," Jazzi assured her.

Jazzi walked into the living room with its two love seats and coffee table in the center. A desk sat against one wall. Jazzi glimpsed a legal pad there with a list of names. She spotted a small dining table for four in a little nook by the stairway that led up into the kitchen. A partially open door off the living room was ajar and Jazzi could see that that was a bedroom.

There was one thing in the living room that stood out besides the furniture. A large paddleboard was lodged against the one loveseat. It was gray with tan stripes and an orange nose. It was an epoxy paddleboard, probably lightweight.

"You're eying one of my obsessions," Brie joked. "I don't have a deck pad, so I need to wax the board before I take it out again."

Jazzi noted the board's leash lying over Brie's side table. The leash would attach the board to Brie's ankle or her thigh. If she fell off, she could use the board to float. It was a safety measure.

"The kitchen's not very big," Brie said. "But come on up and join me while I dish out supper. The thing I don't like about this place is that I have to go up and down the steps to bring food down to the table. But it suits me. I don't have guests that often."

"The place is different," Jazzi said as she followed Brie up the stairs. "I like it. Many townhouses these days are open concept. This is much cuter."

Brie had decorated and furnished the unit in mostly neutrals—tan love seats, taupe and dark brown patterned rugs. The rich wood trim and doors along with the wood furniture made the space cozy. The sailboat photos on the wall added color. Jazzi also noticed the vase of flowers on the counter in the galley kitchen.

"You like flowers?" Jazzi asked.

"I do. I always stop for a bunch at a flower garden at least once a week."

A hint of lemon drifted from the saucepan on the range top. Brie dropped the pasta into a boiling pot of water.

Jazzi said, "That smells wonderful."

"I hope you like it. What would you like to drink? Wine, lager, a non-alcoholic beer? I've been filling the fridge with those since I've been dating. Open the fridge and pick what you want."

Jazzi chose a Coors Edge.

"You're the first one to take one of those. Are you a tee-totaler?"

Jazzi had to laugh at that image. After all, she did run a tea bar. "I can be. I like to keep a clear head especially when I'm driving. But I enjoy a glass of wine now and then too. I also know tea aficionados who like a slug of bourbon in their tea."

Brie chuckled. "Score one for teetotalers."

In no time at all, the angel hair pasta cooked and Brie spooned it onto dishes with transferware cabin scenes. She carried the plates while Jazzi set a wine cooler for Brie and her beer on the table. Taking her phone from her jeans pocket, she switched it to silent and laid it to the side of her plate. Brie's was already beside hers.

Brie had gone back up the stairs for silverware and the napkins. After she returned, they clinked their bottles together and took a few swallows. Then they sat and Jazzi could see Brie was eager to start their conversation.

Brie pushed up the cuff of her long-sleeved mustard-colored mesh shirt before she picked up her fork. Her blue eyes targeted the plate in front of her.

Jazzi ate for a minute or two, then complimented her hostess. "This is delicious."

That comment seemed to open their conversation. Brie began with, "I set up a meeting with my bio dad for tomorrow evening. The meeting will be at his house. I don't know if I'll meet his family too."

"Do you have a choice?" Jazzi inquired, not sure how blunt she should be.

"I don't know. Maybe. Why do you ask?"

"You might want to meet with your dad first and get the lay of the land."

"He said when he married, his wife had two kids. He adopted them. It would be a lot to meet everyone at once. What if his wife doesn't like me? What if I don't make a good impression?"

Jazzi stopped eating and placed her fork on her plate. "Stop," she warned. "You can't do this to yourself. Sure, you want to be prepared. But, Brie, if you think about everything that could go wrong . . . Don't do that. Think about what could go right. Focus on what you want to know. I wanted to know why Portia gave me up."

"Your bio mom's name is Portia?"

"It is. That was my main question for her. What's your main question for your dad?"

Rolling pasta onto her fork, Brie decided, "I do want to know why he gave me up. My mom died in childbirth. I want to know about her . . . if I look like her."

"Those are all legitimate questions," Jazzi said. "And I hope you learn the answers."

With her wine cooler bottle sweating on the table, Brie took her napkin and placed it under the bottle. "Let's talk about something else for a little while."

"Whatever you'd like," Jazzi agreed, knowing Brie was nervous about her meeting and spending many waking hours thinking about it.

Brie pointed her fork at Jazzi. "You should try this dating app I'm registered with."

"No thanks. I'm busy enough. Dawn and I have adopted a kitten. He'll keep me busy when I'm not working."

"You know, in the summer tourist season, there are lots of

choices. Using the dating app is more convenient than happy hour at the pub."

Jazzi shrugged. "I stop in at The Wild Kangaroo sometimes with Dawn during happy hour, but it's not my scene."

"That's even more reason for you to use the app."

Suddenly Brie pushed the sleeves of her shirt up both her arms. "Is it hot in here, or is it just me?"

"I think it's the pasta," Jazzi said. The temperature in the townhouse was comfortable with a breeze blowing through open windows.

Jazzi glanced across the table at Brie, spotted her left arm and froze. There was a bruise on her wrist, a large one, and it looked fresh. Was that the reason she'd worn long sleeves?

Brie caught her looking, and there was no avoiding the question.

"That looks nasty." Jazzi kept her voice measured and her thoughts from jumping to conclusions. "Did something happen at work?"

"No, not at work. Something happened on my date over the weekend. It was just a mishap."

"A mishap?" Jazzi prompted, trying to keep her voice calm.

"It was an accident . . . really," Brie insisted.

Jazzi considered pushing further for an explanation when Brie's phone played.

Jazzi saw the name flash on the screen—Nolan Johnson.

Brie snatched up the phone, said "Excuse me," and went deeper into the living room near the front door.

Jazzi couldn't overhear, and she really didn't want to. Whatever happened on Brie's date wasn't her business. Yes, she and Brie might be becoming friends, but it wasn't Jazzi's intention to intrude.

After Brie returned to the table, she sat with a sigh. "I went out with Nolan on Sunday and he wants to go out again."

"You don't want to see him again?" Jazzi couldn't help but wonder if it had something to do with that bruise.

Brie shook her head, her hair flopping this way and that. "He's a golf pro and just doesn't seem like my type."

"The type to settle down?" Jazzi asked.

"Yes. I think he's a player. That's not the kind of man I want to date, at least not anymore."

Just how did a woman tell if a man was the type of man who wanted to settle down? The only way to know was through lots of conversation and hours together.

But maybe Brie had a better handle on a man's psyche than Jazzi did. Maybe.

After Jazzi parked in the garage, she hurried up the stairs and inside the apartment with bags from the pet store. She had stopped there before going to Brie's for supper. She'd hoped she'd picked up all the supplies the kitten would need. After another day, once they were sure the kitten was free of fleas, she could let him out and settle him into his new surroundings. For now, she and Dawn were taking turns spending time with Zander in the bathroom. That was the name they'd chosen for him.

She slipped off her shoes and laid a huge bag with a litter pan and a bag of litter on a chair in the kitchen. The other she carried to the sink in the bathroom then sat cross-legged on the floor, her harem pants folded under her. Dawn had taken Zander to the vet that morning and he'd been cleared for kitty diseases.

Now the little fluff ball came tromping over to Jazzi and climbed up onto her lap. She brushed his cheeks with her thumbs. He seemed to like that so she did it more. His green eyes sparkled when he opened them and she tossed a little plastic ball. Racing after it, he tumbled tail over ears as she laughed. It was so good to have a kitten again. She knew he'd grow quickly, but she was going to enjoy every minute of his kittenhood. She'd bought supplies for a litter box and she'd take care of that in a little while, after they had quality time together. The ball forgotten, he came over and sat on her knees looking up at her, meowing.

"I suppose that means you're hungry."

One of his ears twitched and he meowed again.

"I see. You're going to be one of those responsive types."

His dish from his previous meal was empty. She picked it up and stood, careful to step around him. She shuffled the bags to the toilet seat, then washed the dish in the sink. When she pulled a can from the bag, she said to him, "I found you two varieties of kitty food. Hopefully you'll like both of them. What are the chances?"

Popping open one of the cans, she used her finger to mash some up in the dish. She mixed a little bit of water in it. He seemed to have trouble drinking from his water dish, and the vet had suggested adding water to the food. He meowed while she set it on the small vanity and washed her hands. After she set it on the floor, she sat again to watch him.

He ate like a pro. She wondered how long he'd been foraging on his own. The vet had said he *was* about six weeks old. He had some scratches on his little pink paws, so there was no telling where he had been or even where else he had been hiding.

Suddenly the door to the bathroom opened and Dawn peeked her head inside. "I'm back. How was your dinner?"

Zander was busy eating.

"Dinner was good. I'll ready Zander's litter box and we can talk."

In the kitchen, Dawn took a diet soda from the fridge. "I told my parents about our new ideas. They gave me that eyebrow-raised-we-don't-know-if-it-will-work look, but I told them I think it will. I just hope Delaney can get that runway model for a book signing."

Jazzi took the plastic litter pan from the bag and placed it on the floor. Then she opened the bag of litter and poured some in. "My dinner with Brie went okay, I guess. She's nervous, really nervous about meeting her bio dad. I told her she has to relax. If she doesn't, she won't even seem to be herself when she meets him. She didn't know if she'd meet the rest of his family at the same time, but I told her I thought it would be better if she didn't . . . if she just had a conversation with him, at least to start. She has to decide if she just has questions or if she really wants a relationship with him."

"That's why I haven't searched for my bio parents," Dawn said. "I just don't know how involved I want anything to be."

"The conversation between us got intense for her. So she talked about her new dating pastime. I'm a little worried about her."

"Why?"

"Have you ever heard of Nolan Johnson?" After all, the community of Belltower Landing was in reality a small town. "He's a golf pro. I'm not sure where."

"Maybe he's a vacationing golf pro," Dawn suggested. "He could be working at one of the resorts or at that private club on the other side of the lake."

"I suppose."

Apparently Jazzi had some worry in her voice because Dawn asked, "Is there a problem with him?"

Jazzi and Dawn talked about mostly everything. She didn't hesitate now to reveal, "Brie went on a date with him. She had a bruise on her wrist. When I asked about it, she said it was just a mishap. But I don't know. I told myself to butt out. Whatever happened is *her* business. At least, I suppose it is. Yet I feel that we could become friends, and if she's in trouble of any sort—"

"Don't you think she'd tell you?"

"No, I don't. That's the whole history of #MeToo. Women don't speak up when they should."

Dawn took a swallow from her soda. "Maybe it *was* just a mishap."

"Maybe. But she says she doesn't want to go out with him

again. He phoned her while I was there. She says he's not her type. It could be best if she stays away from him."

Jazzi spread the litter granules evenly in the plastic box. "We'll have to get Zander a bigger box as he gets older, but this should be okay for now. Are we going to move him out of the bathroom tomorrow?"

"Maybe after we're done working for the day if we don't see any evidence of flea dirt or fleas. The vet thought he must have been sheltered somewhere to be as clean as he was. We should really put up a flyer in the bookstore, don't you think?"

Jazzi frowned and her heart sank at the idea. "Yes, but I hope nobody claims him. I like the idea of being a cat mom."

Dawn pulled out a chair at the table and sat. "Speaking of good ideas, I forgot to tell you. I emailed Precise Packaging today. I received an answer late this afternoon. Their packaging consultant assures me he can produce economical products to serve our purpose. His graphic artist will draw up sketches for boxes for us to approve." Dawn had set her phone on the table and now she took it in hand and opened it. "This is his estimate for quantities, depending on the sketches we choose. Some will be bigger boxes than others. I told him a bell tower, a kayak, and a canoe, at least to start."

"We can delve into our emergency fund to make this happen," Jazzi said. "I think it might be worth it, especially for our online store. We can start with the lowest quantity and see what happens."

"He said we're looking at a three- to four-week time frame from approval to having the boxes. That's pretty quick."

"If we build up our online business that could keep us going through the quieter months."

Jazzi lifted the litter box and couldn't help returning to their previous conversation. "Brie said she's meeting with her bio dad tomorrow. I think I'll check with her after the weekend. At least she'll know she has our support."

"And Nolan Johnson?"

"I'll just listen to whatever she wants to tell me. All we can do is support each other, right? Women power."

Dawn gave a nod and repeated, "Women power."

On Monday morning, Jazzi took a sunrise bike ride, watching the sun break the horizon beyond the lake and forests. The cool breeze tossed her hair as she pumped her legs to climb hills and allowed downward inclines to increase her speed. The ride was as satisfying as yoga and meditation or church . . . at least for her.

After she stored her bike in the garage and climbed the outside steps to her apartment, she looked forward to spending time before work playing with Zander. They'd attached an old-fashioned sleigh bell strap from the Christmas Shop, open all year, to the kitchen door knob. That noise kept Zander away from the door.

She tried to open the door quietly in case Dawn was still in bed. Her roommate didn't share her early morning exercise routine. No sooner had she slipped off her trainers, scooped up Zander, cuddled him in the crook of her arm, and was slipping her finger into the cottony white fur around his ears when there was a loud knock at the kitchen door.

Jazzi deposited Zander on the sofa away from the door. Nevertheless he promptly jumped down to investigate a mouse toy by the coffee table leg.

Jazzi quickly opened the kitchen door and stood shocked at who she found there—Oliver! No words came to mind. They weren't friends, per se . . . definitely not *dropping in* friends.

"Hey," he said with that quick smile she'd glimpsed often at The Wild Kangaroo. He was dressed in stonewashed jeans that had slits at the knees. His two-toned red and white Henley shirt emphasized his broad shoulders and sturdy biceps. His blond hair looked damp, and his blue eyes were twinkling as if they held a secret.

Jazzi was excruciatingly aware that she'd just returned from a bike ride. She needed a shower. Her white tank and pink shorts had seen way too many washings. What was Oliver doing here?

Taking a bolstering breath, she was finally aware of the box he was carrying . . . with the holes in it.

"Who dares to darken our door at this hour?" Dawn called, opening her bedroom door. She crossed the living room in her summer pj's and flowered robe, looking not altogether awake.

"Guilty," Oliver said.

Dawn's eyes went wide when she spotted and recognized him. "Aren't you going to ask him in?" Dawn asked Jazzi. "It looks like he brought us a present."

Jazzi felt mortified that she was letting Oliver stand there. She still couldn't seem to find her voice. Clearing her throat, she finally invited, "Come on in."

Oliver strode to the small kitchen table and set the box there. That's when Jazzi heard the soft mewing sound from inside.

Curious, she crossed to the table and stood beside Oliver. She was aware of the foresty scent of his aftershave. "I'm afraid to ask what you have in there."

He glanced at Jazzi and then at Dawn with a wicked grin. "I heard you found a friend the other night. I think this is his sister. I found her on Thursday holed up in one of the empty boxes behind the pub." He opened the box and inside sat a particularly precious all-black kitten with the same furry cheeks and fluffy tail as Zander.

"Since Tom Lee and I are friends—we kayak together sometimes—I took her to him. I heard about your found kitten from him. Anyway, Tom kept her for me, tested her, and gave her a flea treatment. I kept her sequestered until this morning."

"And now?" Dawn inquired, already reaching into the box to pet the cute little being.

"Well . . ." Oliver drawled. "I'm a big believer in uniting siblings."

Jazzi suspected there was a story there because of the way he was looking at the black kitten, then transferred a caring gaze to her brother.

"My guess is they got separated from their mother," he decided. "I thought yours might be lonely since you're both in the store a lot. I figured they could be mates, and keep each other company."

"I don't know if we have enough room for two." Dawn looked unsure as she picked up the black kitten. Zander had come over to investigate and was sitting on Jazzi's bare foot.

"You have more room here than most apartments," Oliver observed. "I paid the vet bills. She's all yours if you want her. If not, I'll keep her but I'm afraid she'll be lonely with the hours I work, and I don't live onsite like you do."

Dawn stared at Jazzi. "I can tell you want to keep her."

Jazzi knew she was no expert at hiding her feelings. She never had been. "Yes, I'd like to keep her but you have to be sure too. Sometimes two cats are as easy as one. Sometimes not. More cat food, more litter, more snuggles, and more companionship."

Oliver's gaze met Jazzi's and held for a few moments. "Her name is Freya. It's the name of the Norse god of love and beauty. It also means noble lady. I thought she could grow into it."

"You're into Norse mythology?" Dawn asked as if she didn't believe him.

"I have a few Scandinavian as well as Australian ancestors," he joked.

"It's a beautiful name. Let's put her on the floor and see if they remember each other," Jazzi suggested.

Dawn set Freya on the floor at the table's edge. Zander made a beeline for her. They smelled each other all over, and then he tumbled Freya over to her side and began washing her little face.

"Aww!" Dawn was obviously just as lost as Jazzi. The two kittens were theirs.

Jazzi wagged her finger at Oliver.

He chuckled. "If I find any more, I promise I'll keep them."

They were all watching the reunited siblings bathe each other when Jazzi's phone played "As It Was" by Harry Styles.

Oliver's eyebrow twitched up.

Jazzi gave a shrug and took a few steps deeper into the living room when she saw Delaney was calling. At the same time she was about to say hello, she heard sirens and vehicles race down Lakeview Boulevard outside. It sounded as if they were headed away from the lake to the east side of town.

"Hi, Delaney."

"Jazzi . . . Jazzi . . . I can't believe—" Delaney was stammering and didn't at all sound like herself.

"What can't you believe?" Jazzi asked, worried now at the sound of her friend's shaky voice.

"I came over to Brie's this morning to see how her weekend went. I found her."

Jazzi's heart skittered and her chest tightened. A cold chill inched up her back.

Delaney confirmed the foreboding Jazzi felt as she cried, "Brie is dead!"

Chapter Four

Keep your distance. Keep your distance. Keep your distance.

The mantra had been playing in Jazzi's head all day as she'd shelved inventory, waited on customers, took phone orders, and pretended the day was a normal one.

It wasn't.

As Delaney sat in Jazzi's and Dawn's apartment that evening, close to tears, Jazzi felt that wide gap of distance she'd attempted to manage all day from Brie Frazier's murder was diminishing. Relating exactly what had happened this morning was difficult for Delaney. It was all too fresh. Jazzi felt it becoming fresh for her too.

Is this how her mom had been drawn into solving murders in Willow Creek? Daisy Swanson had helped police in the small town solve ten murders. No one in Belltower Landing knew about that history, and that's the way Jazzi wanted to keep it. Yet as Delaney relayed what she'd seen, Jazzi had more and more questions.

Jazzi had brewed tea and iced it. She brought three glasses with a small pitcher of sugar syrup to the coffee table. Dawn had laid out a plate with peach muffins from their store's bakery case, but none of them seemed to feel like eating.

Delaney added sugar syrup to her tea and stirred. Freya was nestled in the corner of the sofa with her brother, napping. Sliding to the back cushion, Delaney stroked them as they snoozed.

"I won't ever forget what I saw." Her voice caught and she looked down at the kittens once more.

"Did you say that the door to Brie's townhouse was open?" Jazzi asked, tucking her long hair behind her ear as she thought about what that meant.

"The door looked as if it hadn't closed properly when someone had left."

"Maybe they left in a hurry," Jazzi suggested. If Brie had let someone inside, that meant she'd known whoever it was.

"I knew it was murder before the detective said it was a homicide," Delaney said. "Brie had marks around her neck. She had no pulse. She was cold. As soon as I saw her and touched her wrist, I knew it was too late for anything I could do. I called 9-1-1 and just sat there, staring at her."

"Oh, Dee," Dawn sympathized. "I'm sorry you went through that."

"It was almost worse after the police arrived." She reached for her tea and took a few healthy gulps.

"In what way?" Dawn inquired.

Jazzi had known police detectives who were good guys, but they all had one focus, finding the killer. She imagined Delaney had been targeted with hard questions.

"They interviewed me for two hours at the station. I felt like a criminal. They asked how I knew Brie. What was I doing there? How long have we been friends? Who were her other friends? Did I know anyone who wanted to hurt her? They asked the same questions over and over until I finally gave up trying to hold it together and broke down sobbing. Then they let me go. But they told me they might call me in again."

"They were testing you to see if your story was consistent." Jazzi didn't just know this from movies she'd streamed or books she'd read. She knew it from experience.

Dawn shot her a questioning look and fiddled with a silver ear cuff above her pierced ear. "All of this makes me so uncomfortable. A killer is roaming somewhere in Belltower Landing. Maybe we need more security up here at the apartment. The store has an alarm and cameras outside and inside, but all we have here is a dead bolt and a locked doorknob."

Jazzi had considered that when she'd opened the door to Oliver that morning. Had it just been that morning? "We need a peephole. We always meant to put one in."

"At a minimum," Dawn said.

"The thing is," Jazzi murmured, "Brie most likely knew her killer."

Both Dawn and Delaney turned toward her, looking shocked.

"If neither the front door nor the back door was damaged, and no windows broken, then Brie let whoever did it inside." That determination was an easy one to make.

Now that they'd moved away from the trauma the scene had caused Delaney, more questions had zipped around in Jazzi's head. Still . . . she didn't know if she should ask them. She didn't want to upset Delaney further.

However, Delaney seemed to need the opportunity to express herself in a safe place. Her false eyelashes fluttered as she wrung one hand against the other. "Brie's place was messed up, not like someone ransacked it, more like she struggled with whoever did it. A light was knocked over. Her paddleboard lay on its side. The ottoman was out of place. Thank goodness I didn't touch anything."

The kittens had awakened and crawled over to Delaney's lap. They snuggled near her hip. Jazzi wasn't going to ask about

Brie's paddleboard leash. The mantra played in her mind again—
Keep your distance.

She was going to concentrate on Tomes & Tea and the new
kittens. End of story.

The following morning, Jazzi slid out of bed trying to shake
off her sleep-deprived fogginess. Her bedroom with its whitewashed furniture, colorful lilac and blue patterned bedspread
and curtains, usually brought her morning joy and pride that
she'd stepped into adulthood and was going to succeed at it.
Last night, though, she'd spent most of it petting Zander, letting him romp on and off her bed with his sister, trying to find
solace in them. Having no energy now, she knew she had to
shake this mood to greet her customers. After dressing in a
raspberry and white flowered sundress, she fed the kittens,
slipped on white ballet-style flats, and softly rapped on Dawn's
door.

Dawn called, "Come on in." Her roommate looked sleep-
deprived too.

"Did you manage any sleep?" Jazzi asked.

Dawn brushed her bangs from her eyes. "Some, but when I
woke up, I couldn't grasp the reality of what had happened."
She looked Jazzi over. "Are you going down to Tomes already?"

Jazzi nodded. "I need something to occupy my hands if not
my head. I'll check in new inventory."

The kittens rushed over Jazzi's foot on their way into
Dawn's room. Jazzi lifted Freya and set her on Dawn's bed.

Dawn pulled the kitten into her lap. "I'll see you downstairs."

Jazzi could hear the breaking sadness in Dawn's voice.
"Downstairs," she agreed.

After the bakery delivered maple walnut muffins, and Jazzi
filled the baked goods case, Erica arrived. They hugged hard.

Soon Dawn joined them and the morning propelled itself forward.

It was after one thirty when Jazzi slipped off her work apron and took her lunch break. Often she ate in the back room, but today she needed motion. She stepped outside into a beautiful May day. The sky was pale cornflower blue with amazing puffy white clouds that floated lazily overhead. Although she'd pushed troubling thoughts away all morning, now vivid pictures of Brie—like photographs—clicked through her awareness. She didn't want to push them away. She'd enjoyed her time talking to Brie, and had instinctively known they could be friends.

Jazzi considered walking to the marina and buying lunch from one of the many food trucks gathered there. Instead, though, knowing she couldn't ignore her sadness and grief for Brie, she decided to sit somewhere quietly without a lot of ruckus around her. She crossed the street to a deli, bought half of a turkey-and-Swiss sub and a bottle of water, then started for the green.

Strolling along the sidewalk under the maple and oak trees, catching the scent of mown grass and a hint of moisture from the breeze over the lake, she found her way to the path leading to the bell tower. Teak and stainless steel six-foot-long park benches lined pathways across the green. The bell tower stood in the midst of it all, stretching three stories high. Phineas Harding had designed it. Built of brick, it was twelve feet wide and twelve feet deep. Eight-foot arches cut through the tower from front to back and side to side. A round clock faced Lakeview Boulevard and the belfry rested on top of that.

Halfway across the green, Jazzi stopped, then walked farther. She settled on a bench close to the stretch of gravel path that bordered the lake, a good twenty yards from its shore. She'd learned the surface area of the lake was sixty-three-hundred acres. She spotted outboards, pontoons, and a few small sailboats traversing the smooth blue-green water.

This was what she needed.

She opened her water bottle, took a few swallows, and set it on the bench beside her. Then she opened her sandwich.

She'd taken a few bites and let the peace of the place surround her when a man in a light gray suit and a spiffy navy tie came from around the back of the bench and looked down at her. "Are you Jazzi Swanson?"

Jazzi considered the man and thought he looked familiar but she couldn't place him.

"Who wants to know?" she returned, not being flippant, merely wanting to be cautious. Could he be a friend of Dawn's parents? He looked to be in their age group.

His brown hair with a few swaths of gray ruffled when he ran his hand through it. His brown eyes were serious as he stared down at her. "I'm Detective Sergeant Paul Milford from the Belltower Landing P.D."

She studied him again carefully until he sighed and pushed back his jacket revealing his shield attached to his belt.

Now she remembered seeing his photo in the town's newspaper, *The Landing*. "I'm Jazzi," she admitted.

"Someone at the bookstore saw you head over here. She told me you like to come here to think. May I sit?" He motioned to the bench.

He must have spoken to Dawn or Erica, maybe even Audrey if she'd arrived to help with the afternoon to over-supper shift. "You can sit," Jazzi agreed. "How can I help you?"

"I needed to talk to you because Delaney Fabron told me that you met with Brie Frazier twice within the past week."

"I did," Jazzi said, not saying any more. She'd learned from experience not to answer more than was necessary. Her mom had told her that many times. After all, she didn't know this detective or exactly what he wanted. She was going to find out, though.

"I'm making a timeline." His look was direct. "I need to know Brie's activities during the days before she died."

When Jazzi was quiet, he lifted one hand, palm up. "I know who your mother is. I know that she's an amateur sleuth who helped the police in Pennsylvania solve a few murders."

"Ten," Jazzi filled in.

His eyebrows shot up.

"My mom helped solve ten cases."

Detective Milford leaned back into the bench and looked a little more relaxed. "I need to be honest with you, and I want you to be honest with me. Will you be?"

"I want you to find out who killed Brie," Jazzi said.

"Then talk to me," he coaxed. "Delaney said you hadn't known Brie long."

"Delaney introduced us, so to speak," Jazzi acknowledged. "I suppose she told you what the meeting was about?"

"She said that you were adopted, that Brie was adopted, and she wanted to talk about that."

Deciding she could be straight with the detective, Jazzi told him about her meeting with Brie and Dawn, and then about her supper with Brie last week.

"We connected," she said, "as many adoptees do. She was searching for her birth dad. She was concerned about the face-to-face meeting with him. She had emailed with him and was going to meet him on Friday night. She didn't know if she'd be meeting just him or him *and* his family. She was anxious about it."

"That's pretty much what Miss Fabron said. I realize if what you say is true, you didn't know Brie Frazier long."

"If what I say is true?"

"Miss Swanson, you know I have to verify everything."

Jazzi shrugged. She knew that was probably so.

He hadn't taken out a notebook and pen or anything like

that, but from his intelligent sparkling eyes, Jazzi figured he was remembering everything she'd told him.

"Did you only talk about adoption? I mean, when women get together, don't they talk about other things too?" he prompted.

The detective had a quirk of a smile on his lips. He was fishing and she might as well give him something. "Brie also talked about dating."

"Guys she dated?"

Jazzi considered Nolan Johnson, but she only knew what Brie had said about him, and that she'd had a mishap . . . and that bruise wasn't anything important. Since Jazzi didn't really know this detective or how he operated, she decided to be circumspect.

"Did Delaney tell you that Brie was using a dating app?" she asked. He really should know that about Brie.

"No, she didn't. We don't have Brie's phone or her laptop. The killer must have taken those. Do you know if she'd been dating much?"

"I think she'd been using the app the past few months. She was serious about finding the right man. She wanted to settle down and have a family." Jazzi's throat suddenly became thick and she swallowed a few times. The detective waited patiently until she continued. "That's why she especially wanted to meet with her biological dad. She wanted any medical information that could be pertinent."

"That makes sense," he said. He looked out over the lake too, maybe trying to make a quiet connection with Jazzi.

Now it was her turn to ask a question. "Has there ever been a murder in Belltower Landing?"

"I'm not sure about that," he confessed. "I just came on the force last year, to help with a hit-and-run investigation. When I was offered a position here, I decided to stay. After all, who doesn't want to live in a resort town? I kayak now almost every weekend. How about you?"

"I paddleboard mostly. My roommate's family has a pontoon boat. We go out on that now and then. But the store keeps us busy."

"I imagine so."

When she looked into the detective's eyes, she had the feeling he knew a lot more about her than she wanted him to know.

He reached into an inside pocket and took out a business card. He handed it to Jazzi. "I want you to call me if you hear anything else, or if you remember anything else. I intend to catch Brie Frazier's killer."

No sooner had the detective left the bench when someone else sat down beside Jazzi. When she turned, she saw it was Parker. His dark brown brows were drawn together and he was frowning.

"Hey, there," he said.

"Hey yourself. What are you doing here?"

"I was at the store when the detective came in. I followed him over here."

"Trailing a detective? You could get arrested for something like that, I suppose."

Parker shrugged. "I wanted to make sure you were okay. He said he wanted to talk to you, and Audrey told him where you'd gone. I didn't like the idea of him singling you out someplace where there were no other people around you who could watch over you."

"Parker," Jazzi chastised him.

He held up his hands in surrender. "I know, I know. You can take care of yourself. We're not still living in the Dark Ages. But sometimes I think we are, here in Belltower Landing."

She couldn't help but smile. "The detective was just doing his job, trying to figure out the timeline for Brie's activities and all of that. He knew I'd met with her twice."

"Did he give anything up?" Parker asked.

"You've been listening to too many true crime podcasts. No, he wasn't forthcoming, though he did say they don't have Brie's phone or laptop."

"Interesting," Parker mused. He was wearing an oversized yellow T-shirt with the marina's logo on the front. He had a small outboard he took out onto the lake anytime he could. He liked to fish.

"What did you want to talk to me about?" Jazzi asked.

"The virtual reality idea for promotion."

Her appetite returning, Jazzi took a couple more bites of her sandwich. "I'm listening."

"Tomes and Tea does carry virtual-reality kits for kids."

She nodded and wiped a smear of mustard from her lip. "We do. I think we have one about dinosaurs and one about volcanoes. There are interactive books that go with them."

He stretched his long legs out in front of him. "There are a couple of ways you could take this. You could set up a virtual-reality station for kids and have them take part and then also highlight all the books that might go with that particular subject, like dinosaurs or volcanoes or whatever."

"Saturday morning sessions?" she suggested.

"You could do it anytime, any day of the week. It's summer . . . school's out. As long as you publicize it the right way, you could get enough kids in to make it worthwhile. When they bring their parents in, then they see all the selections. Get my drift?"

She nodded. "I do. Our other option?"

He shrugged. "Set up virtual reality for adults. You know there are great fantasy virtual reality games. You could have your whole section of fantasy novels highlighted. That would draw in adults and kids, especially teens."

She punched him lightly on his bicep. "You are particularly full of good ideas, especially if Delaney can't convince that runway model to help us." She crumpled up the paper her sandwich had been wrapped in and stuffed it into the bag to take along to put in the trash. Then she picked up her water bottle.

"And . . ." Parker drawled. "You could always date Theo." Parker's gaze seemed to be targeting her especially seriously.

She couldn't believe he'd care if she dated Theo, or anyone else for that matter. They were friends, after all.

Neither of them said anything. Parker knew where she stood on the subject of dating. More tourists appeared on the green as they enjoyed the view. A group was gathered around the bell tower arches, peering underneath, possibly waiting for the 2:00 p.m. bell chime.

Jazzi studied them. She expressed her thought aloud. "Has anyone actually ever gone up into the bell tower?"

Parker looked that way. "Everything is mechanized, but my dad once told me there's a locked trap door with a ladder that pulls down. It's only used for emergencies. The mayor holds the key."

Unlike Jazzi, Parker had lived in Belltower Landing all of his life, except for his years at college. He'd traveled across the country for that to attend Stanford.

Her attention was suddenly drawn to a landscape gardener who made sure the town green was pristinely cared for. He was edging grass along one pathway, his Weedwacker whining.

Jazzi checked her watch. "I have to get back to Tomes."

Parker stood when she did. "I'll cross over with you."

A few minutes later, Jazzi and Parker stood at the crosswalk of Lakeview Boulevard when Parker asked her, "Do you think the detective will figure out who killed Brie Frazier?"

"That's hard to say. What if Brie was dating someone who was a tourist? That person could have left town and no one would ever know."

The stoplight, one of the few on the boulevard, changed to green. They crossed, with Jazzi glancing to the right and left at the fuchsia Knock Out roses growing in the center strip. Across the boulevard, they stopped under the dogwoods shading the street. In the spring their pink blooms invited tourists to walk the streets and admire them.

Stopping outside of Tomes & Tea, Jazzi admired the storefront. It was painted a seriously deep forest green. The multipaned window display, like a large bay window, held vertical panels on the bottom and smaller square panes in a double row above the top. That display invited customers inside. The assortment in the window now boasted every self-help book imaginable. A smaller display to the side showcased books about children coping with their feelings. Double doors, the trim around the glass panes painted in that deep forest green, carried the historical flavor of other shops on the block. A foot-high placard across the top of the bookstore and tea bar's front proclaimed TOMES & TEA under dentil trim molding. A stack of books decorated one side of the name while a teapot tipped on the other.

Casually, Parker touched Jazzi's arm. "Don't think too much about that detective. I'll catch you later."

Jazzi gave Parker a good-bye smile and went inside the store, wondering if life would ever seem normal again after what had happened to Brie.

The store was relatively busy. Although Jazzi still had a few minutes of her break left, she was ready to get back to work. As she passed Dawn at the tea bar, her partner said, "I checked on Zander and Freya when Audrey arrived. They're fine. They finished their lunch and were napping on the sofa." Dawn motioned to a table at the rear of the store. "Delaney's back there. She's still upset."

Imagining how Delaney felt after finding Brie's body, Jazzi said, "I'll talk to her before I circulate."

After a nod, Dawn served a customer a cup of steaming-hot black tea and a maple-walnut muffin.

Jazzi smiled at another customer who was studying a Catherine Steadman psychological thriller. "Are you finding what you're looking for?"

"I am. She's a new author for me. I just have to choose one."

Glancing at the bookshelves, assuring herself everything was in its place, Jazzi made her way to the table in the back. Delaney was staring down into a cup of hot tea as if hoping it could soothe her thoughts. Jazzi knew tea could soothe the body. She wasn't sure about thoughts.

Delaney was wearing a terra cotta–colored shorts and blouse set. Her lip-plumping lipstick matched, and her false eyelashes made shadows on her cheeks. She appeared to be dejected and sad.

Jazzi laid her hand on her friend's shoulder.

Delaney jumped, startled.

"I didn't mean to scare you," Jazzi apologized. "How are you doing?"

"Lousy. I can't forget what I saw."

There was no need for Delaney to explain what she meant.

Jazzi sank onto the chair across from her. "Is there anything I can do to help?"

Delaney raised her gaze to Jazzi's. "No, afraid not. If anything, I want answers. Do you think Brie's murder had anything to do with her looking for her bio dad?"

"I'd hate to think that," Jazzi admitted. "I think it's more likely the murder might have more to do with the dating app she was using."

"Do you think someone was catfishing her, and she found out and confronted them?"

Catfishing was a downfall of communication on the Internet, especially on dating apps. Someone manufactured a fake profile to lure unsuspecting men or women into a relationship for a nefarious purpose. Could Brie have gotten caught up in that? Anyone could be susceptible when they were looking for someone to love.

"It's possible." Jazzi met Delaney's gaze. "And it's likely Brie was smart enough to figure it out. The detective told me they don't have her phone or laptop. But they'll find answers."

"Do you really think so?" Delaney's eyes were misty.

"I do." But although Jazzi said the words, she wasn't sure she meant them.

Chapter Five

At closing Jazzi received a text from Parker asking if she and Dawn wanted to meet at The Wild Kangaroo for a late supper. After checking with Dawn and finding out she was busy, Jazzi texted Parker back.

Live music tonight, right?

There is. Meet me there? Seven thirty?

She texted a smiley emoji.

At seven thirty she stepped into The Wild Kangaroo and saw Parker had snatched a table for two near the bar. She didn't always like sitting there because it was noisier, but tonight with live music it wouldn't really matter.

"I ordered cheese fries and crab sticks to get us started," he said. "You can check the menu. I didn't know what to order for you to drink."

She slipped into her seat. "I'll try lemonade for now. I heard about their new sunset creamsicle drink. It sounds delicious. I'll save that for later."

"It has whipped-cream vodka in it, doesn't it?" Parker asked.

"One night a week, I have to let my hair down, right?" she teased.

And she had let her hair down. It flowed to mid-back, straight and glossy. She'd flat-ironed it into a smooth style with the very ends waving. She'd dressed up a bit tonight in lime-green bell-bottoms, a yellow spaghetti-strapped tank, and a tie-dyed bolero jacket. Maybe she just wanted to uplift her mood. She didn't know. After all, she felt like wearing black. But her attitude had always been to soldier on.

Parker's gaze drifted over her. "You look nice."

It was something a brother would say, and Jazzi smiled. She was glad she and Parker were friends.

The waitress brought them their crab sticks and cheese fries and took their drink orders.

After ordering cheese and bacon rolls, Jazzi glanced around. There was loud chatter and voices everywhere. The place had filled up fast. Music usually started around eight thirty.

"Have you heard anything about the group who's playing?"

"They're supposed to be good." Parker gave her a sly smile. "They're called the Snob Barrel."

She laughed out loud. "Okay, let's hope they sound better than their name."

Parker downed a few cheese fries. "Everybody comes to be social and just have background music while they talk, don't you think?"

After she dunked the golden crispy fried crab stick into a soy dip, she shook her head. "I don't know. It depends if they treat the night like happy hour, or if it's just a place they come to with their friends."

"I've been thinking about those dating apps," Parker admitted.

"Are you thinking of creating one?"

"No. I've decided they should have background checks attached to them. They're only safe if the user actually uploads a true profile. What if there was a way to create an app that somehow utilized background checks?"

Jazzi shrugged. "Even then, not everything that can be hidden in somebody's past would show up. How thorough could that be?"

Parker chose a crab stick and spritzed it with vinegar. "And there would probably have to be a charge."

"As well as fostering advertising for the app?"

"How do you know about that?" Parker asked.

"I know someone who started a podcast. Once he started gaining subscribers, it took off because sponsors signed up."

"Computer matchup dating services were once the rage. These apps have taken over. I can't believe someone as attractive as Brie Frazier had to use one." Parker blushed a bit as he said it.

"I haven't dated that much, Parker, but I do know it's hard to connect with guys. Using an app or not."

"I haven't dated much either. But we haven't dated much for different reasons."

"What's *your* reason?" She picked up a cheese fry and ate it.

"I'm socially incompetent."

"You are *not*," Jazzi protested vehemently. "You can talk to anybody."

"I can talk to anyone about computer stuff. Everyday stuff? I'm not so great."

She shook her head again. "I don't believe that."

"Let's face it, Jazzi. I'm a nerd. During my teen years, I mostly lived in my room with my computer. And truth be told, I still spend a lot of time that way."

Jazzi waved a crispy crab stick at him. "I guess the question is, do you want to spend it that way? Or out alone in your boat? Or do you want to mingle with a crowd of people?"

"Not a crowd. I do enjoy book club, though."

"See? Everybody needs friends who get them. The book club accepts you."

"You mean they accept my quirks," he said self-deprecatingly.

She chuckled. "We all accept each other's quirks, don't you think?"

They settled in with their appetizers, chatting when it felt right, quiet and just listening to the surroundings in between. After a jostling group of four men came in and sat at the bar, Jazzi noticed Oliver was tending it. That wasn't usual, but maybe tonight with music, his duties were a little different. He tried to be everywhere, she knew that.

Oliver seemed to know the men who were sitting there. Suddenly her ears perked up. She heard the name Nolan more than once.

Jazzi leaned her shoulder closer to Parker's. "Do you know any of those men sitting at the bar?"

Parker took a look at them. "No, I can't say I do. They could be tourists. Oliver seems to know them. My guess is they come and go in here a lot."

"I heard the name Nolan," she admitted.

His eyes grew wide. "Do you know somebody named Nolan?"

"I know someone named Nolan Johnson, but not personally. Brie dated him."

"Someone from one of those apps?"

"Yes."

"You mentioned him for a reason, Jazzi. What's up? What do you know about him?"

"I know Brie didn't want to date him again. He called her the night I was there for dinner, and she made some excuse."

"That's not unusual with the dating apps, from what I hear."

"No, I know. It's just . . ."

"This is *me*, Jazzi. Spit it out. It's just what?"

The look on Parker's face was totally serious. She knew he didn't gossip, and neither did she. This was something she could run by him and get his opinion on. "Brie had a bruise on her wrist."

"And? She could have knocked herself against something. She was out on her paddleboard a lot, right?"

"Yes, but she said it was a mishap. It happened on her date with Nolan."

"What kind of date was it? Out on a boat? Something like that? Anything can happen."

"I know. Maybe I'm simply too suspicious."

"Are you watching *Forensic Files* again?"

She smiled. "No, I've switched to British mysteries."

Parker stared over at the bar. "There could be more than one man in Belltower Landing with the name of Nolan, you know."

"I know, but he seems to be about the right age."

"Did you tell the detective about him?"

"No. I didn't want to get him in trouble if nothing actually happened."

"You mean maybe nothing abusive happened."

"Yes. But, like you said, on a boat anything can happen . . . or on a paddleboard."

The waitress came over to their table with the cheese and bacon rolls they'd ordered.

Jazzi decided nothing ventured, nothing gained. She nodded to the second man at the bar with red hair. "Do you know him?" she asked the waitress.

"Sure, he comes in here a lot. His name's Nolan Johnson. He's one of our regulars for happy hour. Do you want me to introduce you?"

Quickly Jazzi shook her head. "No, I was just curious. Thanks. The cheese and bacon rolls look really good."

"They're always good. Oliver makes sure about that. Enjoy them. The music starts soon."

The yeasty aroma of the rolls had Jazzi's mouth watering.

The Wild Kangaroo's rolls weren't only topped with cheese and bacon but were stuffed with provolone and bacon too.

"What are you going to do now that you know Nolan Johnson is sitting over there?" Parker asked. He watched Jazzi pick up a roll and smell it as if it was fine perfume.

"I'm not going to do anything. I had my curiosity quenched. Let's dig into these."

At Parker's probing look, Jazzi heard that mantra in her head again—*Keep your distance*. That's what she was going to do. And now she knew one of the men to keep her distance from.

"You are an interesting Gen Z specimen," Parker announced, like a proclamation, as she took a large bite of the roll.

"How so?" she asked after she swallowed.

"You like books and tea, conservative as well as flashy clothes, you paddleboard, you cook for you and Dawn now and then, and you like cats, especially kittens. You're digitally aware, but you're not constantly on your phone. I've even seen you poring over old maps. You know, the kind that fold up?"

Jazzi almost sputtered. "Parker, you can't fit any Gen Z woman into a box. You should know that by now."

"But I can, Jazzi. That's just it. You're the first woman I've met in a while who cares more about ideas than clothes, who cares more about friends than what they think of her. You had the courage to look for your birth parents and start a business."

"Dawn started the business with me."

"Yes, she did," Parker agreed. "But she's still attached to her parents. She cares about their approval."

"Don't we all want our parents' approval?"

"I suppose," he said, finishing the last crab stick. "But I think whoever raised you, raised you to be an independent thinker, and that's a good thing. And speaking about being an independent thinker, I believe you should convince Dawn to let me develop an app for Tomes and Tea. Just imagine how that will connect you to your customers. I'm willing to develop one if you want me to."

Jazzi picked up her glass of lemonade and took a long sip. "I think too much is happening at once."

Guitars began strumming on the other side of the bar.

Parker said, "We can't see very well over here."

"No, but we can listen."

Parker sent her a glance with a smile that told her something she didn't want to know. It might be that Parker Olsen liked her for more than being a friend.

Two hours later, Parker insisted on walking Jazzi back to her apartment.

"There's a killer out here somewhere," Parker had said. Jazzi knew she shouldn't be foolish so she agreed. Up on the landing, she asked, "Do you want to come in?"

"And meet the kittens?"

"That's the reason," she said. "Dawn might be home too."

Once they were inside, Jazzi had two kittens cavorting around her feet.

Parker leaned down and picked one up, staring Zander in the face. "You're going to protect your cat moms, aren't you?"

Zander meowed at him, and Parker laughed. Then he set down the kitten, and Zander and Freya ran off toward Dawn, who was lounging on the sofa.

After he said hi, Parker looked at their door. "You still don't have a peephole."

"We're going to put one in," Jazzi assured him. "I have a drill down in the storeroom. I can figure it out."

Dawn protested. "When I was at my parents' tonight, my dad said he'd put one in for us. He'd put a sturdier dead bolt on the door too."

"We can do it ourselves," Jazzi told her.

Parker gave Jazzi a look, and she remembered what he'd said about Dawn being close to her parents. Parents like to be protective. She knew that. She'd been fighting against her mom's protection for a few years now.

"Okay," Jazzi said with a shrug. "If he wants to do the dead bolt."

"He does. But I told him he has to let us know when he's coming so we can put Zander and Freya in one of the bedrooms. Did you see anyone you knew at the Kangaroo?" Dawn asked, curling up her knees on the sofa and settling back in the corner.

"We did. Kaylee and Derek came in, so we sat at a table with them for a while. It was nice. You should have come."

"My parents wanted to talk to me."

"About the bookstore's plan for promotion?" Parker asked.

"Well, that's part of it. My mom doesn't understand how social media influencers work. She doesn't realize how important it will be if Delaney coaxes that runway model to come to the store to sign her books. No, my parents wanted to talk to me about opening a second Rods to Boards store, maybe in Ithaca. My brother's going to manage it. They wanted me to do it. I hate to disappoint them. I like to please people, especially my parents. But Tomes and Tea is important to me. Our store, not *their* store. My brother can handle business on their side. He can be the inheritor of their franchise if that's what it develops into. I don't really want anything to do with that. I've got to find my own life, just as Jazzi has."

Jazzi didn't believe she was a role model for that. She was trying to find her way just like any zoomer was. She was fortunate . . . even blessed . . . that she'd been given the opportunities she had.

Parker had come in and pulled out a chair at the little table.

He turned it around and sat facing Dawn. "Have you given up the idea of connecting with your birth parents?"

"I have for now. For one thing, I don't want to upset my parents even more. But the second thing is—look at what happened to Brie."

Jazzi shook her head. "I really don't think that has anything to do with her birth dad." Though she did remember that email address and the fact that Brie had met with him. *Could* that have had something to do with what happened to Brie? She didn't want to think so.

"Are both of your parents against finding your birth parents?" Parker asked.

"Mom's against it more than Dad. They confuse me sometimes. They say they want me to be happy, but then when I make a decision on my own, they have all these reasons why it might not work out. Even Dad wants me to take over the outfitters business someday. It doesn't make sense to me. My brother's into it. He knows every product and every account."

Like with Jazzi, the Fernsbys' first-born child, a son, was their natural child. Dawn had been adopted. Jazzi's older sister Vi was a natural child. Part of Jazzi understood exactly where Dawn's parents were coming from.

"They don't want you to feel like you're adopted. They want you to know that they see you the same way they see Farrell, right?"

"I guess so. I understand how much they love me. I also understand that they want to be enough for me, and that's why they don't want me to go searching."

Jazzi had lost her adoptive father to cancer by the time she'd searched for her birth mother. That had a lot to do with her search. Everybody's life was messy. Dawn's was no different.

Jazzi was about to say so when her phone played "As It Was." Taking it from her pocket, she studied the screen. "It's my mom," she said and cringed.

"Don't you want to talk to her?" Parker asked.

"It's not that. I bet I know why she's calling. She's heard about Brie's murder. She knows people . . ." Jazzi started to say, and then stopped. There was no reason to tell Parker and Dawn that her mom knew detectives in the small town of Willow Creek, that she'd worked with them, had barbecues with them, and called them her friends. Jazzi had no doubt whatsoever that they had told her about the murder in Belltower Landing.

"Do you really think she heard about the murder here?" Dawn asked.

"Yes."

"Are you going to tell her that you knew the victim?" Parker asked.

"I've always been honest with my mom. I'm not going to stop now. But I'd better go to the bedroom to take it. Parker, I'll see you later, okay?"

He held up his fist for a fist bump and she gave him one and then disappeared into her bedroom. After Zander followed, she shut the door.

The neon green and blue LED lights glowed in the bookstore's cubicles as Jazzi, Dawn, and Delaney sat at the back table. The Edison lights above the sales counter shone brightly as Delaney opened her laptop and began to prepare for a Zoom video meeting.

Dawn pulled her chair up next to Delaney's and Jazzi's as Delaney clicked on the link. Dawn nudged Delaney. "Is this really going to happen?"

"The odds are good," Delaney said with a short quick smile and a flutter of her eyelashes.

Jazzi knew their friend was feeling proud of herself that she could help make this meeting with Emilia Perez happen.

There was a ding of a notification. Delaney pressed a button on her laptop and there, in vivid color, Emilia Perez smiled at them.

"Hi, Emilia," Delaney said. "Meet my friends Dawn and Jazzi. They own Tomes and Tea."

As Jazzi studied the screen, she realized Emilia Perez was truly strikingly beautiful. Her dark brown hair was parted in the center, high off her forehead. Each side was finger waved away from her face. Her brows were demure yet dark, her eyeliner flowed into her cat-eye markings. Her nose was narrow and her lips, a perfect rose bow, were plump and glossy. She was wearing a white short-sleeved dress with black jewel accents. It was obvious she worked out from the muscles of her shoulders. The beauty mark on her left cheek was a signature one and she didn't try to cover it. Jazzi knew from Emilia's stats that she was five-foot-eleven and regal in her bearing. If crowns were made for women, this woman would take the prize.

Emilia smiled broadly, and her black onyx earrings shone as she turned her head. "Hello, Dawn and Jazzi. Delaney has told me all about you."

"It's a pleasure to meet you," Jazzi said, meaning it. "We're so grateful if you're willing to help our bookstore."

"You sound surprised," Emilia said with a laugh. "I do book signings all the time. I'm in the middle of a tour now."

Dawn chimed in, "We know your book has made the best seller list. That's why we're so eager to have you."

"And have me you will, if we can figure out our schedule."

"Tell us what you have available," Delaney suggested. "As a resort town, we're going strong all summer."

"Delaney, you know on the weekends I'm tied up the most. However, I had a bookstore back out of a book signing, something about a problem with the roof. I don't even think you know about that yet."

"When was it scheduled for?" Delaney asked, looking at the calendar on her phone.

"It's in a month on a Friday. I hope that isn't too short notice to promote it well."

Jazzi leaned forward, excited in spite of herself. "That date is absolutely *perfect*. It coincides with our town's Welcome Summer Festival on the summer solstice. We should have even more traffic than usual."

"Especially if we get the word out there far and wide," Delaney said. "We'll put together a special promo for Emilia's Instagram feed and yours. We should have a really successful signing. It will certainly bring interest to the store, beyond the confines of Belltower Landing."

"I'm looking forward to it," Emilia said. "Delaney will be our go-between. She'll take care of my travel arrangements and the time you want me there. I have to go now, but she'll keep me informed and I'll keep her informed. It was a pleasure meeting you both. Now go take some pictures of the store inside and out, and post them on your Instagram feed along with the fact that I'll be doing a book signing at your store. Four weeks is a short time, but it's also enough time to jazz up excitement for the event."

After a wave at the three of them and a winsome good-bye, Emilia clicked off.

Dawn hopped up from her chair. "I can't believe it. I can't believe she's actually going to do it." She gave Delaney a hug. "Thank you, thank you, thank you."

Jazzi hugged Delaney too. "She's absolutely beautiful, isn't she?"

"Inside and out. Sure, she cares about followers and sales, but she also genuinely wants to help you."

Erica came in from the storeroom and saw they were grouped together around the laptop. "It's time to open, girls."

"Emilia Perez is going to come here for a book signing in

four weeks," Dawn told her. "We're going to put this store on the map."

Erica laughed. "I never doubted it. I'll open the door."

Jazzi was aware that one book signing with somebody famous wasn't going to be enough to assure success, but it was a start. They needed a strategy and they'd have to develop that too. Jazzi hadn't been naïve enough to think a bookstore would take care of itself. She knew online sales had cut into the numbers for brick-and-mortar stores. On the other hand, brick-and-mortar stores were becoming relics. That meant a store with the right amount of events and promotion could make a success of itself, and she intended to see that happen. Maybe she'd been asleep at the wheel up until now, simply trying to become an adult rather than a business owner. That was going to change.

After tea was brewing and the store opened, Dawn said, "I'll stay in here and take care of the customers. You and Delaney shoot the photos. You know what Emilia needs."

Dawn didn't like to be the front woman, and she knew Jazzi enjoyed taking photos with her phone.

Delaney said, "You take some outside. I'm going to take photos in here before it gets crowded. I'll do panoramic photos so people can get a hint of what the store is like. The lights will make things pop. But I'll need pics of the two of you together too."

Jazzi agreed. The outside photos probably weren't as important as the inside ones. But Jazzi could take enough that Delaney could send whatever she wanted to Emilia.

First Jazzi went across the street and started clicking from different angles—the bay window, the side panels, the windows up above. The store was unique and she wanted to show that off. But she also wanted any of Emilia's followers and their own who were seeing the feed to understand the geographic location and how Tomes & Tea was cuddled in between other stores. Lakeview Boulevard with its Knock Out roses was pretty in itself. You never knew what would tickle followers' imaginations.

After she finished across the street, she took close-up shots of the window with its children's display inside. She was contemplating what she should take next when she heard a familiar voice over her shoulder.

"Hi, Jazzi. It's unusual for you to be out here instead of inside."

Theo Carstead's eyes twinkled at her as she turned to face him. "Photos for promo," she said easily, noticing again how handsome he was with that cleft chin and unruly hair. "Are you looking for something to read?" she asked.

"I am. Believe it or not, I like to hold a book in my hand instead of looking at it on an e-reader. I'm into books about planes now, and I think I'd like to become a pilot."

"The wild blue yonder," she said. "I don't know how I'd feel being in a small plane out there with blue and white all around me."

"The instruments do the flying now. You wouldn't have to be afraid. I found someone who's teaching classes at the regional airport. I'm starting them next week. I just want to investigate all the types of planes I could possibly fly. Anyway, I won't hold you up. But while I'm here, how about going with me for that drink? Maybe tomorrow night?"

Like a chime in her head that kept replaying, Jazzi remembered what her friend said about Theo's connection to Evan Holloway. She also knew Emilia's book signing wouldn't be enough to raise the profile of Tomes & Tea. Shouldn't she just say yes to Theo?

Taking all of it into consideration and tired of thinking about it, she answered Theo, "Sure. Let's have a drink together. Should I meet you at The Wild Kangaroo?"

"Seven thirty."

"That's good," Jazzi said, and waved as Theo went into the bookstore. She was gazing after him when a little girl suddenly barreled into her and wrapped her arms around Jazzi's knees.

"Hi, Jazzi."

Pocketing her phone, Jazzi looked down to see Sylvie Bianchi. "Hi there, Sylvie. How are you today?"

Addison, a staunch member of the store's book club, said, "She's determined to find a book about baby rabbits. She thinks she wants one. I'm trying to dissuade her."

Jazzi laughed. "Maybe a book will do it. Maybe *two* books."

Addison wagged her finger at Jazzi. "You're just trying to sell books."

"You might want to think about the cost of a rabbit hutch and food and also the bunny getting loose in your house."

Addison laughed, her long blond hair blowing in the wind. "You could have a point."

Jazzi gave Sylvie a hug and then straightened, looking into the bookstore where Theo had gone.

Addison took a step closer to her. "What's wrong? You look worried."

"I am. I might have just done something I shouldn't have."

"Confession is good for the soul," Addison advised, as she took Sylvie's hand to make sure she stayed by her side.

"Remember we talked about my accepting a date with Theo Carstead?"

"Yes," Addison drawled.

"I just did, and I feel as if I did it under false pretenses. It's not like me to think the end justifies the means. Maybe I should break the date."

"Wouldn't that be worse?" Addison asked.

Jazzi pulled her braid over her shoulder and fingered the end. "It could be. I don't know. I have until tomorrow night to think about it."

"Before you wear yourself out thinking about it, why don't you take a photo of me and Sylvie out front? I'll post it on my Instagram feed and you can post it on yours too. Then you won't just have a picture of a bookstore."

"I wonder if I could get all of my customers to take selfies out front," Jazzi mused.

"Now you're thinking like a woman who wants to promote her store."

Chapter Six

Soon after sunrise the next morning, Jazzi convinced Dawn to go paddleboarding with her. In late May, the weather was perfect for time on the water. Exploring one of the lake's channels near the forest, they spotted red-winged blackbirds, watched the sun rise high and sparkle on the lake, and readied themselves for a Saturday of mingling with customers, selling books and tea, and shooting more photos to promote Emilia Perez's book signing. Jazzi also had something else more serious on her mind—her date with Theo Carstead tonight. She still felt guilty about agreeing to meet him.

Her feet positioned parallel about hip-width apart and centered between the edges of her board, Jazzi paddled in rhythm with Dawn. They were heading back toward the launch area for kayaks, canoes, and paddleboards.

Dawn called over to her, "The SUP community is having another overnight excursion over the Fourth of July. Are you interested?"

The stand-up paddleboard community had a club that sponsored events and excursions, also challenges to raise money for charities. "I'm going to pass this time," Jazzi said. "We'll be busy with events until the end of June. "July could be just as busy."

"Maybe you'll be dating Theo," Dawn said wickedly.

Jazzi just shrugged, feeling uncomfortable talking about her date. What if she did have drinks with Theo tonight and decided she wanted to see him again? How did asking him for a favor fit in? "We'll see how tonight plays out." Shifting her paddle from the water to her board, she dropped down on her knees, and then sat, intending to float to shore.

Dawn did the same.

Jazzi had her eye on three common loons near the shore when Dawn pointed toward the canoe rental stand where a food truck was parked. "Look over there."

From the logo on the side and the yellow and purple colors on the truck, Jazzi knew it belonged to Casper Kowolski. He sold delicious fish tacos, burgers, and fries. When water enthusiasts came back from a morning of kayaking, boarding, or canoeing, they were hungry, and he was there for them. Dawn had parked her SUV in the parking lot where the food truck sat now. However, Dawn wasn't offering the suggestion of a fish taco for breakfast. She was pointing to the official police SUV parked near the food truck. They'd have to pass right by it to take their boards and paddles to Dawn's vehicle.

After Jazzi paddled the board in with her hands, she unhooked her leash from her ankle and slid off the board. Making sure her dry bag that protected her phone was secure on her hip, she picked up her board and paddle and carried them onto the shore.

Jazzi was wearing a yellow and orange sun shirt along with yellow shorts. Her black swim shoes protected her feet against the gravel and sand along the shore. She glanced at the food truck where Detective Milford was talking to Casper Kowolski as she and Dawn carried their boards to Dawn's SUV. They were drying off their boards before putting them on the rack when the detective came over to Dawn's vehicle.

After a cursory good morning and a return greeting from Jazzi and Dawn, he took a look at the rack on the SUV that held the two boards. He was wearing a linen camel sports jacket today, but he still looked hot and sweaty. As if he was making an off-handed comment, he said, "It must be convenient that Dawn's parents own an outfitters store."

Dawn grinned at him. "I get a discount."

At that, he targeted Jazzi. "What about you? Do you get a discount too?"

Some paddleboards were inflatable but both Jazzi and Dawn owned hard boards. Dawn's was pink and yellow, and Jazzi's was a Bahamian blue and green.

Jazzi cast a hard look at the detective. "Does this have something to do with Brie's murder?"

He didn't look surprised that she'd been direct with him. "It could. Did you buy your board outright?"

"No. I bought Dawn's used board at a good price. It's teak, if you want to know."

When Jazzi had detached her leash from her board, she'd wrapped it around her arm. Now Detective Milford motioned to it. "Tell me about the leashes you use with your SUPs."

Dawn looked confused but Jazzi suspected where this questioning was headed. Dawn used a coiled leash but Jazzi's was straight, the same as Brie Frazier's had been.

"You're obviously asking for a reason," Jazzi said. "Was Brie's straight leash the murder weapon?"

His eyes narrowed as he tried to hide his surprise. "Why do you ask?"

"Because I saw Brie's board and leash in her living room the night I had dinner there. The leash was lying over the end table. I know she was strangled and the leash just lying there like that . . ." Her voice trailed off and she felt her throat tighten.

"I can't discuss the investigation." The detective had a stone face that was supposed to be expressionless.

Jazzi supposed it was, but she saw a tiny twitch at the corner of his eye. He might not be talking about the investigation, but he had just confirmed for her that Brie had been strangled with her paddleboard leash.

Hesitating at the red door of The Wild Kangaroo that evening, Jazzi brushed her damp hands down the sides of her blush-colored skirt and straightened the shoulders of her silky cream blouse. She'd added swingy coral earrings that could peek out between strands of her black hair. She'd also used a brush of mascara and subtle lip gloss tonight. She was nervous. She didn't know exactly what she wanted to say to Theo Carstead.

She was simply going to have a drink with him, and see what happened next. She might not even mention Evan Holloway . . . or she might.

Deciding that indecision didn't look good on her, she swung open the red door and stepped inside the pub. A cold blast of air-conditioned air hit her.

Oliver was speaking to a server near the entrance. He said, "I told Chad to go home. He had too much sun today and looked ready to drop. I'll help you cover tables three and four."

Glancing up and spotting Jazzi, Oliver lifted his hand in greeting. Then he came a step closer and pointed to a table near the bar. "Somebody's waiting for you. I told Theo I'd keep an eye out for you."

Giving Oliver a nod and a smile, she spotted Theo and crossed to his table. He gave her a wide smile and motioned to the chair across from him. "I saved you the best seat in the pub."

Sinking into the silver metal chair, she laid her small clutch with her phone on the table and smiled back. If she was looking for a hot guy, Theo was it.

The waiter came over to take their order. "Watermelon sangria," Jazzi said.

"You're one of *those*," Theo gibed after the waiter left.

"*Those?*" Jazzi asked.

"Fruity and light. The bartender keeps them that way for the tourists."

"I'm not a tourist, but I do like fruity and light."

Theo had ordered a mojito with an extra shot of rum. Jazzi felt she had to say, "I admit I'm not a party girl."

"I've heard that." Theo's coy look unsettled her.

"Really? What else have you heard?" After all, she'd never known that anyone discussed her reputation in Belltower Landing.

"Just that you keep to yourself and your book club friends."

Considering what he'd said, she agreed. "I do. Not much time for anything else if I want to bike and roam on my SUP."

"I prefer working out to balancing on a board."

He was acting as though she should admire him for that. She did admire anyone who kept to an exercise regimen, but Theo seemed to be saying it for effect.

The waiter brought their drinks and set them on napkins in front of them. Jazzi took a slow sip of hers. As she did, Theo watched her.

"Good? Yes?" he asked.

"Perfect," she answered, aware of Oliver carrying drinks to a nearby table. Short-staffed, he'd pitched in to help. Nice.

She didn't look his way but Theo must have been aware her attention had wandered. He leaned in closer to her. "Tell me about your taste in music."

She could. She could tell him about her playlist on her phone. She could tell him she listened to everything from oldies to sixties rock to Coldplay to Ed Sheeran and Harry Styles. But that would be a get-to-know-you conversation that led into real friendship. She simply couldn't pretend that she was interested in him so he'd do her a favor. She just couldn't.

She looked him straight in the eye, took a breath, and blurted out, "I met you here under false pretenses."

He looked confused, then sat back in his chair and studied her with slitted eyes.

"That's not like me, Theo. I don't do things like that. You asked me out and I guess you expected someone who wants to date. I can't say I do, but I *can* say I'm trying to save my business partnership."

His eyes widened and his mouth turned down in a frown. She could see his perfect white teeth when he asked, "What does that have to do with *me*?"

His cheeks had grown ruddy and she wondered if he was embarrassed. *She* certainly was. She summed up the problems with their store as quickly as she could.

"We need influencers to help us. We need our social media to blow up. We need to give the bookstore a chance to succeed. Dawn and I are best friends. I don't want to lose her, not as a friend and not as a business partner. We have the same vision, and that's everything."

"I get that. But I still don't understand what it has to do with me."

"One of my book club friends told me that you know Evan Holloway, and he's going to be performing at the summer festival."

Theo was a smart guy, and the light seemed to be dawning in his eyes. Unless that was the glitter of the little hurricane lamp on the table. But she doubted it.

"You want me to hook Evan up with your bookstore."

"All Evan would have to do is stop at our store and post on his social media accounts that he did. Just imagine how that would enhance our image. He could sign autographs, maybe, if he brought photos along, and each customer who received a signed autograph could take a selfie with him or with us, whatever Evan would want."

She stopped. She knew this wasn't what Theo had expected. He actually looked crestfallen, and maybe a little angry.

"Theo, I'm sorry. Just forget about my request. I'm simply not interested in dating anyone now, especially if that man is only in Belltower Landing for the summer."

Theo mumbled, "I should let you pay for your own drink."

"I intended to pay for my own drink anyway."

Growing quiet, he looked down at his napkin and then back at her. "Why didn't you string me along to get an appearance from Evan?"

"I couldn't do that to you. I had to be honest with you. My mother taught me better than what I was going to do."

Suddenly Theo stood, took bills from his pocket and plopped them on the table. After a disappointed look at her, he didn't say good-bye. He simply left.

Jazzi rubbed her fingers across her forehead under her bangs, and then leaned her chin on her hand. She looked at the drink and wasn't thirsty for it. She knew better than to think alcohol was going to make her feel more like herself. She should not have accepted Theo's invitation no matter what anyone had encouraged her to do.

Since there wasn't any music tonight, customers came and went. The pub was relatively settled in when Oliver came over to her. Her heart did a little skip or maybe that was her couple of sips of sangria. She should stick to tea.

"Everything okay here?" he asked, his look sympathetic.

"I'm fine. I just did something stupid and I regret it."

He motioned to the chair across from her. "May I sit?"

"Sure."

"I overheard some of that."

She dropped her head into her hands and rubbed her face. After she peeked out at him, she said, "Now I'm totally embarrassed."

"Why are you embarrassed?"

That Australian accent could convince her to tell him anything. "Because I don't like to make anyone feel bad, and I certainly don't want to deceive anyone. That was a stupid idea from start to finish."

"To save Tomes and Tea?"

"No, to try and coax Theo to help me save Tomes and Tea because he knows somebody famous."

"Why didn't you go along with your original plan?"

Jazzi fingered her clutch, almost wishing her phone would vibrate and she could stop the conversation to answer a text or take a call. Finally, though, she admitted, "My college boyfriend strung me along instead of being honest with me. I wouldn't do that to someone. I can't do that to someone. In the long run, it hurts more."

The look Oliver gave her was a combination of admiration and curiosity. It made her heart do another skip. "Let's change the subject so I can forget about this fiasco."

"As fiascos go, this was a pretty minor one," Oliver reminded her.

She managed a half smile. "I have something I want to ask you. Do you know Nolan Johnson?"

Oliver turned around, checked the bar as if he expected to see Nolan there. "I have a nodding acquaintance with him. Why?"

"Do you know where he lives?"

"Okay, that's two questions about him. So now I have to know why you're asking."

"You know about Brie Frazier, right?"

Oliver's brow furrowed and he rubbed his stubbled jaw. "The woman who was murdered?"

Pushing strands of her long hair over her shoulder, she realized she hated people thinking about Brie as a headline. "Yes. I was getting to know her. She was dating Nolan before she died. I thought about talking to him."

"Because . . ." Oliver's prompt convinced Jazzi that he was perceptive rather than simply curious.

"He was one of the last people to see her the week before she died. I'd like to talk to him, that's all."

"That's a gutsy move. He could shoot you down as quickly as Theo."

"I haven't done it yet." She had to convince herself that speaking to him would be gutsy, not stupid.

"I have a feeling you will. Nolan lives in a condo near the golf course."

Now she knew where to find him. Did she want to find answers? Or did she want to take the safe route and tell the police?

Shelving new arrivals the follow morning, Jazzi felt as if she needed another cup of black tea to wake up. She'd been awake late into the night thinking, analyzing, and feeling. Still, she forced herself to concentrate on shelving correctly the new batch of memoirs that had arrived. Some were more like biographies. Others were thoughts about a lifetime.

Erica suddenly appeared beside her. Audrey's mother studied Jazzi with compassionate brown eyes. Usually they held warmth and humor, but right now, they were concerned. Often both Jazzi and Dawn confided in Erica. Jazzi knew that before Erica came to work this morning, she'd attended Sunday Mass at the Holy Family church. Erica's spiritual life wasn't something she spoke about. She didn't have to. Wisdom and peace seemed to emanate from her.

"Dawn told me your date with Theo didn't go so well last night."

Jazzi sighed. She wasn't sure how much she wanted to say, but Erica was a mentor in the ways of life.

"Did Dawn tell you what happened?"

"Not really. She glossed over the details. Is there anything you want to tell me, maybe need to get off your chest?"

Erica had raised four kids. Jazzi was surprised the woman didn't have more gray strands in her hair.

"You know I accepted a date with him when I wasn't sure I should have."

"Yes, you needed his professional acumen."

Jazzi had to smile at that description. "I suppose that's one way you could put it. The other was I was taking advantage of a situation and I shouldn't have."

Erica shook her head. "I don't know, Jazzi. I don't think that's true. You're a young woman still learning the ways of the dating world and life. Learning about business practices too. Dawn did say that you confessed to Theo why you had accepted the date. What happened after that?"

"He got up and left. I don't blame him. I'd have been angry too. What if a guy accepted a date with me if I asked him, just so he could get a discount on books?"

This time Erica laughed. "I'm glad you have a sense of humor about this."

Jazzi flipped her braid over her shoulder. "I don't know what I'm going to do if I run into him again."

"You're going to say hi. If he snubs you, he snubs you. If he doesn't, you can talk again. Don't make it the end of the world, Jazzi."

"Learn from my mistakes and move on?"

"Possibly. Every situation is different."

Suddenly Jazzi's phone pinged, signaling a text had come in.

She slid it from a pocket of her apron. "It's Dawn. She says there's someone at the tea bar who wants to talk to me."

"Do you want me to finish shelving these books?" Erica examined the cart.

"That would be great. Thanks. I'll be back."

As Jazzi approached the tea bar, she spotted Dawn speaking with a woman who looked to be around sixty. She was round and homey-looking in a navy-blue mid-calf dress. The short sleeves capped plump arms. The woman's hair was gray streaked with white, and she wore a serious expression as she pushed her tortoiseshell-rimmed glasses up her nose. As Jazzi took a second look, she saw that the woman looked tired, with blue bags under her eyes.

Dawn quietly made introductions. "Jazzi, this is Estelle Frazier, Brie's mom. She'd like to talk to you."

Jazzi felt taken aback. Brie's mom? Pushing her surprise aside, Jazzi said, "I'm so sorry about Brie, so very sorry."

Coming a step closer, Estelle patted her arm. "I know, I know. We're all in shock. I know you had dinner with Brie, and I'd like to talk to you about that. Do you have a couple of minutes?"

Jazzi glanced over the store. Audrey was waiting on a customer, Erica was shelving books, and it looked as if Dawn was free. Dawn nodded to her and mouthed, "Go ahead."

Jazzi invited Estelle to one of the small tables and asked if she'd like a cup of tea.

"Hot tea would be wonderful," Estelle said.

"We have Earl Grey today, or a peachy white tea."

"The peach sounds great," Estelle said, and sat heavily into one of the white enameled chairs.

Giving a sign to Jazzi that she'd heard, Dawn was already pouring the tea. Jazzi crossed to the baker's case and pulled out two lemon poppyseed muffins. Having something to pick at to eat and to drink might help Estelle feel more comfortable. Jazzi couldn't imagine what she wanted, but she'd soon find out.

Dawn carried the cups of tea to the table while Jazzi brought the muffins. She sat across from Estelle and stared into the woman's sad eyes. "I don't know what to say," she began honestly. "I just can't imagine what you're going through."

Brie's mother fluttered her hand as if Jazzi's further condolences weren't necessary. "I'm going through grief. That's for sure. But I'm worried about something else."

Surprised, Jazzi forgot about the tea she'd been about to sip. "What are you worried about?"

"The police won't tell me anything." Now there was a resolve on Estelle's face that superseded her grief.

"What do you think they have to tell you? They have an investigation going on, and I imagine they have some suspects."

"Oh, they should have suspects all right."

Estelle tore the muffin in half. Jazzi saw hot anger in her eyes. "Do you think you know someone who might have wanted to hurt Brie?"

"I know why Brie came to you." Estelle stirred her tea absently with the little wooden stirrer. Steam rose from the cup as it cooled down. "She told me she spoke to you about finding her biological father."

"She did. She was supposed to meet with him."

"Yes, she was. And she did. His name is Joseph Covino. He's wealthy. He has a large estate on the east side of the lake, but he also has children and they might not want to share it."

Jazzi pushed her palm against the hot paper cup because she suddenly felt chilled. "I don't quite understand."

"I have the feeling those kids of Mr. Covino's didn't want Brie to be part of their family. And the police won't tell me if they've questioned them. I don't know what to do."

Putting it all together, Jazzi realized Estelle had to blame someone. Joseph Covino's children were handy targets. "You want Brie's murderer brought to justice. I certainly can understand that. But you have to let the detective do his job."

"He could at least tell me if they've questioned the family." Estelle pressed her lips firmly together.

"Investigations don't work like that," Jazzi said, finally picking up her cup of tea again. "They keep everything buttoned up so there are no leaks. With anybody they question, they hear their testimony over and over again to make sure there are no inconsistencies. They look twice at anybody who isn't consistent."

The older woman studied Jazzi. "You sound as if you know about this."

"I read a lot of mysteries," Jazzi said with a shrug, instead of mentioning that her mom had been involved in murder investigations in Willow Creek.

Dawn had finished serving a customer at the tea bar and now she joined Jazzi and Estelle. She looked down at Estelle. "You must tell us if there's anything we can help you with."

"There is one thing," Estelle said, looking down at the muffin, and then over at Jazzi. "Can you and Dawn come to the memorial service? Delaney is coming. I'd like more of Brie's friends to be there. It would be a great support for me and her father. He's walking around as if he doesn't know what to do next. He goes into a room and can't remember why he's there. He won't talk to me about it, though, so I'm not sure how to help him."

Jazzi reached out and held Estelle's hand. "I know it's not the same thing but I lost my adoptive father when I was a teen. All you can do is be there when he wants to talk. Be there if he needs you to listen. I kept my grief inside for a very long time, and that wasn't healthy. I think that grief is finally what encouraged me to search for my birth mother."

"Brie was searching for her biological father to get family

history, at least that's what she told me." Estelle seemed sure of that fact.

Nevertheless, when Jazzi didn't respond, Estelle asked, "Or was there some other reason? Did she not like the way me and her father raised her?"

Jazzi shook her head. "Nothing like that. But adopted children have questions. Yes, she probably wanted to find out the medical history if she intended to have a family someday, and it sounded like that's what she was intending. But I'm sure she wanted answers too."

Estelle looked down at her tea and studied the inside of the cup. But there were no tea leaves there to give her answers. "I wonder if that's what got her killed."

Chapter Seven

Jazzi watched and listened Tuesday evening as the book club members chatted about the books they'd read—from motorcycle mechanics to historical sagas to psychological domestic thrillers. However, there was an undercurrent of a situation and a particular name not mentioned. The circle around the tables grew quiet as Jazzi distributed cups of peach iced tea and Erica opened a container of cookies she'd brought to share with the group—macadamia nut with white chocolate chips. Addison had brought a pretzel and cereal mix snack that she often made for her daughter.

Kaylee passed the salty snacks in one direction while Derek passed the cookies the other way. After he'd taken two, he finally broached the subject on their minds. He asked Delaney, "Have you heard any more from the detective?"

Delaney's stylishly uneven and wispy hair along her cheek hid her face as she ducked her head and stared at the romance she'd brought along still resting in her lap. When she raised her gaze to Derek, her eyes were swimming with tears.

Immediately Derek stammered, "I'm . . . I'm sorry. I never should have asked."

Delaney raised her hand to stop his apology and took a tissue from her jeans pocket. She swiped her tears away. "This keeps happening. I think I'm fine and then . . ." She sucked in a breath. "The detective has questioned me three times now and hasn't told me a thing, even though I've asked him so many questions. His eyes become slitted, he purses his lips, and doesn't say a word, simply asks another question."

Erica, who always mothered them all, reached over and squeezed Delaney's arm, giving their friend comfort.

In the quiet that followed, however, Dawn blurted out, "Brie was strangled with the leash from her paddleboard."

There was an almost unanimous gasp from the group.

"Dawn!" Jazzi was totally taken aback by her roommate's lack of sensitivity.

Turning to Jazzi, Dawn asked, "Don't you think they should all know?"

If the detective had wanted to keep that detail from the public, he wouldn't have broached the subject of leashes with her and Dawn. The coroner's report would certainly reveal it. Still . . .

Not everyone might want to know details like that.

Giselle was quick to say, "I don't want to know. I don't even want to *think* about what happened. I hesitated coming tonight because I didn't want to hear about Brie's murder, let alone talk about it." Giselle's heart-shaped face showed her obvious upset as she closed her eyes. Her heavily gray-shadowed eyelids seemed to proclaim the somberness of the moment.

When she opened her eyes again, she took them all in and stood. "I've two early jobs in the morning. The houses have to be cleaned before the owners come home later in the day. I'm going to go." She stood, picked up her purse that she'd laid on the table, and crossed to the door.

Dawn hurried after her.

Jazzi could hear Dawn apologizing to Giselle.

Taking in the rest of the group at a glance, Jazzi asked, "Does anyone else feel the same way? We won't talk about Brie's death if that upsets you."

"We have to talk about it," Parker determined. "A killer is roaming around out there somewhere. The more we know, the better it is for everyone. Burying our heads in the sand is too dangerous, especially if someone Brie dated did this."

"We don't know that," Jazzi reminded him as Dawn returned to the group looking sheepish. Jazzi considered what Estelle had told her about Brie's biological father and his family.

"I agree we don't." Parker studied Jazzi. "But crowd-sourcing knowledge has solved murders before. Exactly what do *you* know?"

"Not much more than you do. But Dawn and I ran into Detective Milford after we went paddleboarding."

"He was talking to Casper Kowolski at his food truck," Dawn informed them.

"Why Casper?" Parker wanted to know.

Jazzi suspected the reason. Should she say it? Was Parker right about crowdsourcing knowledge solving murders? What if it could?

In the middle of most nights, she concentrated on everything she knew about Brie and her belongings in her townhouse. Last night, as if all of it had jogged her memory, she remembered the legal pad on Brie's desk and the list of names on it.

She said quietly, "Casper's name was on Brie's list."

"What list?" Audrey moved forward on her chair. "You didn't mention a list before."

It wasn't something that had stood out to Jazzi as important, although she'd figured the police had confiscated it if the list had still been on Brie's desk.

"Brie had a list of men. I think it was a list of the men she'd dated. Some names had been crossed out. Casper's was one of them. Since the police are questioning Casper, I'm sure they have the list now. They certainly have everything from her townhouse that can give them a lead."

"That's if they know how to do their jobs," Addison muttered, surprising Jazzi. "Our police force mainly stops speeders, clamps down on DUIs, and handles domestic fracases."

"That's true," Audrey agreed.

"Who else was on the list?" Kaylee asked. Her lioness dark brown curls seemed as wild as her tone with the question.

Jazzi still wasn't sure that crowdsourcing was the answer. What if the list of names was leaked and residents looked at the men with suspicion. Reputations could be ruined.

Still, there would be some merit in asking the group about Nolan Johnson. "Nolan Johnson was one of the most recent men Brie dated. His name had been crossed out too."

"Tell them about Brie's bruise. Did you tell Detective Milford about that?" Dawn asked.

"No, I haven't," Jazzi admitted, not sure Dawn's revelation was going to help anything.

"What bruise?" Kaylee wanted to know.

Still Jazzi hesitated.

Parker attempted to allay her fears about the wrong info getting out. "Jazzi, I'm sure this group can keep anything confidential that we feel is necessary."

Jazzi did trust these friends. But Dawn had proven over and over that sometimes she had no filter. Parker's gaze was considerate and assured her she could trust him and the rest of the group.

"When I had dinner with Brie, I noticed a bruise on her wrist as if someone had grabbed her hard. She'd had a date with Nolan Johnson and explained the bruise had come from a mishap. That was it."

As serious as she'd ever seen his expression, Parker kept his eyes on her. "Did you tell the detective this?"

"No."

"You have to, Jazzi. It could be important."

Looking at her friends and their worried faces, she realized that bruise could be a clue. "I'll stop in and see Detective Milford tomorrow."

The following morning, Jazzi stood in front of the electronic door at the Belltower Landing police station. The building was a historic one that had been brought up-to-date over the years. It was a two-story brick structure. There were headers—large decorative trim boards and moldings under the eaves and around the rectangular long windows. Each window also boasted an apron. An arched-brick side portico led into the facility, giving it much more character. Jazzi had heard that town officials, including the mayor, worked from offices on the second floor. Phineas Harding had designed the building when the resort town had started to take off, according to historical folklore.

Jazzi went inside the lobby and found a long, glassed-in reception desk to the right that was two-sided. Within the glassed-in area two doors led out of it, maybe into offices. To the left, Jazzi spotted a lineup of green vinyl chairs with two small black tables between them. A black door to the rear of the lobby probably led to more offices, maybe an interrogation room? She assumed the jail was also located at the rear of the building.

A police officer was seated at one sliding reception window and a woman at the other. She had headphones on. Maybe she was the dispatcher?

Jazzi approached the police officer, and he opened the window. She said simply, "I'd like to see Detective Milford. It's about the Brie Frazier murder."

The officer, whose badge said TAYLOR BLPD picked up the phone beside him and pressed a button. Less than a minute later, he pointed to the chairs and said, "Take a seat. He'll be out for you."

Most of the time, Jazzi did what she was supposed to do. She'd gotten good grades for herself and to earn her parents' approval, as well as listened when they gave her advice. With law enforcement, it was a given that she should do what they said. Crossing to the chairs, she sat and took out her phone, thinking she'd have a long wait. She was scrolling through her social media feeds when that big black door to the rear of the lobby opened.

Detective Milford headed straight for her. "Miss Swanson? This is a surprise."

"I think I have some information you might want."

With a raised brow he motioned to that big black door. "Let's go to the back and talk."

He must have put his sports jacket back on to come out and fetch her because the collar was turned under in the back. He did have an image to portray, she guessed. She also supposed for a murder investigation he was spending long hours here.

The door led to a hall with rooms to the right and to the left. He took her to the second room on the right, opened the door, and motioned her inside. She switched her phone to silent and slid it into her purse. After she followed him inside, she took a chair at the table. It was as big as a card table, and he sat on the other side.

He didn't try to engage in chitchat. He simply asked, "What do you have to tell me?"

"You said you don't have Brie's laptop or her phone. Will you subpoena her phone records?"

"We will. But that will take some time." He'd folded his hands on the table and now he looked down at them, and then back at her. "Miss Fabron said Brie mostly used her laptop for work. She thought Brie had a personal electronic tablet in addition to her missing laptop and phone. We didn't find that either. Do you have any idea where she might have kept it?"

"No idea at all," Jazzi said. "Do you think the killer took it?"

"What do you think?"

The detective's stare seemed to laser through her. It made her nervous. She supposed that's what he intended. "If he took her phone and laptop, he probably took the tablet too."

"You assume it's a *he*."

"Some strength would have been needed to strangle a woman. Am I right about that?"

"Did you Google the strength it takes to strangle someone?"

Jazzi decided not to answer.

"I'm going to ask you again, Miss Swanson. Why did you come today? To ask me questions or to give me information?"

She knew she was hesitating even while she was here. Finally she admitted, "I thought if you searched Brie's townhouse, you'd find the list of the men she'd dated."

He kept silent for a few moments. Then he turned aggressive again. "Is there something about a list I should know?"

"It was a list of men on a legal pad. If you found it, I believe it was a list of men she'd dated. She had gone out with a man the weekend before I had dinner with her. She said his name was Nolan Johnson."

The detective's body posture still told her he was examining every word she said. "Why do you think that information is important?"

"Because Brie had a bruise on her wrist. She was wearing a long-sleeved top the night we had dinner and I wondered why. When she pushed up her sleeve, I saw the bruise on her wrist."

"Did you ask her where she got it?"

"She said she'd had a mishap on her date."

"And the man's name was Nolan Johnson?"

"Yes."

"You've known this all along," he stated in a berating tone.

"Yes, I have. As I said, I had dinner with her and learned about it then."

"Then why didn't you tell me when I talked to you before?"

"Because I knew nothing for sure. Why would I sully a man's name without proof?"

"That's simple, Miss Swanson. The man could be a killer."

"Maybe, maybe not. Maybe it was just an accident. I know what gossip can do. I know what rumors can do. I wasn't going to be part of that. But I'm here now and I guess you should be glad about that." She stood, more than ready to leave.

He stood too. "Maybe I have more questions," he said gruffly.

"Do you?" she countered.

"Do you know anything else you're not telling me?"

She thought about the names she'd glimpsed on Brie's list. *Did* the detective have it? She knew he wouldn't confirm or deny. But she also remembered what Estelle had told her. "Brie's mom came to see me."

At that, he scowled. "Why would she do that?"

"She knew Dawn and I had talked to Brie about being adopted. She's worried, Detective. She's worried that someone in the Covino family might have hurt Brie. I suppose you're looking into them too?"

"I can't discuss the investigation," he said evenly, as if she hadn't heard him say that before.

"I understand," she acknowledged. Then she turned around and walked out of the room.

He didn't follow her. When she left the police station, she wondered if the detective would talk to Nolan Johnson and the Covino family. Could any of them be the killer?

Jazzi was using the eraser on the Tomes & Tea whiteboard on Thursday. Today their specials were peach crumb muffins and lemon ginger tea.

Erica came up beside her. "I might have to take some of those muffins home with me. I like everything from the Dock-side Bakery, but they are spectacular."

"We might have to call over there to see if they can supply more midday if they're that good." Jazzi hadn't yet tried one, but she believed Erica's assessment.

"Have you heard from Theo?" Erica asked with that concerned-mom look.

"I doubt if I will. I handled that so badly."

"But you were honest with him. That counts."

Jazzi doubted it. As she finished writing the specials on the board, Erica said, "I'm on the sales counter this morning. Dawn told me to put a flyer for Emilia Perez's book signing in every purchase bag."

"I expect the poster for the window to come special delivery this morning. We'll put it up as soon as it arrives. The copies of Emilia's book that I ordered came yesterday. I'll work on the display this morning. When Delaney comes in, I'm sure she'll give me ideas on how to make it even more eye-catching."

"I'm not sure you need ideas. You know how to display books."

Erica could always be counted on to be complimentary and positive. Jazzi appreciated that.

"Should I open our doors?" Erica stepped back to study the whiteboard.

Jazzi checked her watch. It was 9:59. Just as she answered Erica with a yes, the bell tower chimed ten o'clock.

Jazzi repositioned books on tables and shelves as she headed through the space to the storeroom. Once there, she pushed a carton she'd opened yesterday onto a dolly, wheeling it into the center of the store. She considered which table she'd use for Emilia's book display. They had a square one that could work. If she covered it with a royal-blue tablecloth, the look would be striking with the white cover of the book and the bold red lettering on the cover that stated *Runway Queen*.

After positioning the dolly where she intended to set the table, she swerved the box of books from it. Turning, she was about to wheel the dolly to the back when she heard her name called.

"Jazzi Swanson, don't run off. I need to talk to you."

The male voice was angry and determined. Audrey was panting as she ran to catch up to his long-legged stride.

"This man asked where you were."

"I'm right here," Jazzi said calmly and faced the man who'd asked her location. She recognized him from the night she'd seen him at The Wild Kangaroo. "How can I help you?"

"You can help me by staying out of my business. You can help me by keeping your mouth *shut*."

Audrey's face expressed shock and she was immobile. Jazzi slid her hand into the pocket of her royal-blue work apron and fingered her phone. "I might be able to help you if I knew what you were talking about."

If she was reasonable, maybe Nolan Johnson would be too. His red hair was gelled in place. He wore a white polo shirt and shorts. Although a frisson of panic rippled up her back, she stood her ground and squared her shoulders.

"As if you don't know. I know you had supper with Brie because I called her while you were there."

"Yes, Brie told me you called, Mr. Johnson."

"Of course, she did. You women don't know how to keep anything to yourselves. You think all the world has to hear about your private business. *You* talked to Detective Milford, didn't you? You're the one who gave him my name."

Jazzi kept quiet. Did Nolan know that for sure, or was he guessing? "I think you should leave."

"Or what?" When he took a few steps closer to her, Audrey gasped.

Jazzi removed her phone from her pocket.

He stared at it. "You'll mind your own business if you know what's good for you and your bookstore."

With that threat, Nolan Johnson spun around and strode away.

Thankful that only Audrey, Erica, and Dawn had witnessed the scene rather than her customers, Jazzi put her phone to her ear.

"What are you going to do?" Audrey asked, looking as shaken as Jazzi felt.

Dawn and Erica had joined them as Jazzi answered, "I'm calling Detective Milford."

She called the direct line that she'd entered into her phone after he'd given her his card. He answered on the first ring. "Milford."

"Detective, it's Jazzi Swanson. Nolan Johnson just came into the shop. He as much as threatened me. Even if I learn anything else, I won't come to you if you won't protect my privacy."

As Detective Milford stammered that he hadn't told Johnson she was the one who told him about Brie's bruise, Jazzi closed her eyes and wished none of this had ever happened. She wished Brie was still alive. She wished she wasn't involved. She wished she was skimming the water on her paddleboard, gazing at the waves and the horizon, away from the detective and murder and anyone who would want to hurt a beautiful young woman like Brie.

Chapter Eight

Every fifteen minutes the next day Jazzi made an announcement in the bookstore. "Take a selfie in your favorite spot in Tomes and Tea and post it on your social media. Show your post to Dawn and you'll receive a souvenir bag of our Belltower Blend tea."

Today was explicitly *Selfie Day*. Delaney had offered the idea to prepare customers for the big events coming up— Emilia Perez's book signing, Evan Holloway's concert, and the regatta weekend soon after. Delaney's thoughts were practical. If Tomes & Tea customers were used to taking selfies in the store, the habit would spill over to the big events. Jazzi hoped she was right. She knew the tea souvenir boxes that were ordered would help promote the store too, but they wouldn't be ready for another week. Along with the selfie posts with #tomesandtea, the shop's visibility would be raised.

As Jazzi straightened the books in one of the cubicles, a woman came up to her with a girl of about ten beside her. She had bright red hair and freckles, as did the child. Mother and daughter?

That was soon confirmed when she said, "Kelsey and I love your bookstore. She especially likes those lights in the shelves."

Kelsey nodded. "Mom said I should ask you about the book I want."

Jazzi crouched down to the child's height. "If we don't have it, I'm sure I can order it. What are you looking for?"

"I want *The Friendship Code*," she said, her head bobbing with certainty. "It's number one in the Girls Who Code series. It's about girls who like computers and friendship."

Jazzi grinned at Kelsey's complete knowledge of the book she was searching for. "Do you like computers?"

"I do," she acknowledged in an adult tone. "Mom says I know more about them than *she* does."

"That's true," her mom agreed.

"Come with me." Jazzi headed to the appropriate shelf. "We have the first three books as well as activity books for coding."

"We can take a selfie with the books," the woman told her daughter. "I'll post it on Instagram."

As mother and daughter found the book and took a selfie, Jazzi reminded them, "Don't forget to show Dawn and pick up your free tea."

The words were no sooner out of her mouth when she felt a hand on her arm. To her surprise when she turned, she was staring into the face of Rupert Harding, the mayor of Belltower Landing. Around fifty-five, he had a mop of white-gray hair, longish and expensively cut. Even so, it made his head appear very round. The lines under his eyes and around his mouth told her his job had its more serious aspects than simply sitting behind his desk.

A descendant of Phineas Harding, Rupert liked to stand out. Today he wore a tangerine-colored knit shirt and a tan fishing vest with hunter-green linen slacks. They were not made for fishing. His Italian leather loafers hadn't seen water either, but he was sockless as if he was ready to go wading on a moment's notice.

As usual he was accompanied by his nephew, Charles Harding, who was his chief of staff. Charles was around thirty-five. Unlike his uncle and boss, he wore his dirty blond hair cropped short. His white oxford shirt and navy slacks seemed like a uniform.

Both men were staring at her as Charles said, "We need to talk to you."

That sounded ominous, Jazzi thought. She motioned to the room's corner near the stock and break room, away from the activity and any customers.

"Do you really believe your *selfie* gimmick will even bring in business?" the mayor asked.

She was sure this visit wasn't about her store's events. "It is today. Would you like a cup of tea or a muffin?"

Charles vehemently shook his head, but Rupert just lifted his hand in dismissal. "Not today."

"My uncle received a complaint about you," Charles blurted out.

"Really?" Jazzi returned. "Who complained?" She couldn't imagine that anyone had brought up her name to the mayor. Had she jaywalked too many times?

Rupert took over. "Miss Swanson, Nolan Johnson complained. He said you sullied his name. Nolan stays for the summer at a premier Belltower Landing resort. His golfing expertise brings tourists to town to learn his techniques. He even holds teaching seminars that fill up the conference room at the community center. Believe me, we don't want him taking his following to another resort town."

Jazzi was almost speechless. Almost. The mayor was berating *her* when the man in question had threatened her.

Holding on to her very long fuse, she took two deep breaths.

"Mr. Mayor, I appreciate the position you're in. But maybe Mr. Johnson didn't tell you that he threatened me. I gave the detective pertinent information. That should not have brought the man to my store where he thought he could bully me."

Charles sidled closer to her. She didn't like the smell of his clingy cologne, and she took a step away.

Charles scowled. "You took Nolan's comment the wrong way. You're too sensitive. After all, you put the man's character in question. How would you like to be called into the police station and questioned?"

"I had my interviews with Detective Milford. I told him the truth."

The mayor became more conciliatory than his chief of staff. "I'm sure Nolan did too. I just want you to be aware that your actions can cause unfounded rumors. We wouldn't want that to happen, would we? Be aware, Miss Swanson. That's all."

With that last admonition, the mayor and his chief of staff swept out of the store.

Jazzi felt like . . . pulling a few books from the shelves and throwing them.

But adult that she was, she stood right there and counted to one hundred. Still, smoke must have been puffing from under her French braid because Erica brought her a cup of tea. "It's raspberry vanilla. It could help you think sweet thoughts."

Jazzi wrinkled her nose at Erica but accepted the tea.

Parker, who apparently had been browsing, crossed to Jazzi with a perplexed expression. "That was the mayor."

The surprise in Parker's voice almost made Jazzi smile. But she was still perturbed enough to throw a few books. "I think he was here to warn me not to talk to Detective Milford about any residents he believes are prominent."

"Excuse me?" Parker asked with annoyance.

Jazzi explained what the mayor and his nephew had to say.

"You're upset, and rightly so. Maybe you should just stay away from the investigation," Parker advised her.

"I intended to do just that."

Parker picked up on the tense right away. "You *intended* to?" His tone was worried.

"The thing is, Parker, how effective can the investigation be if the mayor steps in? How will Brie get justice that way?"

Although Jazzi didn't drive much in Belltower Landing—she usually walked or rode her bike—she drove her Mini Cooper at least once a week to make sure all ran smoothly. Today she drove with Dawn to the Forsythe Family Funeral Home and Crematorium. "Have you ever been here before?"

Dawn nodded. "Once when my paternal grandfather died. It's quite a complex."

A long driveway spread in front of a white pillared portico. They parked in a lot beside the two-story main building.

Dawn spread her arms wide toward the structure. "That's the original funeral home. The Forsythe family added the chapel and other rooms as well as the crematorium that stretches to the east. Corey Forsythe, Alan Forsythe's son, lives on that second floor." She raised her hand toward the floor's balcony. "I think it would be creepy to live there."

Or spiritual, Jazzi thought. They were both silent as they considered living above the funeral parlor and what they were about to participate in.

Last evening, Estelle Frazier had phoned Jazzi to check if she and Dawn would be attending Brie's funeral today. She'd said, "Delaney will be coming. But she's falling apart like I am. Of course, Harry will be with me. But he's so broken up about Brie's murder, he's zoned out. If I cry, I doubt if he'll notice. He's in his own sad world. I need someone there for support. The service will be so hard. I don't want to fall apart."

"Will there be a private viewing?" Jazzi had asked, knowing funeral services could take many forms.

"Yes, I . . ."

Jazzi had heard Estelle's voice crack.

After Estelle had composed herself, she'd said, "I'll manage that with Harry, but it will just be the two of us in the funeral home's chapel. Two of your friends volunteered to be pallbearers, Parker Olsen and Derek Stewart. One of Harry's poker buddies will help too and the funeral home will provide the others. They'll carry the casket to the room for the service and lay it at graveside. I just . . ."

As Estelle stopped to find her voice again, Jazzi waited. "My doctor said he could prescribe something to calm my nerves," Brie's mother had confided. "I don't want it. I want to be alert and remember what's happening. Harry took something last night. He looked groggy this morning. He prefers to try to sleep through this awful time."

Jazzi could somewhat understand all of the emotions Estelle was feeling. She could understand Harry Frazier's too. Jazzi had been a preteen when her adoptive father had died of cancer and she'd been devastated. She'd wanted to go to bed and pull the covers over her head. But her mother and sister wouldn't let her. Still, for years, her grief had been a quiet but deep sadness she hadn't dealt with . . . not until she'd decided to search for her birth mother. Somehow she'd wanted to fill that hole in her life that had almost swallowed her.

She'd told Estelle, "Dawn and I will be there. You can count on us."

Remembering that promise, Jazzi fit her keys into her purse and she said to Dawn, "Let's go inside."

The double doors at the side entrance led into a well-equipped lobby with a patterned area rug over a polished wood floor. A few people sat on the right side on love seats positioned around a dark wood coffee table. A round pedestal table surrounded by caned chairs was located on the other side.

Dawn nudged Jazzi. "That's Corey Forsythe, Alan's son."

The finely suited man welcomed everyone as they came in the door and said, "The service will begin in ten minutes if you'd like to sign the guest book and make your way to our reception room."

As Corey suggested, Dawn and Jazzi signed the guest book. Following Corey's direction, they went to the large room with upholstered high-back chairs. At once it was easy to see many men and women were dressed in black. Brie's friends, however, a younger crowd, had worn an assortment of colors. Jazzi had chosen a violet and white patterned blouse with a dark violet pencil skirt. Dawn had worn navy linen slacks and a pale blue short-sleeved sweater.

No sooner had they stepped into the room than Estelle, who must have been watching for them, stood from her seat in the front row and came to the rear of the room. Her face looked ravaged with grief. In a black dress with her face pale and eyes glistening behind her tortoiseshell glasses, she looked absolutely lost. She pointed to the front of the room. "Come sit in the front row with us."

The man seated on the left aisle in the first row had his head bowed.

"Harry can't even look at the casket," Estelle said. "The young woman Brie worked with, Lara, is sitting beside him, Delaney beside her. We don't belong to a church per se, that's why we're having the service here. Apparently Mr. Forsythe handles many funerals."

Jazzi attended the Community Chapel that was ecumenical in nature. But not as often as she'd like. She patted Estelle's shoulder. "Let's sit. I'm sure Mr. Forsythe will celebrate Brie's life."

During the service, tears rolled down Estelle's face while her husband sat stoic. She reached over and held on to Jazzi's arm so tightly Estelle's pudgy fingers had white knuckles.

Mr. Forsythe spoke about Brie's outgoing nature and made Brie's sunny personality evident as he relayed stories from her childhood and teenage years that Estelle must have related to him. After he finished, he read Bible verses the Fraziers had chosen. He ended with, "We will proceed to the graveside service at Mount Cedar Cemetery. First, however, take a few moments to share your memories of Brie with each other."

The room was quiet until a few minutes later when lowered voices became louder chatter. Parker and Derek came over to Estelle and her husband to give their condolences once more. Jazzi assumed the man around Harry's age who stopped to speak to him was his poker buddy who'd volunteered to be a pallbearer.

Jazzi didn't think she'd ever seen Parker in a suit before, though she knew he probably wore one for his consultation gigs. She mentally shrugged. Maybe not.

Dawn must have been thinking the same thing because she joked to Parker, "Did you have to buy a suit?"

Moving toward them, allowing a woman Estelle knew to step close to her to talk, Parker gave them a slow smile. "I have a few suits. When I'm not in Belltower Landing, I let my business persona take over."

"He hobnobs with some influential CEOs," Derek gibed. Then he lowered his voice. "They know he can burn through their systems' firewalls."

Jazzi took a longer look at Parker. He was humble, never stating outright how much he'd accomplished at the ripe old age of twenty-seven.

Suddenly Jazzi heard a loud male voice to the left of them. Harry was facing off with a taller man who wore a dark navy pin-striped suit, white shirt, and navy tie. The funeral director was standing with them, looking worried. The tall man didn't look much older than Harry, but the two men were opposites in appearance.

As Estelle approached the object of Harry's ire, Alan Forsythe leaned close to her to tell her something. Maybe who the man was who had Harry upset? Jazzi noticed his regal bearing of him as well as the style of the short-cropped gray hair. Something about his nose and jawline and his blue eyes seemed familiar. Estelle looked terribly concerned, even stiffly distant. That was unlike Estelle from what Jazzi had seen of her.

Harry's friend pulled him away as Estelle said in a frosty polite voice, loud enough for Jazzi to hear, "Thank you for coming, Mr. Covino."

Covino? Brie's biological father?

Jazzi could hear Harry muttering to his friend, "He gave her away. He shouldn't even be here."

Estelle turned to Jazzi as if she needed her support. Uncertain, Jazzi stepped up beside her as Estelle introduced her to the man. "Jazzi was one of Brie's friends."

"Jazzi," Mr. Covino said with a small smile. "Please call me Joseph. Brie told me about you. She said because of you, she decided to meet me. Thank you." He shot a disappointed look at Harry. "You'd think on this day Brie's two fathers could be civil."

Harry had stopped grumbling but stared at Joseph Covino as if he was certainly an interloper.

Joseph turned back to Jazzi and Estelle. "I only knew Brie a very short time."

Catching sight of the tears in the man's eyes, Jazzi felt for him. How awful to begin to get to know a daughter, to start to relate to her, then to have her snatched away.

Estelle's expression became sympathetic as if she understood. Her husband had made the first meeting more uncomfortable than it had to be. She reached her hand up to Harry to draw him into the conversation, but he took a step back.

With a sigh that spoke of his weariness and grief, Joseph gave up on enlisting Harry's understanding. "I know this isn't the time or place to have a conversation about Brie. I wanted my two children to come with me today, but they didn't want to intrude on your private moments. I wish you'd both . . ." He directed a glance to Harry. "I wish you'd both come to my home so we could have a real conversation. I learned things today about Brie that she didn't have the chance to tell me."

When no one seemed to know how to respond, Joseph asked Estelle, "Can I have your phone number? We really should get together at some point."

Estelle didn't hesitate when he took out his phone. She rattled off her number and he tapped it in.

"I will be in touch," he assured her. Then he stepped away as if he didn't want to cause more commotion.

Jazzi would like to hear Joseph Covino's story. It would have been important to Brie.

As Estelle moved close to her husband, Jazzi saw that people were heading out of the room. Parker and Derek had joined Corey Forsythe at the casket.

Jazzi suddenly caught sight of someone else she recognized—Detective Milford. He watched Joseph Covino leave the room and he turned his gaze toward Harry and Estelle. Just what had the detective thought about what had happened? More important, had he known suspects on his list might be here today? Who was he watching most carefully?

Late that evening, the marina was a plethora of sights, sounds, and smells. Boats from pontoons to cabin cruisers came and went from their slips, engines revving and sometimes horns blaring. Far out in the lake Jazzi could spot sailboat masts. The scents of damp grass and fish rode on the breeze, but they mingled with food truck aromas—from savory to sweet—funnel cakes, barbecued ribs, hot wings, tamales, sweet potato frites, and cup-cakes.

After Tomes & Tea closed, Jazzi had met Delaney in front of the community center. A boardwalk stretched in front of the center to the areas around the marina and boat supply store. The boarded area had been laid to be a gathering place. At night residents could play music, mingle, and catch dinner from the food trucks that lined up across from the marina. For the Welcome Summer Festival, Jazzi guessed there would be evening events planned that would bring scores of residents down to the space.

Delaney was still wearing the clothes she'd had on for the funeral . . . white slacks, a bright pink blouse, and a white shrug. Before meeting Delaney, Jazzi had stopped at her place to change into a short halter-necked sundress in a gauzy teal material. They strolled toward the food trucks without talking and Jazzi suspected they were both thinking about the funeral service.

Delaney finally spoke. "It was so sad, wasn't it? I can't believe Brie isn't in my life anymore."

Jazzi bumped her shoulder against her friend's. "I learned more about Brie today. It sounds like she always had an outgoing personality."

"She could be a party girl the past few years," Delaney admitted, adjusting her crossover bag on her shoulder. "I've never known her dad to be as volatile as he was today."

"I think he scared Estelle. I wonder if he knew Joseph Covino's story—why Brie was adopted—if that would make a difference. Did Brie tell you anything about it?"

With a sorrowful expression, Delaney shook her head. "Maybe she thought I wouldn't understand that type of abandonment. Now I wish she had told me."

"There are always regrets when we lose someone."

"I forget that you know about that."

At the food trucks now, they decided what they were ordering for supper. Several picnic tables were occupied but a few were vacant. It was the type of balmy June night when being outside was a pleasure.

Delaney chose a truck where she could order falafel. Jazzi gravitated toward the waffle truck. The cook put two waffles together to form a pocket. Then the pocket was filled with anything from omelets to sweet desserts. Jazzi ordered the omelet-filled waffle pocket with bacon and broccoli.

Delaney who was mostly a vegetarian laughed. "Do you think that's healthy because of the broccoli?"

"Yes." The simple answer brought a laugh from them both.

Once they were seated with drinks and food, Delaney studied her falafel wrapped in pita bread with tomatoes, cucumbers, and a topping sauce. She picked it up and took a bite. Jazzi did the same with her waffle.

After wiping her fingers, Delaney took a drink from her water bottle. "I want to add some enhancements from Tomes and Tea to the Welcome Summer celebration."

"How?" Jazzi wiped a spot of cheese from her lip.

"It would be an advantage for your shop to donate two or three baskets filled with bookstore items and teas for the silent auction."

"I think Dawn will agree to do that. Everyone who bids will see the tea in the new boxes as well as the books. Maybe we could do a romance basket, a thriller basket, and an activity book basket."

"Add some pamphlets about items you'll be promoting, maybe for the virtual reality games. Tourists often buy items on vacation they might not buy the rest of the year. You want to do anything that will pull them into your store to look. Are you making sure your website address is printed on the tea boxes?"

"For sure."

After they finished eating and stowed their trash, they started walking back toward the community center. Jazzi asked Delaney, "Do you want to stop at the green?"

"I don't know," Delaney said. "I'm still feeling sad. I don't know what I want to do."

"Why don't you come back to the apartment with me? You can play with the kittens. Maybe we'll play a board game. You know, old school."

Delaney smiled at that. "Kittens and a board game sound good."

Chapter Nine

The next morning around ten, Jazzi was surprised to see a text from Theo Carstead. **Meet me at the bell tower on your break?**

Hmm. What could Theo want to discuss? She should find out. Maybe they could be friends after all. She texted back. **At two?**

He sent a thumbs-up emoji.

Before she slipped out of the store, she told Erica she was going to take a walk and she'd be back in half an hour. Erica gave her a probing look but didn't ask questions. She did seem to have a sixth sense. She'd probably developed it with her kids.

Lakeview Boulevard was busy with tourists dawdling as they enjoyed the weather and the relaxed atmosphere. So much in Belltower Landing this time of year was all about the tourists, pleasing and catering to them.

Jazzi crossed the boulevard at a light and headed for the green. Often anyone who worked in the shops and downtown businesses brought takeout with them to the benches for lunch or breaks. She'd buy a wrap at the deli after her meet with Theo.

He was waiting by the arch at the bell tower, dressed in jeans and a red tee. Jazzi tried to gauge his expression. He wasn't smiling but he wasn't frowning either. His unruly hair waved over his brow and dipped over his hazel eyes.

As she approached, he stood straighter and motioned to the closest empty bench. She joined him there and they sat side by side about four inches apart.

"This isn't awkward at all, is it?" Jazzi quipped.

At that Theo tried to suppress a smile. "Not much. Look, I understand somewhat why you don't want to date. I'm not much more than a tourist here for the summer."

"I'm glad you understand. I truly didn't intend to mislead you." Studying Theo's cleft chin, she thought again about how handsome he was . . . how it would be easy to be attracted to him.

His shoulder brushed hers as he turned toward her on the bench. "The bottom line is that you were honest with me. I can respect that. So I made a call to Evan Holloway's publicist."

Her jaw almost dropped. Finally, with her senses coming alive again she asked, "You did?"

This time Theo gave her a full smile. "I did. I spoke to Phil about Evan's schedule when he comes to town for the Welcome Summer Festival. He'd left time for Evan to check out the shops. In other words, to be seen as an ordinary guy. So they can fit in a visit to Tomes and Tea. It will be some time in the afternoon on Saturday. They'll give me a heads-up right before it happens."

"Oh, Theo, thank you! That's wonderful news." She wanted to hug him but didn't think that was wise given the circumstances.

After his eyes studied her for a few moments, he said, "You'd better soup up your music history section on your shelves. Evan's thoroughly immersed in it."

"I can do that. In fact, I have the opportunity to pick up

books at an old house. There's a whole library of books on all subjects. The owner was a history buff. Who knows what I might find."

"Do you want company? It could be a joint venture. After all, you might need someone to carry the books."

As she studied Theo, she wondered if they *could* be friends simply for the summer. After all, he'd done her and her shop a huge favor. Dawn was going to be thrilled, and Jazzi was grateful to propel Tomes & Tea to a new level. "Sure, you can come with me. We might even find a valuable book in the lot. You never know."

"No, you never know," Theo agreed. "It sounds like fun. Text me the deets when you have them."

She would. She found she was even looking forward to the outing.

"This is only one of his estates," Estelle whispered to Jazzi as they made their way from the circular driveway to the huge double front door of Joseph Covino's residence. Even driving up the lane from the road, Jazzi could see the immense lake house with its creative stonework, peaked roofs, glass, and decks. It was everything a lake house should be and more.

Last night Estelle had phoned Jazzi and said, "I received an invitation from Joseph Covino to meet with him at his house, but Harry won't go with me. I asked Delaney but she has client meetings tomorrow. Will you come with me? I want to find out more about him. Brie would have wanted that."

Jazzi hadn't been so sure what Brie would have wanted, yet she knew Estelle needed to do this. So here they were at this beautiful house on Lake Harding. The property achieved privacy by being bound by arborvitae hedges.

One side of the mahogany double doors opened and Joseph stood there with a somber expression. "I'm so glad you could come. Come in."

Jazzi and Estelle walked into the ceramic-tiled foyer. With a welcoming gesture, Joseph motioned them through a wide arch into the open concept layout. Gazing straight ahead, Jazzi at once was enthralled by the cathedral ceiling and the wall of glass at the other end of the great room that faced the lake. A formal dining room to the right of the great room also looked out over a deck.

Muted voices came from the kitchen area. Turning that way, Jazzi caught sight of a svelte blonde who could have been around fifty. She wore plenty of makeup to hide the lines Jazzi guessed were there. With her was a young man around Jazzi's age. He had a deep tan and almost white long hair, probably bleached by the sun. He wore his hair tied back with a leather band. With his head bent to the woman beside him who was younger, he looked like an older brother telling his sister a secret. That was confirmed when Joseph introduced his family.

Beaming toward the kitchen, Joseph beckoned to his wife. "Connie, come meet Estelle Frazier and Jazzi Swanson. Estelle is Brie's mom, and Jazzi was her friend."

The three of them came from behind the marble-clad kitchen island. Connie extended her hand to Estelle but there wasn't any particular warmth in her eyes when she said, "I'm sorry for your loss."

It was an automatic condolence.

"These are Connie's children—mine too—Damon and Andrea." Joseph capped his stepson's shoulder. "I have the pleasure of working with Damon every day. He joined me at my investment firm two years ago."

"It took him a few years until he trusted me," Damon wisecracked.

His mother admonished him. "Damon!"

"You know he's right, Mom," Andrea chimed in.

Joseph smiled at his stepdaughter. "Andrea is still trying to find her path."

"I found it," Andrea snapped, her purple highlighted bob swinging along her cheeks. "I'm going to design pontoon boats."

"Good luck getting a job," Damon quipped. "It's a good thing Joseph can keep you in designer bikinis."

"What about your Tesla?" she shot back.

Connie looked embarrassed, the first genuine expression Jazzi had spotted on her face.

"Come on, you two. We'll let Joseph have some privacy with his guests."

"You don't have to leave . . ." Joseph began.

"We have court time scheduled," his wife said, crossing to Joseph and giving him a kiss on the cheek. "We'll see you later. I'll whip up some of those espresso martinis you're so fond of when I get back."

And just like that, after a flurry of good-byes, Joseph's family left.

Dressed casually today in jeans and a pink polo shirt, Joseph looked right at home in his surroundings. With the ease of a good host, he directed Estelle and Jazzi to the modular arrangement with the sofa and chaise near the windows. He took the comfy-looking massage chair at the fireplace. "They're always on the run," he said of his family. "Some weeks I hardly see them with my work schedule."

Up until now Estelle had been quiet, obviously taking in the Covinos' lifestyle. "You should make time to be with them. You never know when that time will be taken away."

He nodded. "Yes, I suppose you're right. I never expected to find someone to love when I was in my fifties. I should appreciate Connie, Andrea, and Damon more."

"How long have you been married?" Jazzi asked.

He didn't seem bothered by her question. "I married Connie eight years ago. I adopted her kids officially around six years ago."

"When we adopted Brie," Estelle said, looking sad, "I was

told that her mother died in childbirth. There were no relatives who could take care of her so she was put into the foster system. Harry and I had been trying to adopt for a few years, and we found her. It was wonderful. *She* was wonderful. Can you tell me what happened? Why she was put up for adoption?"

The silence was oppressive until Joseph rubbed his hand over his face. His history was obviously difficult.

"I was a graduate student at Princeton when my girlfriend, Gilda North, got pregnant. She lived in Belltower Landing. We'd spent a few weekends here. I married her and I told her I'd stand by her. But she died in childbirth. Her parents had been killed in an accident. She didn't have anyone. My mother and father were divorced and traveling separately. I didn't know what to do. So I gave up Brie. It's not a pretty story, and I should have taken more responsibility then, but I didn't. It's good to know Brie had a good life with you. Even though I was happy with Connie and my new family, I felt guilty all these years. I had moved here and I couldn't stop thinking about my little girl and what happened to her. When I turned sixty, I subscribed to that adoption website that fostered reunions. I couldn't believe it when I connected with Brie . . . that she'd been looking for me too."

"She told me you emailed a few times before she came to meet you."

"That's right. Then we met here and we spoke for hours. We connected. I started to love her that day."

Jazzi couldn't help but ask, "Did Andrea, Damon, and your wife meet Brie then?"

"No. But they did during my next meeting with her the following morning for brunch. Andrea seemed to connect with her, though Brie was older. It always takes Damon longer to warm up to people, but I'm sure he would have loved Brie eventually."

Although she shouldn't judge from first impressions, Jazzi wondered about that.

There were framed photos of Andrea and Damon on all the tables and on the bookshelves—pictures of them on boats, in kayaks, and swimming. Joseph noticed Jazzi looking at the photos.

"I like to have reminders around of what a fortunate man I am . . . to have this family. But . . ." He hesitated and he turned to Estelle. "Do you have a photo of Brie that I can frame and hang? I'd like to have one here. I had every intention of changing my will to include her, and I told her that. I wanted her to be my real daughter, not someone I'd met and then let pass through my life. I told her I'd give her my medical records, but I never had a chance to do that, either. I'm so sorry about that. I've been calling the police every day to find out if they have any leads. But they don't."

"Maybe you calling them will make more of an impression than me calling them," Estelle said, obviously certain of that fact.

What Joseph had said about including Brie in his will had caused Jazzi's chest to tighten. What if that was the reason Brie had been murdered?

Still feeling embarrassed about her pretense with Theo, Jazzi agreed to let him drive her to the property where she could choose the books she wanted before the rest went to auction. He pulled up in a flashy yellow BMW convertible that had a slightly green tint to it.

She slipped into the leather seat, catching the scent of his cologne—musk and patchouli. "Cool color car." She suddenly realized being a DJ for important clients must pay well.

"It's called Sao Paulo yellow. I wanted something distinctive."

"Do you know where we're going?" She'd given him the address but wondered if he was familiar with the area.

"GPS is great for that," he quipped.

She laughed.

"No parties out here, if that's what you mean."

Jazzi soon saw that "out here" was a drive into the forest about fifteen miles away from the center of Belltower Landing. She hadn't really explored this area where several multimillion-dollar properties were located. As they drove, Theo talked about some of the parties he'd helped rev up with his deejaying expertise in Reno, Las Vegas—and Nashville, where he'd met Evan Holloway.

"He's really an upfront guy," Theo assured her. "He'll take his visit to your store seriously. He loves to interact with fans. He'll never forget those days when he started out with an audience of ten."

They talked about music. Theo listened as she revealed how she'd refined her taste in music from her preteen years in Florida to high school favorites in Willow Creek to her college years in Delaware. By then they were driving up a winding road through white pines, birch trees, and soaring oaks.

The two-vehicle road they'd driven on ended in a wide driveway with a four-car garage. The house, built in the 1930s, was traditional yet rustic, wood atop stone that rose three stories high.

Theo whistled. "What a beauty."

"I'd seen photos," Jazzi said, "but they could never capture *this*. The house is pretty much empty except for the library," she added. "The owner believes books should be available to everyone, especially the classics. He already donated stacks to the library but they didn't have room for more. He doesn't want to see the rest trashed. Dawn's parents hooked us up. I can take what I want to sell."

"Are you going to need a truck?" Theo joked.

"Actually no. Apparently boxes are available in the house and the owner will have them delivered to Tomes and Tea."

"That's service."

"From what Dawn told me he's an old-fashioned guy. He just

wants his property handled well. The real estate agent will be staging the home this week, then it will be put on the market."

At the thick, wide, oak-paneled door, Jazzi rang the bell. She could hear it echoing from inside the house.

The door opened and Jazzi faced a man who Dawn had described as old . . . in his seventies. "Mr. Thurgood Denten?"

"Yes, indeed," he responded. "You must be Jazzi. I spoke to the Fernsbys about you and their daughter Dawn."

"Dawn's managing the store today, so I brought my friend Theo with me to look over the rest of your books."

"Splendid," Mr. Denten said, now shaking Theo's hand. "I have vinyl records in the collection too. I don't suppose you'd be interested in those? The library didn't want them."

"I'm certainly interested," Theo said. "I have a huge collection of vinyl."

"Feel free to take what you like. Even my grandkids don't want them. Let me show you to the library."

The house was as magnificent inside as it had been outside. Those large Palladian windows let in tons of light. The foyer's terrazzo floor led into a hallway. To the right was a massive living room with floor-to-ceiling windows that looked out onto the forest and the land to the side of the house. Mature bushes and shrubs dotted the landscape from holly to hinoki cypress to blue spruce at the border. Since Jazzi's grandparents had owned a nursery, she recognized many trees, plants, and shrubs.

The left led to another living space with a monumental fieldstone fireplace. Beyond that, Jazzi glimpsed a gourmet kitchen with top-of-the-line appliances and a huge breakfast nook. The hand-cut stone finishes, the rich wood floors, and the high ceilings made the home grand. But as they entered the library, Jazzi didn't think anything was as grand as this. It was two stories. A wooden staircase led up to the mezzanine-like area that also had shelves of books. A massive carved desk sat downstairs in front of more bookcases filled with tomes and tomes. Jazzi couldn't wait to start looking through them.

As soon as Mr. Denten said, "I'll leave you to it," and left, Theo turned to Jazzi. "This place has more books than your bookstore."

Jazzi could spot the empty shelves, the gaps where books had been taken out to send to the library. "Imagine growing up with this." Her voice was filled with awe. She was automatically drawn to a shelf with leather-bound volumes. She pulled one from those that had slipped to the side as if one or more had been taken away from the shelf.

"Have you ever read *Treasure Island*?" she asked Theo.

"Afraid not. Books weren't a big part of my childhood. I suppose somebody read you *Goodnight Moon*, or whatever the latest thing was back then?"

He was teasing but she answered seriously, "One of my favorite bedtime stories was *Good Night, Baby Bear*. A mama bear finds the perfect spot for them to go to sleep for the winter but baby doesn't want to fall asleep."

"And did *you* fall asleep?"

"It must have worked. I'm a normal kid, right?"

He laughed. "I remember music. My dad played everything—Miles Davis, the Beatles, Dave Brubeck, Rihanna, Eminem, even Faith Hill. You know her song 'Breathe'?"

"I do. I'm all over the place now with Spotify—country, pop, alternative. As a preteen, I was into Maroon Five and Adele. Then later Ed Sheeran, and of course Taylor Swift."

He laughed. "Of course."

She'd moved to another shelf that was a mixture of hardbacks and paperbacks. "Oh, Mary Stewart!" she said with admiration. "*This Rough Magic . . . The Crystal Cave.* I might have to keep that one for myself."

"No clue," Theo said as he moved toward wider shelves that held vinyl albums. He started fingering through them, then pulled a few out. "You really don't care about the vinyls?" he asked.

"No, not for Tomes and Tea. You can take what you want. There used to be a store where I lived called Guitars and Vinyl. The store was filled with plenty of guitars and lots of vinyl. I used to go in there now and then. My mom knew the manager. I had a small vinyl collection at one time, but when I left for college I sold them back."

Before she turned to go up the stairs to the second floor of shelves, she studied the desk. "Look at this desk. My stepfather would love this. He crafts his own furniture."

"Is it anything like this?" He looked at the engravings on the drawers.

"No. He does mostly kitchen islands with reclaimed wood and granite, that type of thing. He's good. But that feels like an entire life ago." Before she started up the stairs, Theo put his hand on her elbow.

"You're fun to be around. Are you sure you're not dating anybody?"

"I'm really not." Looking into Theo's handsome face, she actually thought about dating him. He was a good conversationalist, and they were having an okay time. Still . . .

She remembered the hurt after Mark had broken up with her. She remembered the death of her adoptive father to cancer and how hard that was to get through. She remembered how she'd felt after she found out her biological father had been killed in service in Afghanistan. Her heart just didn't want to take the lumps and bumps a relationship would bring her. It was as simple and as complicated as that.

Chapter Ten

In the storeroom at closing time, Jazzi sorted a new supply of romance novels that would fill bookshelves in Tomes & Tea tomorrow. She considered the books she'd selected at the Denten house. They'd either fill shelves in one section or she'd spread them throughout the store.

Engrossed in her plans, she wasn't prepared for Delaney practically flying through the storeroom door in tears. She seemed harried as well as grief-stricken.

Usually Delaney dressed impeccably but this evening her hair looked windblown, the boat neckline of her peach blouse listed to the right, and her lipstick was smudged. Even her beaded necklace with a gold medallion was turned askew. Over her arm Delaney carried a denim jacket with fringed sleeves and hem, not her style at all.

"Oh, Jazzi, you're not going to believe what I found!"

Jazzi held Delaney by the shoulders. "What's wrong?"

Delaney raised up the jacket. "Brie came over to my place the day before she died."

"I know. Is that why the police have brought you in for questioning so often?"

"I suppose . . . and because I found her. I probably had the most contact with her of anyone."

"What happened when she visited you?"

"Nothing much. I don't think she wanted to be by herself at her place. I wasn't sure why. Now maybe I do know why." She lifted the jacket again.

"I don't understand." Jazzi still didn't know why Delaney was upset or why she was here.

Delaney shook the jacket at Jazzi. "This is Brie's. She forgot it. I found it in the back seat of my car. She'd tossed it there when we went for lunch. I didn't notice it until this afternoon. It had slipped to the floor. It still . . ." Delaney choked up then went on. "It still smells like her perfume."

Jazzi hugged Delaney tightly, hoping to give her comfort, but Delaney pushed away and raised the jacket between them again. Then she pulled a wadded piece of paper from the pocket of the jacket. Handing it to Jazzi, she whispered, "I don't know what to do with this."

"Did you look at it?"

Delaney nodded. "Read it."

From the sound of her friend's voice, Jazzi knew she probably didn't want to read it. Carefully unwadding the smashed paper, Jazzi pressed her finger around the edges to straighten it. The paper was pale green and, from the perforation at the top, looked to be from a tear-off notepad.

It read:

We don't want or need you in our family. We know you just want our dad's money. You won't get it. Leave us alone so no one gets hurt.

The note was unsigned but it was obvious who had sent it or delivered it to Brie. "Did Brie talk to you about this?"

"No." Delaney carefully laid the jacket over a stack of boxes. "Brie seemed distracted when she stopped by," Delaney revealed. "I was working and hadn't intended to take a lunch break but she convinced me to do it. She seemed uptight and didn't eat much for lunch. We went to Vibes and ate outside. She got hot and took off her jacket."

Jazzi sank down on a chair at the break table. Vibes was a popular lunch spot overlooking the lake not far from the marina. It was one of Brie's favorite spots apparently . . . and Delaney's too.

"Then she just left it in your car?" she asked Delaney.

"Yes."

"I wonder if the note was hand delivered." Jazzi suddenly let the paper drop onto the table. "It's evidence."

"Do you think someone in the Covino family hurt her?" Delaney seemed to be horror-stricken at the thought.

"It looks like it's possible, doesn't it?" Jazzi didn't want to think about it any more than Delaney did. But it definitely was a possibility.

Suddenly Jazzi knew what they had to do. "There's nothing *we* can do about this." She rose from the chair and went to the tall cupboard in the corner of the storeroom that stood next to the mini-fridge. Reaching inside, she plucked out a ziplock bag from the box. Using a napkin from a holder on the table, she picked up the note and pushed it into the open bag.

She zipped it closed. "We're taking this to the police station. Detective Milford can handle it. Our fingerprints are on it, but they have yours. They can always take mine if they want to eliminate me."

"Eliminate you?" Delaney asked.

"Yes. They can check whatever other prints are on the note. Come on, let's walk it over now."

In the store window the next day, Jazzi rearranged the book display, knowing she had to keep it fresh. She turned when she felt someone approach. It was Erica.

"Did you come to help?" Jazzi teased over her shoulder.

"Do you need help? I have teas sorted for tonight."

Tomes & Tea would be open later than usual that evening. They were having a tea tasting. Customers could come in and go from teapot to teapot where Dawn, Audrey, and Erica would pour tea for them to taste. Customers who texted their preference to Jazzi's burner phone, used for this purpose, could win a twenty-five-dollar gift card. It kept customers and Jazzi's sales force chatting and interacting.

"No, I don't need help here. Traffic should pick up late morning when the lunch crowd stops to browse."

"And buy," Erica said. "Sales are up. June is usually a good month."

Jazzi straightened. As her hair flowed over her shoulder, she repositioned the book about children's feelings and how to elicit and accept them.

She faced Erica, and the older woman laid her hand on Jazzi's arm. "You're worried whether Dawn will sell out her share of the store."

Yes, she was. Could she keep the shop afloat on her own? Could she interest someone else in a partnership? She didn't want to, but she had to be realistic about it. "I'm more worried about keeping sales thriving in fall and winter. If we see an increase in customers with our online business, we might be okay. It doesn't matter what season it is for the customers to buy books and tea online. They just have to know that we're here. We'll need incentives for them to use us. That's what we need to think about."

"Have you brought this up at a chamber of commerce meeting? We can't be the only small business having this problem."

Jazzi knew the problem with bringing it up there. Some businesses were only open for the tourist season. "I'm sure we're not the only ones. The question is always how much do we gear our store's attention toward the tourists and how much to Belltower Landing's residents who are our bread and butter."

Erica leaned closer to Jazzi and kept her voice low. "Do you think the murder will affect the town's tourist trade?"

How awful to have to even think in those terms. "I don't know. We haven't been inundated with the press since it happened. Delaney said there were news vans at Brie's town house. I don't know if Estelle has been bothered by them. Unfortunately the press won't shine a light on Brie's murder for long. They'll hop to the next crime that captures their interest."

Erica's brows raised and she looked perplexed. "I guess you've been paying attention to news cycles."

Yes, she'd paid attention to news cycles in Willow Creek, Pennsylvania, too. She'd had to keep her eye on them since her mom had often been involved in them. But not so much here until now. Even so, the town had some rich high-caliber news makers, and the press followed *them*.

When Jazzi didn't respond, Erica kept her voice low. "Delaney told me about the note she found in Brie's jacket. Has the detective contacted you?"

Jazzi had been astonished that he hadn't. "No, but I left a note with the baggie, and Delaney sent him a text telling him where she found it."

"Hmph," Erica grunted as if she expected better from the police department.

"For all we know, Detective Milford might have so many leads he can't follow them all."

"You're giving him the benefit of the doubt. The older I get, the less I do that. Someone might have to make some noise."

Was Jazzi willing to make noise? Not now. The less she was involved, the better. That's what she'd told her mother when she'd called. Jazzi was sticking to it.

Attempting to forget Brie's murder wasn't easy, even though Jazzi was busy. She didn't even take a break as she selected the teas to brew for the tasting—Darjeeling, orange pekoe, White Symphony, oolong, along with herbal blends. Dawn had ordered a surplus of baked goods to sell. Customers sipping tea would certainly choose a cookie or a muffin to accompany it.

Jazzi was rushing here and there, filling in wherever she was needed when the tasting started. She carried the extra phone in her pocket to be aware of texts coming in. Audrey had chosen random numbers for the winners of gift cards. Herbal tea sample cups and tea kettles on hot plates lined the tea bar. A printed sign stood in front of each pot naming the tea for sampling. Audrey poured brews of honeybush, mango, and strawberry pomegranate into small sample cups. They'd had a full store of tourists today.

Book club friends came to the tasting as well as tourists and regular customers. Parker raised up his teacup to Jazzi and winked. She knew he was rooting for the success of Tomes & Tea as well as her and Dawn.

At one point, Addison sidled up beside her. As Jazzi made sure the tea station was ready for pouring, she asked, "Where's Sylvie tonight?"

The soft point of Addison's chin quivered a little when she answered Jazzi in a low voice. "Mark and I had an argument. I told him I needed an hour or two to myself. I love Sylvie but sometimes spending twenty-four hours a day with a three-year-old makes me want to join a convent for a week."

Jazzi couldn't help but smile. "What are the chances of that?"

Addison's wide hazel eyes glimmered with dismay. "Zilch. I could never leave Sylvie with Mark for a week. The sink would be piled with pizza boxes. Sylvie wouldn't have a clean shirt in her closet, and Mark might head for a monastery."

"Maybe you and Mark need a date night once a week."

"And you'll babysit?"

"Sure. I bet Sylvie would love playing with the kittens."

"You are a gem, Jazzi. I'll talk to him about it."

Suddenly Dawn was rushing toward Jazzi, her expression stormy as she checked over her shoulder toward the entrance. "Nolan Johnson is here. Should I tell him to leave?"

Jazzi looked toward the front of the store. The redheaded man was headed toward her, dressed casually tonight in jeans and a beige polo shirt. He didn't appear angry—no lines on his forehead . . . no frown on his lips.

Body language was a reliable gauge of a person's mood. "It's okay, Dawn. Let's see what he wants."

"I'll keep my phone handy," Dawn assured her.

When Nolan reached her, he asked, "Can we move to a quiet corner?"

Studying him again, Jazzi made the decision to hear him out. "Okay." She motioned him to the rear of the store. Both Dawn and Parker were watching. Parker's raised brows said he wouldn't be far away if she needed him. She wouldn't, if *she* could help it.

As soon as they reached the book cubbies at the back of the store, Nolan began, "I want to apologize for the way I reacted when I came in before. I spoke rashly. Detective Milford told me you felt threatened. I never meant for you to feel that."

"You were upset," Jazzi conceded, hoping to encourage him to say more.

"Yes, I was. I'd never been questioned by a detective before. He made me feel like a criminal."

"That's his job."

"It must be my red hair," Nolan gibed with self-deprecation, "that made me so irate."

This was a different man than the one who had threatened her. Which was the true Nolan Johnson?

When he noted Jazzi's studying glance, he sighed. "Look. All I wanted was to date Brie. For some reason she shut us down. When I found out she'd been murdered, I was devastated."

"You really cared about her?" Jazzi felt the necessity of probing as much as she could.

"I did. And then the detective called me in to the station. The idea that he thought I could hurt Brie made me livid. I shouldn't have taken it out on you."

She wasn't going to state the obvious, but *no*, he shouldn't have. Should she tell him about the mayor's visit? No point to that. Instead she was blunt and asked the question that had been on her mind. "How did Brie get that bruise on her wrist?"

Nolan was quiet for a moment. "We went for a canoe ride. She lost her balance and I caught her wrist. That's it. I was afraid she'd end up in the water, and I grabbed her hard. I never meant to hurt her. There was nothing more to it than that."

Nolan's explanation was plausible. Did she believe him? She wasn't sure. But for now she'd take his explanation at face value. An olive branch wouldn't hurt. She certainly didn't want to make an enemy of him.

"Tell me, Mr. Johnson. Do you like tea?"

He gave her a small smile. "Call me Nolan. I'm willing to try tea. I don't think it will replace my Cabernet in the evening, but you never know."

Jazzi showed him to a tasting table. Who knew? He might convert from wine to tea.

But she doubted it.

Estelle had called Jazzi the night before and asked to meet her at the Silver Wave Eatery for a late lunch today. She'd said she needed to get out of the house away from her husband's morose grief to somewhere a bit pleasant. Jazzi couldn't refuse. Yes, she needed to be at Tomes & Tea more than ever, but she'd learned at an early age to place people as her highest priority.

The Silver Wave indeed had an upbeat atmosphere. Decorated in silver and blue with a wall-sized mural of the lake and an outboard hopping over a wave, the restaurant served a solid selection of American cuisine at inflated prices.

"Lunch is on me," Estelle repeated as Jazzi searched the menu for a reasonably priced selection.

"You don't have to do that, Estelle."

"I insist. I asked you here to pick your brain. I know I'm taking you away from work."

"I *do* get a lunch break," Jazzi reminded her with a smile.

Estelle sent Jazzi a sad smile back. "I know you're placating me. I appreciate it. I wish Harry and I could support each other like we should. But he's just walled himself off. I can't reach him." Estelle gave her glasses a push higher on her nose in frustration.

"Would he consider going to a grief counseling group with you?"

"I doubt it. His parents, when they were alive, showed very little emotion. He said he never wanted to be like them. He was a great support for me when we couldn't have children. He was always open and loving with Brie. But now he seems to have reverted to his parents' cold behavior."

When the waitress appeared to take their orders, their conversation stopped. They both ordered salad plates with scoops of chicken, tuna, and egg salad on baby greens.

Jazzi picked up her glass of ice water with a slice of lemon floating atop the ice. She took a few sips, thinking about how to restart the conversation. Finally she asked, "What do you think would help your husband?"

"I'm not sure anything will." Estelle folded her plump arms on the table. "It is possible that if the police catch the killer, Harry might have a little peace."

"I'm sure they're working as hard as they can to find the killer."

"Do you think he left DNA?" Estelle wanted to know.

Jazzi brought her fishtail braid over her shoulder and fiddled with the end. How much did she want to discuss her thoughts with Estelle? On the other hand, who better to consider as a sounding board?

"The detectives certainly won't tell us anything about that. Are you sure you want to talk about this?"

Nodding vigorously, Estelle assured her, "I do."

"From what we know, Brie was strangled with the paddleboard leash that she'd tossed somewhere in the room. If the killer grabbed that, the murder wasn't preplanned. If it wasn't preplanned, he or she wasn't prepared."

Estelle frowned. "That means DNA had to be on that leash. But DNA won't do much good if the killer doesn't have a record."

"That could be true," Jazzi agreed. "On the other hand, if the police narrow down suspects and swab them, they can find a match."

"What if they swab the wrong suspects?" Estelle's eyes were shiny with intelligence and curiosity as well as grief.

"There is another way. The police can submit DNA to ancestry companies and possibly find relative matches. Then they can search the family to find someone with a connection to Brie. But that takes time."

The waitress brought their orders and again they ceased their conversation. Jazzi and Estelle both picked up their forks. While they ate, Jazzi told Estelle about Nolan Johnson and what had happened with him.

Estelle dug into her egg salad. "Do you believe him?"

"I don't know. There's another problem with finding DNA in Brie's townhouse. Anyone she dated could have been there with her and left DNA."

"But not on the leash," Estelle pointed out.

"Maybe, maybe not."

Jazzi was surprised at how clinically Estelle could talk about the murder. But a mother did what a mother had to do.

"Did Brie mention receiving a note from the Covino family?"

"From Joseph?" Estelle asked.

"No." Jazzi told Estelle about the note Delaney had found.

"I hope that detective is looking into Joseph's wife and her children."

Like anyone in their situation, Estelle wanted to pin the murder on *someone*. That note seemed to make Connie's kids prime suspects. "Again, it all takes time," Jazzi said.

"The killer could leave town and get away with it!"

"I doubt that. Let me run a few names by you. See if you recognize them . . . if Brie ever mentioned them. Casper Kowolski, Gregg Rizzo, Vic Finch. Did Brie ever talk about any of those men?"

Estelle thought about the names. "I don't recognize them, but I know who you should talk to—Brie's friends from work, especially Lara Bogart. Lara might know. Delaney was Brie's closest friend but she spent lots of time with Lara at work. I can give you the organization's office number."

Almost finished with her meal, Jazzi took out her phone. Estelle pulled out hers from her handbag. Jazzi had entered the number into her contacts with the name of the organization when her phone vibrated. She'd switched it to silent for her lunch.

The text was from Detective Milford. **Meet me at the station at four p.m. I've questions about the note you left me. Confirm.**

Jazzi sighed, then she told Estelle, "The detective wants me to meet him at the station at four. Maybe I can learn something from him."

Then she confirmed to him that she'd received his text and she'd be there.

The bell tower was chiming four o'clock when Jazzi again stepped into the lobby of the Belltower Landing Police Department. Immediately she noticed Delaney sitting on one of the vinyl chairs.

Delaney rushed over to Jazzi. "Did he call you in too?"

Jazzi knew who *he* was. "He texted." She gave Delaney a huge hug and Delaney held on.

Finally pulling away, Delaney asked her, "Do you think he'll question us together? You didn't find the note, I did. Maybe he'll separate us."

"Easy," Jazzi said. "Let me check in and . . ."

The big black door to the rear of the lobby opened and Detective Milford came striding toward them. "No need to check in," he told Jazzi as he held his hand up to the clerk in an I've-got-this gesture.

"Come on." He motioned Jazzi and Delaney to follow him.

They walked down the hall but this time he led them to a conference room. There was a long table, no video setup that Jazzi could see. Not exactly an interrogation then?

After they were all seated, the detective began. "Tell me about the note. Give me your story."

"It's *not* a story," Delaney protested.

"Where did you find it?" His tone was even, as if he was controlling his temper.

Reading Detective Milford's body language—tight shoulders, stern expression, his hands balled on the table—Jazzi kept quiet.

"The crumpled paper was in Brie's jacket pocket," Delaney explained.

"Why did *you* have her jacket?"

Even to Jazzi that question sounded like an accusation.

"We were friends," Delaney explained. "We went to lunch together. She got hot at the restaurant, removed her jacket and then left it in my car."

He turned his laser-like gaze to Jazzi. "How did you get involved?"

She decided to keep her answer short. "Delaney and I are friends. She was upset. She came to me to show me the note."

"And upset women talk," he muttered.

Instead of being offended by his attitude, Jazzi decided to go on the offensive with the nature of the note Delaney had found and what it might mean. "Have you questioned the Covinos?"

Detective Milford leaned back in his chair and gave her a hard stare. "I had to question the two of you to make sure the note was genuine."

Jazzi felt annoyed that he could believe it wasn't. "Did you seriously believe we would try to give you fake evidence?"

He lowered his hand to the table and tapped his fingers. His brows drew together and his shoulders were still stiff. "This is a murder investigation. Absolutely anything is possible."

"*Are* you going to question the Covinos?" Jazzi asked calmly.

His gaze stayed steady on hers. "I will, but there was another robbery last night. I've got a lot on my plate."

To Jazzi it seemed Brie's murder should take precedence, but if the detective was also being pressured to solve the robbery cases because high profile residents were involved, he had a public relations dilemma for sure.

"You can go," he told them both, his tone curt.

When Jazzi stood, so did Delaney. Neither spoke as they crossed to the door.

However, Jazzi stopped when he said, "Miss Swanson, I *will* find Brie Frazier's killer."

If that was a promise, Jazzi hoped the detective could keep it.

Chapter Eleven

In a back corner of Tomes & Tea on Monday, Jazzi adjusted the virtual reality goggles over her eyes. Last night she'd downloaded the cell phone app she needed to make the system work. The experience with the world atlas virtual reality would be amazing for an eight- to ten-year-old. She was witnessing images of continents appear before her eyes. There was also an interactive book and a kit where a child could actually dig up a dinosaur relic.

Although thoroughly engrossed in the experience, she felt a tap on her shoulder. Removing the goggles, she found Parker staring at her with a broad smile. He was dressed in black jeans and a gray Henley shirt with a picture of a boat and the words I'D RATHER BE FISHING printed above it. His dark brown hair looked freshly trimmed.

"It's amazing," she decided.

"I told you it would be." His expression was smug.

Last evening when he'd dropped off the VR system for her to assess, he'd told her, "Kids and adults alike will be intrigued."

"Your idea to set up a virtual reality station for customers to try is a good one. We could have a day of it. I don't want to relegate floor space to it on an ongoing basis," Jazzi explained. "But having a virtual reality event once a month might work. We'll have to see how many customers we can draw in."

"Once they use the system, they'll want to try it again," Parker assured her. "But you have to make clear they need an up-to-date smartphone to do it. The system takes a lot of storage space."

Thank goodness she had Parker to walk her through the specifics. Not only that, last evening while they played with the kittens and the little rascals had climbed all over them, she'd explained about her visit to the police station and how bothered she and Delaney had been by it.

Was the detective going to investigate Joseph Covino's family?

As Jazzi laid the VR system on a nearby bookshelf, Parker helped her disassemble it. "I came by for another reason too," he admitted. "It might help you get clarity about the investigation into Brie Frazier's murder."

"What?" She was interested in spite of her warnings to herself to stay away from it.

"How would you like to play tennis some morning?" He asked it as if it was something she did often.

"Tennis? I haven't played tennis since college. Why would I want to disgrace myself on the court?" She couldn't keep the laughter from her question.

"You might have a good reason for dressing in tennis whites."

She knew some of the resort courts around Belltower Landing required whites, though there were public courts too. That reason better be a good one.

"I know Andrea Covino," he revealed. "She teaches beginners at the tennis club."

Why hadn't he told her this last night? Maybe because he hadn't wanted to give her the chance to become more involved through his acquaintance with Andrea? "Are you a member of the tennis club?"

"I am. I don't have to be sociable while I'm playing tennis."

Parker always sold himself short. It wasn't easy for him to make conversation with people he didn't know. He felt awkward and unsure, although he was probably the most intelligent man she knew. If given the opportunity to go boating, paddleboarding, hiking, and possibly playing tennis, he was there.

"I even play with partners now and then. I've played with Andrea."

That was news. News she wanted to take advantage of? How could she not? Maybe Estelle would feel better if Jazzi at least spoke with Andrea Covino. If Jazzi ran into her by planned accident . . .

"How do you know when she'll be there?"

"I know her schedule. She's often teaching beginners in the early morning. I'm sure I can sign up for a court nearby."

Before Jazzi could think about it any longer, she nodded. "Let's do it."

Minutes later, she was watching Parker stop to talk to Dawn as he motioned to the shelves where Jazzi stowed the VR system. She imagined he was telling Dawn about that. It was amazing how he had no problem conversing when anything tech oriented was involved. On the other hand, wasn't that true of anyone? It was easy to talk about something that interested you personally.

As she waved to Parker on his way out, she noticed Oliver Patel sitting at a front table with a muffin and a cup of tea. He was dressed in cargo pants and a striped yellow and white T-shirt. Turning her gaze away from him, she continued to box up the VR system, concentrating on pushing the goggles into the box. She wasn't aware of Oliver until he came up beside her.

Her fingers fumbled on the package. "Good morning, Oliver."

"G'day."

He had a curious look in his blue eyes that had her wondering why he was here . . . other than tea and a muffin. "Slow morning?" she asked him. He didn't stop in often.

"I was kayaking with a friend and decided a spot of tea was perfect."

"And your friend?"

"He works at the Lake Edge Hotel. He couldn't take more time this morning. Fortunately for me, my workday doesn't start till around eleven."

"What kind of tea did you order?" She had to admit she was curious about him.

"Black tea . . . always black tea. Nothing fancy for me. How are the kittens?"

"Growing," she said with a smile. "Their bellies are rounding, and they tumble around like they own the place."

"They probably do."

When Oliver smiled, the lines of his sharp stubbled jaw eased. He actually looked a bit unsure as he waved at the box in her hand. "Did Olsen set you up with that?"

"Yes. I'm considering having a demo day. Do you think it will draw in kids and parents?"

"No worries with that. You could sell a truckload, and anything attached to the system."

"I'm hoping."

He waited a beat. "Are you and Olsen together?"

Jazzi blinked twice. "You mean like dating?"

"Just wondered if you're paired up."

She was quick to respond, "No, we're not. We're good friends. We have been since I worked in Belltower Landing during summers in college."

"You worked here?"

"I did. Dawn and I were friends and I worked with her at her parents' store, Rods to Boards. That's where I met Parker."

"I see."

She wondered if he did. She and Parker did things together like eating at The Wild Kangaroo, but those weren't dates.

As if he was thinking along the same lines, Oliver said, "You and Olsen often grab a bite at the Kangaroo."

"I grab a bite there with other friends too—Dawn, Delaney, Derek, Audrey."

Oliver held up his hand to stop her. "I get it. You have lots of mates."

"I do. Don't you?"

He shrugged. "I have two very good friends. That's all I need."

"Friends are as important as family. I like having a lot of them."

"Because you miss your family?"

"Sometimes."

His expression gave her pause. Was there sadness there about family? "Do you miss your family?"

"Not so much."

That might be a topic for another occasion. She swept her gaze away from Oliver toward a group of four women who had come through the door and were chatting loudly.

Oliver noticed them too. "I won't hold you up." He took a few steps away. "I'll see you around."

Her conversation with Oliver was an unusual one. Was he thinking of asking her out? And if he was, just what would her answer be?

Jazzi preferred the lake and its sparkling water, forests, and waterfowl to chlorine-scented pools and the hard pavement surrounding them along with many swimsuit-clad bodies. But they had their purpose, providing exercise and entertainment, especially for kids.

Jazzi had taken her break midafternoon to visit the town's public pool. It was located near Belltower Landing's largest strip shopping center. Jazzi had ridden there on her bike. Earlier, she'd called the number Estelle had given her for the office where Brie had worked along with Lara Bogart. Lara had been easy to reach. This afternoon she was teaching a class at the pool for a group of children who were spending a week in the resort town.

Jazzi dismounted from her bike and parked it in the bike rack. After securing it, she plucked her water bottle from her rear basket and carried her helmet with her to find Lara. They'd texted selfies so they could recognize each other. In the shallow end of the pool an auburn-haired woman was paddling around with three children, a girl and two boys who looked to be around eight or so and had neon-colored foam noodles under their arms. Jazzi guessed these kids were non-swimmers getting used to the water.

"I'm not afraid of water no more," the little girl told Lara.

"Then I can dunk you," the boy returned with a sly grin.

"No, no, no," the girl shouted, paddling backwards.

Lara held up her hand. "Whoa. No one is going to be dunked. Clancy, you don't like to get your face wet any more than Deb does. We'll work on that next time. Go ahead and get out. Clancy, you go with Rob into the boys' changing room." She pointed to a young man waiting with a group of three more boys. "Deb and Patty, you go with Tanya."

Lara made sure the kids exited the pool safely. It was easy to see she was good with them. She was wearing a coral one-piece racing swimsuit. After she climbed the few steps out of the pool, she stopped by the bleachers and picked up a large beach towel patterned with a dolphin, wrapping it around her waist.

"Is it okay if we sit here?" Lara re-banded her ponytail and shielded her eyes from the sun with her hand. "I'm Lara and I take it you're Jazzi. I have about twenty minutes before my next class starts."

"This is fine. Same time frame for me." Jazzi took a seat on the bleachers, set her helmet beside her, and took a few swallows of water.

As Lara settled in, she pulled a thermos from her duffel bag and took several long gulps. Then she swiveled toward Jazzi. "How can I help you?"

Removing her phone from a case on her belt, Jazzi brought up the page she wanted. "When I had dinner with Brie, I spotted a list of men's names. I think they were the guys she'd dated or was going to date. Can you see if you recognize the names? Did Brie talk about any of them?"

Lara took Jazzi's phone and shaded it so she could see the screen better. "I do recognize the names. Casper Kowolski was one of the first men she dated with the dating app. He has a food truck at the marina."

"Yes," Jazzi agreed. "Did she like him?"

"Brie said he was pleasant enough and friendly. If she wanted another friend, she could see him being that. But I think she minded that he simply ran a food truck."

"Not enough income?" Jazzi preferred to dig to the bottom of Brie's reasoning.

"She didn't come right out and say that, but if she was thinking ahead to wanting a family, she wanted a man who could provide for it."

Jazzi believed a man had to be happy in his work too. "If Casper had plans to open a restaurant, do you think she would have dated him?"

"That might have made a difference to Brie. I'm not sure."

Glancing at the second name, Lara frowned. "I don't know

much about Gregg Rizzo. She did date him longer than Casper . . . three or four dates maybe. Gregg liked sports and that's what they did."

"What was his fatal flaw?" Jazzi's tone was dry.

"Do you think Brie was too picky?" Lara's golden eyes probed Jazzi for her take on the matter.

"You knew her better than I did. But from the sound of it, I think Brie was looking for the perfect man. I doubt if there is one."

Hiding a smile, Lara crossed one long leg over the other. "I can attest to that. But a dating app can offer a wide selection. I haven't tried it. After what happened to Brie, I doubt if I will. I believe Gregg's flaw was that he was falling for her fast. He was a little intense."

"Nolan Johnson talked about golf too much," Jazzi said, "and not Brie's interests. Casper didn't have enough ambition. Gregg fell too fast. What about the last name?"

"Vic Finch?"

"Yes. Doesn't he run a car detailing service?" Jazzi was almost certain Addison had used his service when Sylvie had gotten sick in her car.

"He does. I think he owns it and does quite well. He's reliable and takes pride in his work. Lots of solid clients from what he told Brie."

"But . . . ?"

"But Brie thought he was too controlling. She was quite independent. Didn't like a man ordering for her, things like that. Do you want to see what these guys look like? I followed Brie's social media. She posted most of her dates."

Jazzi hadn't asked Delaney about Brie's social media posts because Delaney had been so upset about everything concerning Brie. "Sure, I'd like to know if I run into Gregg or Vic."

Lara's beach bag was equipped with several pockets. She slid her phone from one. It took a minute for her to bring up Brie's page on Instagram.

As Lara scrolled through Brie's photos, Jazzi saw that Lara had been right about Casper being first. Gregg had been second. He had brown, medium long hair and was quite good-looking. Taking a second glance at him, Jazzi realized the man often stopped in at Tomes & Tea on his lunch hour. He was an accountant, if she remembered correctly. Finally, Jazzi focused her attention on Vic Finch. He had dirty-blond short hair, a wide smile, and had his arm slung around Brie's waist. In the photo, Brie didn't look quite comfortable with that.

Jazzi returned Lara's phone to her. "The photos don't tell us much. They're just those selfie shots you take so there's something to post on social media that day. I guess I hoped for more."

"You hoped one would stand out as a suspect? I imagine the police have gone through Brie's social media too."

Jazzi stood and picked up her helmet. "I'm sure they have. It would be terrific if they questioned the guys and one had a motive."

"There is an obvious motive for any of them." Lara sifted through her bag's pockets again and found a tube of sunscreen. "Jealousy."

Securing her helmet on her head, Jazzi nodded.

That seemed to be an obvious motive, but was it the right one?

When Jazzi swung at the tennis ball early the following morning, Parker easily lobbed it back to her. She was lousy at court play. Parker had a level of expertise that he was definitely tamping down.

"You're being easy on me," she called to him.

When she caught the ball on the edge of her racket and it fell short of the net, she ran to pick it up. She'd dug out white shorts

and a white tank top for this excursion. They'd only been playing about twenty minutes and already she felt as if she needed a
shower. At least with biking, she had a breeze flying past her to
cool her off.

"Smile more, Jazzi," Parker teased. "You don't look like
you're enjoying yourself."

Like her, Parker had dressed in a white polo and white
shorts. Unlike her, he looked as if he'd just stepped onto the
court, all fresh and ready to smash the next ball that soared
his way.

Glancing around at surrounding courts, Jazzi approached
the net. "Isn't it time to find Andrea?"

Parker checked the watch on his wrist that did so much more
than project the time. "Give us ten more minutes and then she
should be finished with her lesson. She usually sits on the sidelines afterwards to down a bottle of water or she goes to the
juice bar. Think you can survive a little more exercise?"

Noticing once more how fit and athletic Parker looked in his
whites, his thick dark brown hair, longer on the top of his head,
a bit disheveled from racing to swat her tennis balls, she realized he was a catch for the right woman—a woman who could
understand his analytical thinking and desire for his world to
be in order.

"I can survive if it means I can talk to Andrea Covino."

"Bumping into her doesn't mean she'll talk." His reminder
was repetitive. They'd discussed the fact that Andrea could ignore their questions.

"I'm prepared. Where is she?" The sun was blinding Jazzi at
the moment.

"Third court over. Don't look. We don't want her to know
we're scoping her out."

Of course Jazzi *did* look, and Parker rolled his eyes. "You
have a habit of doing what I tell you *not* to do."

"She can't see us." They were far enough away that Jazzi knew her estimation of the situation had to be true.

"Andrea is aware at all times of what's going on around her. That's why she's so good on the court."

"Just how well do you know her?" She and Parker hadn't really discussed that.

"Well enough."

Parker's expression was enigmatic, and she knew the subject was closed.

"All right, ten more minutes. Just wait until I drag you on a really long bike ride."

"Not going to happen unless you find one that rolls on water."

She'd give Parker an impatient eye roll this time but he probably wouldn't see it with the bill of her white cap, which she'd bought for this occasion, dipping over her eyes. When she tossed the tennis ball to Parker over the net, he caught it with a grin.

Nine minutes later they met at the sidelines and tossed their towels around their necks. Jazzi picked up her water bottle and took a few quick swallows. Andrea was leaving her court, talking to the teen she'd been coaching. Her student headed inside the building.

Parker touched Jazzi's elbow. "Come on. It's now or never. Just remember, Andrea can seem a little short. It's simply her nature."

Jazzi wondered again how well Parker knew her. "That's not an attractive quality in a teacher."

"Maybe not. But she *is* a tennis whiz. The club is willing to overlook her quirks because of her skill. She could have been great."

Jazzi expected Parker meant Andrea could have been a great tennis player. "What exactly happened?"

"She had an Achilles tendon injury two years ago that took her out of the pros. She's had an attitude ever since."

Instead of sitting on the sidelines, Andrea had headed for the juice bar under the roofline of the tennis club.

Parker explained, "They bring this setup out in the spring through fall. Do you want a green smoothie?"

Jazzi thought about the idea of early morning kale and who knew what else. "No thanks. I'll stick to water."

Tossing her a knowing smile because he knew she'd say that, Parker increased his stride. Jazzi jogged to keep up and slowed as they approached the cold-beverage bar.

Nonchalantly, as Parker, despite Jazzi's objection, ordered a fruit smoothie for her and a vegetable smoothie for himself, he stepped closer to Andrea. "Good workout out there. Your student was lobbing to the left every time and you corrected that."

With a coy smile, Andrea turned toward Parker. "I didn't know anyone was watching, Parker."

Parker didn't seem at all awkward with Andrea. Did playing tennis with her develop that level of comfort? Jazzi would reserve judgment for now. She had questions she wanted Andrea to answer.

With a customary shrug, Parker gave off a noncommittal vibe. Because he wasn't sure what to say next? He didn't banter well with women other than her. That thought discomforted Jazzi.

She stepped up beside Parker and smiled. "I'm Jazzi. I don't know if you remember—"

Andrea didn't let her finish. "I remember you. You're friends with Estelle Frazier."

"I only met Estelle after Brie died. She needed some support."

"I guess so," Andrea conceded.

Although they stood in awkward silence for a few seconds,

Jazzi started with something easy. "Do you know how many times your stepdad met with Brie?"

Andrea bit on her lower lip. "I know of two times—by himself and when he introduced Brie to us. Why are you asking?" Andrea's eyes narrowed suspiciously.

"Estelle and Brie's friends are looking for answers. Her death was awful for everyone. I imagine your stepfather is grieving too."

Andrea admitted, "I guess he is. He's a private person. At first we didn't know what was going on. He didn't prepare us. We didn't know he'd registered on that website. He adopted me and Damon. But we've never been close."

Probably pushing her luck, Jazzi asked, "Did you know Brie before Joseph introduced her?"

Andrea waved to a group exiting the club building. Somewhat distracted, she answered, "Not me. We didn't run in the same circles. Damon said he'd seen her around—singles night at The Wild Kangaroo."

"I imagine you were both pleased for Joseph. Finding a connection like that is huge."

With a sigh, Andrea picked up a green smoothie the barista had pushed toward her—her usual drink, apparently, after court time.

"I'm not that attuned with Joseph. I was around him a couple of years before college, but now I rarely see him. Even in the summer, he's always working. Damon spends a lot more time with him than I do."

"Did you like the fact Joseph was going to include Brie in your family?" Jazzi suddenly felt the warmth of Parker's hand on her shoulder. Did he think she was overstepping?

Andrea must have felt so too. "Look, I'm tired of the twenty questions. Brie's mother is just going to have to live with her questions unanswered. Brie's dead and answers went with her.

I need to go to the clubhouse and freshen up before my next lesson."

Grabbing her drink, sucking on the straw, Andrea didn't say good-bye. She stalked off.

Turning to Parker, Jazzi said, "I guess I struck a nerve."

"Or possibly Andrea is a private person too. Besides, I don't want to believe she had anything to do with Brie's murder."

That's what Parker *wanted* to believe. But what was true could contradict his belief.

Chapter Twelve

The strawberry field, rows and rows of the leafy plants, stretched out in front of Jazzi. Her hands were sticky from picking berries. Even early in the morning, the sun was hot on her pink hat with its large front brim, and sweat slipped between her shoulder blades under her tank top.

"Just think about the strawberry pies I'm going to bake," Erica advised Jazzi and Dawn from the row across from them. "I froze rhubarb so I can make strawberry-rhubarb pies too."

"You spoil us." Jazzi knew Erica baked like Jazzi's mom, great-aunt, and grandmother. Their philosophy saw cooking and baking as a way to show love.

Straightening, Erica adjusted her straw sunhat. "My basket is almost full." She peered over into Jazzi's and Dawn's baskets. "What are you going to do with your strawberries?"

"Share with anyone who wants some." Dawn stooped to another plant. "The strawberries will be great to pick up and eat as a snack."

"If we freeze them," Jazzi added, "we'll have them for strawberry sundaes and smoothies. I might even try baking strawberry scones."

The three of them moved down the rows, unwilling to lose their camaraderie and early morning quiet before starting a busy day at Tomes & Tea.

"It's a shame Audrey couldn't come." Dawn reached into a nest of strawberry plant leaves.

"She stayed overnight with a client's two Papillons. Her overnight pet sitting pays well. How are Zander and Freya?"

Erica had visited the kittens during a few of her lunch breaks. "They own us," Jazzi admitted. "They take turns sleeping with us so neither of us feels deprived."

All three women laughed.

Simply thinking about the kittens' antics curved Jazzi's lips into another smile. "Sometimes when we're in our storeroom, I can hear them scurrying and playing in my bedroom." Her room was above the break room with a door that opened to stairs leading to the bottom floor. She didn't go that way often because she didn't want the kittens escaping to the downstairs.

A noisy gray pickup rumbled over a gravel road near where they were picking. The driver waved. The truck bounded to the building where the farm sold boxes of strawberries and garden knickknacks.

Erica stepped over a few plants to stand by Jazzi's side. "I heard you played tennis with Parker yesterday."

Jazzi tossed Dawn a what-did-you-tell-her look, but Dawn merely shrugged.

"It wasn't a date," Jazzi said.

"Hmm," Erica murmured. "If it wasn't a date, are you going to take up tennis?"

Erica was an expert at ferreting out secrets, and this wasn't even a secret. So, Jazzi might as well fess up. "I was hoping to bump into Andrea Covino there. Parker is acquainted with her and her schedule."

With her forefinger, Erica pushed up the front brim of her

hat and it slid back on her head. Her focus was as laser sharp as the sun. "Did you bump into her?"

"We did. She remembered me."

"You *are* memorable," Erica assured her. "I guess that helped ease into questions you had for her."

"No use denying it. I managed a few. She's not the most open person." Jazzi suspected Andrea's hostility originated from many factors. It could go back as far as her mother marrying Joseph. It could stem from her injury and her life becoming something different than what she'd expected it to be. Maybe Joseph's affection for Brie, happening so quick, had been a surprise. *Was* Andrea jealous? Damon worked with Joseph. Had Andrea's disdain for Brie's entrance into her life turned into murder?

Jazzi wasn't ready to make a leap like that.

"This is like pulling teeth this morning." Erica emitted a huff. "What did you learn?"

Pushing her basket higher on her arm, Jazzi gave in to Erica's interest. "I really didn't learn anything new. Andrea Covino has an attitude. I think she resented Brie's appearance into their lives. Brie would take the focus off Andrea, and I think Andrea likes being anyone's main focus, maybe even Joseph's."

"How could she be jealous so quickly?" Dawn asked. "She only just met Brie once."

"Once was enough if Andrea felt threatened. Joseph had adopted her and Damon. Now someone from his past barges in. If he mentioned to his family about including Brie in his will, Andrea might have felt displaced."

"Damon and his mother could have felt that way too," Erica pointed out.

Erica's conclusion was the right one. "I don't know if the police are considering the Covinos. They should be looking at them as suspects. I certainly would be."

Erica picked up her basket and hesitated. "I know someone on the police force."

"Do you think he'd tell you if they've questioned the Covinos?" Jazzi asked.

"*She* might."

Erica's correction brought a smile to Jazzi's face.

"You should ask that officer if the detective is looking into the list of guys that Brie dated," Dawn said.

Erica swung around to Dawn. "What list?"

Jazzi took over. "When I had dinner with Brie, I glimpsed a list of the men she'd dated, or wanted to date, from the app. Casper Kowolski's name and Nolan Johnson's were crossed off. But there were two others."

As if Jazzi wasn't aware, Dawn gave Erica a nudge. Secret code? These two were coordinating and had already talked about having this conversation.

Jazzi waited in the sunshine, knowing both Erica and Dawn cared about her.

"Are you thinking about talking to these men?" Erica wanted to know. There was disapproval in her voice.

Jazzi remembered comments and questions like these that her own mother had received from friends and family. Like her mother, she was honest.

"It's very likely I could bump into them in the course of a day at Tomes and Tea. That already happened with Nolan Johnson."

Erica looked toward the sky as if she needed divine intervention, then hinted at what was coming. Jazzi decided to accept whatever it was, in the bonds of their friendship.

Still, she wasn't quite prepared for the jolt of apprehension that settled in her chest when Erica reminded her, "Jazzi, you do realize, don't you, that one of those men could be Brie's killer?"

The stark truth settled over Jazzi like a black cloud over-taking the blue sky. Was she really going to pursue having her questions answered? Or would she leave those questions for Detective Milford?

Zander and Freya turned everything into a happy game. Is that what life should be?

Jazzi was unpacking groceries from reusable bags. She dropped one of the empty bags to the floor and the kittens were playing peekaboo both in and out of it. In the next second they'd taken off running to the edge of the sofa. Freya pounced on a toy mouse sending a Hot Wheels car flying. Parker had given it to them believing it was sturdier and more fun than most kitten toys.

Jazzi pushed a carton of milk aside on the refrigerator shelf to allow more room for a caramel-flavored coffee creamer. Then she added the particular brand of orange juice Dawn pre-ferred, to the same shelf. Dawn was having dinner with her brother tonight. She'd suspected he wanted to talk about the idea of opening a satellite store to his parents' outfitter shop. Dawn had promised Jazzi that he wouldn't coax her to become involved in the venture. But Jazzi still felt a grip of apprehen-sion about the siblings' conversation.

Freya found a ping pong ball under a table chair and batted it under the coffee table. Derek had contributed a few ping pong balls to the kittens' toy stash when he'd stopped in to see Dawn one evening and stayed for supper.

Speaking of . . . Jazzi hadn't eaten yet. She'd bought salad fixings. All she'd have to do was wash them in the salad spin-ner, add a pickled red beet egg from the deli, sprouts, hunks of cheese, and slices of carrot. She'd actually baked chicken yes-terday and could add bites of that too.

The salad spinner sat on the counter, still half full of greens as Jazzi arranged hers on a plate. Freya and Zander had run into her bedroom. She'd have to check on them to see what mischief they'd found. After drying her hands, she was about to check on the kittens when there was a knock at her door.

A few days ago, after watching a how-to YouTube video, Jazzi and Dawn had managed to install a peephole in their door. Jazzi didn't know if it made her feel more secure, but she went to look in the peephole before putting her hand on the doorknob.

It took her a moment to recognize Estelle, who was turned away from the door. She must be gazing over to the lake.

Jazzi undid the dead bolt and opened the door. "Hi, Estelle."

Even through the older woman's glasses, Jazzi could spot the dark circles under her eyes. Her grief seemed to round her shoulders. She'd worn a loose print dress, mid-calf and smocked at the top, in deference to the eighty-degree evening. Summer heat was setting in.

Estelle quickly and nervously stammered, "I'm . . . sorry to interrupt your evening. If . . . you'd rather I come into Tomes tomorrow—"

"Nonsense," Jazzi assured her. She glanced over her shoulder to see the kittens on the threshold to her bedroom, but eyeing her.

Gently taking hold of Estelle's arm, she guided her inside. "I have to be careful with the door because of the kittens. That jingling you heard when I opened it was a strap of bells on the door handle. When they hear that, they stay away. Usually."

Once in Jazzi's apartment, Estelle looked around. "This is nice. You and Dawn have decorating skills."

Jazzi shrugged. "We know what we like and we just wanted to be comfortable. Come on in. I hope you don't mind kittens."

"I *love* kittens, but Harry says we're too old for pets." She headed toward the sofa, her tapestry handbag under her arm.

"Do *you* think you're too old for pets?"

Estelle looked crestfallen. "I feel about one hundred right now. Each step feels sloggy. Do you know what I mean? Never mind. You're too young to feel that way."

Suddenly Estelle seemed aware that Jazzi had been preparing supper. She started to rise to her feet. "I've interrupted your meal. I'll speak to you tomorrow—"

"Don't be silly. In fact, have you eaten? I've prepared a salad and there's plenty for two."

Estelle hesitated.

"Really, stay and join me. I have iced peach tea and might even be able to find a bag of barbecued potato chips. My mom sends me care packages now and then and includes my favorites."

It didn't take long for Estelle to agree. "Harry went to a poker game tonight. Poker. Can you imagine? I don't know what he's thinking."

As Zander and Freya ventured toward Estelle, Jazzi crossed to the counter. She pulled two Polish pottery plates from a top cupboard. She and Dawn had found four of them at a flea market and saved them for special occasions. Two had small chips but they were barely noticeable. That's why their budget allowed the purchase.

"It's possible your husband doesn't know what will help him through this difficult time. Do you like baked chicken and red beet eggs?"

"I do. Can I help?"

"No, I have everything ready." As Jazzi took the plates to the table, Estelle left her handbag on the couch and came to sit in one of the chairs.

At the refrigerator Jazzi pulled two bottles of salad dressing from the door. She used honey mustard and Dawn preferred ranch.

"You asked if I think I'm too old for a pet. I don't. I think

I'd like a small pup to walk. That could give me exercise, and someone . . ." Her voice caught. "Someone to care for. Harry doesn't have to be involved."

Jazzi could see that Brie's death was creating a wedge between the couple. It was such a shame they couldn't hold on to each other instead of pushing the other person away.

Estelle went on, "There's an animal shelter on the south side of the lake. I've seen their ads for adoption events."

While Estelle dribbled salad dressing on her greens, Jazzi poured iced tea and took the bag of chips from the pantry closet. She opened the bag and motioned to it. "Help yourself."

Estelle did and soon they were eating in companionable silence while the kittens climbed the sofa and tumbled over the top. Watching them, Estelle gave a small laugh. But then she stopped herself as if that was the wrong thing to do.

Survivor's guilt, Jazzi imagined.

"I had a reason for coming over tonight."

"What was that?" Jazzi asked.

"I hired a cleaning service for Brie's townhouse."

Jazzi knew that there were special cleaning services that cleaned up a murder scene, or even somewhere the police had disturbed with fingerprint dust. Ordinary cleaner couldn't wipe up the powder.

"Did the detective give you their number?"

"No, I called the public information officer. He was helpful."

"I'm glad."

Some police departments had a victim's advocate, but the Belltower Landing department was probably too small for that position.

"The thing is . . ." Estelle began.

"What?" Jazzi prompted when Estelle stopped.

"Brie's landlord said I have to be out of the townhouse by June twenty-eighth."

"He couldn't give you until the end of June?"

"Apparently he needs that time to get ready for the next tenant. And, Jazzi, Harry went there with me today and turned around and left. He said he can't do it." Estelle's voice was quavering now.

"How can I help?" The question flew out of Jazzi's mouth like it belonged in the air between them.

"I asked Delaney if she'd go with me to go through Brie's things, but she said she can't. I think she has a very soft heart even though she pretends to be cool on the outside."

Jazzi believed Estelle was right about that.

"So will you go with me to sort through Brie's things? Please?"

That please was unnecessary. Jazzi's heart went out to this woman. Her own throat closed up as she managed to say, "Yes, I'll help."

Estelle reached over, took Jazzi's hand, and squeezed it.

One of Emilia Perez's books toppled over and Jazzi caught it. "Maybe we have too many stacked there."

Righting the book, Jazzi stepped back and checked the display they'd set up this morning. "I think it's steady now. Delaney wants them all stacked like this to show Emilia has a huge readership. We have to believe she knows what she's doing."

Dawn straightened the placard that sat in front of the arranged books.

Jazzi thought about the customers who would be in and out of the store before the book signing that was a week away. The shiny photo of Emilia, her smile enhancing her beauty, also announced the day, date, and time of the event.

"When anyone buys Emilia's book before the signing, we should take a selfie and flood our social media with those photos. We'll create a buzz. Emilia told Delaney she'll sign the books for anyone who has bought one. It doesn't have to be that day," Jazzi reminded Dawn.

As Erica came by with a customer, she gave the two of them a thumbs-up sign.

"There's our seal of approval." Dawn pointed to the cubicle of shelves to their right and the stack of books on the floor. "On to Shakespeare."

Jazzi had emptied two cubicles in order to arrange copies of Shakespeare's complete volumes but also individual tomes of *A Midsummer Night's Dream.*

"Do you think many residents will attend the play on the green?" Dawn began positioning books on the shelf.

"Two reasons I think they will." Jazzi lifted a book concerning plays during Shakespeare's time, the costuming, sets, and actors, and added them to Dawn's selections. Jazzi had already attached a portrait of Shakespeare above the shelf. "The performance troupe has a group who comes to their plays. Every year since I've been in Belltower Landing, they've performed a play on the green. They have a substantial following."

"And the second reason?" Dawn slipped a mini-figurine of Puck, a character from the play, onto the shelf.

"Evan Holloway. Concertgoers like to wander around before the main performance. I think they'll watch the play to participate in the festival and an evening out."

"Are you going to glitz up?" Dawn's smile was wily.

Jazzi liked color. Glitz, not so much.

"I can lend you something of mine," Dawn wheedled.

In college as roommates, they'd often borrowed each other's clothes.

"If I can't find something in my closet, I'll think about it."

"I have a sparkly white shrug that could go with several of your sundresses."

The proposal sounded attractive, and Jazzi considered the idea. "I'll try it on tonight."

They'd just finished the display when Audrey brought a

young man to the shelf where they were working. He was carrying a large carton.

"Guess what's here," Audrey said. "Ted has our tea boxes." Audrey's face was one wide smile.

Jazzi had planned the boxes with Dawn and Ted.

After he set the carton on the floor, he opened the flaps. The tea boxes were flat. Jazzi would have to square them to fill them with tea.

Dawn stopped at the box and took one of the flat ones out. She quickly shaped it into a belfry.

Jazzi slid her hand to the other side of the carton and pulled out one with a picture of a kayak. "These are terrific. We'll begin filling them this afternoon."

"And I'll photograph them and post the photos to our website," Dawn offered.

After another round of thank-yous and Ted's good-bye, Audrey picked up the full carton. "I'll put this in the storeroom until we get a chance to fill them."

Each of them moved to a different area of the store. Jazzi was helping a regular customer with a biography she was searching for, about a royal, when Jazzi noticed Damon Covino standing nearby. There was no mistaking that severe jawline and stark white-blond hair.

After Jazzi pulled the biography from the shelf and her customer was looking through it, she moved toward Damon. "Can I help you?"

After all, he was in her store, and he was her customer too . . . maybe. She couldn't remember seeing him here before.

He was dressed in navy shorts and a red split-collar polo shirt. He looked ready for a regatta. She would bet he sailed and might be competing in the regatta that would be happening soon.

"Yes, you can help me." His tone was even and restrained.

"Are you looking for a particular title? Audrey can check on the computer to make sure we have it."

He didn't look toward the sales desk where Audrey stood. "I don't need to check your computer. What I need is for you to stay away from my sister."

Jazzi felt the fuse to her temper spark. "Excuse me?"

"You know what I'm talking about. You accosted my sister." He'd stepped into her personal space. His tone was at the least condescending and at the most scary.

"I did no such thing. I asked her how she felt about Brie."

"You just happened to be playing tennis on a court near her?"

Jazzi felt a twinge of guilt. "I was with Parker Olsen."

"There was no reason for you to bother her about a dead girl who wanted better than she had." He spat out his words . . . and they were bitter.

Jazzi felt heat rise up her neck into her cheeks. He had Brie all wrong. Either Damon was blind or wanted to think the worst. Her gaze on his, she gave him the truth as she saw it. "Brie was a healthy, beautiful young woman who had loving parents, a good job, and a bright future. She wanted to get to know her biological father. Tell me, what was wrong with that?"

Damon broke eye contact with her and took a step back. Was he simply a bully who when confronted backed off?

He scanned Jazzi up and down as if really seeing her for the first time. "I guess nothing's wrong with that," he mumbled.

Softening her tone but still wary, Jazzi pointed out, "Once you got to know Brie you might have even liked her."

"Maybe so," Damon agreed, almost automatically to placate her. But it was too late for that now. He shoved one hand into his shorts pocket. "My family would prefer not to discuss any of this with outsiders."

Jazzi hoped Detective Milford would be discussing Brie's death with the Covinos.

When Damon turned to leave, Jazzi didn't try to convince him she wasn't an outsider. She cared what had happened to Brie, and he should too.

But she knew she couldn't make people care when they wanted to stay removed. The whole conversation with Damon bothered her deeply.

Chapter Thirteen

Although there was still a week until the Welcome Summer Festival weekend, that evening Jazzi tried on the lacy white sequined shrug Dawn handed her. She'd chosen an abstract printed haltered sundress in swirls of blue, white and pale yellow. It was relatively backless, and the sheer shrug would be perfect with it.

"I'll glitz you up yet," Dawn crowed, obviously pleased with the look.

The kittens scampered across two other sundresses not as suited for the evening that they were planning.

"What are you going to wear for Emilia's book signing?" Dawn selected a pair of white slingback pumps from Jazzi's closet and held them up.

Jazzi nodded approvingly. "I'm going to wear my work apron."

"There will be a lot of selfies," Dawn said with a sigh. "But I guess you're right. Our logo should be as visible as possible. Emilia will probably be dressed in fire-engine red with winged sleeves." Dawn dropped the shoes into Jazzi's closet.

They had Googled Emilia's runway shows and galas. The winged sleeves were her signature look.

Zander held on to the bedspread as he slid down the side. Freya toppled over him, and they landed on the memory foam rug along the side of the bed.

"I probably have a shiny purse you can use for Evan Holloway's concert. I still have clothes in my old bedroom at home."

When Jazzi had first met Dawn, they'd become instant friends. Jazzi had thought that was because they were so much alike. And they were in many ways, but in just as many ways, they were different. However, that was what made their friendship work. They had fun as well as serious conversations, and they didn't judge each other.

There was a knock at the door.

"Expecting anyone?" Jazzi asked Dawn.

"Nope." As the kittens ran over her bare feet, Dawn added, "Hopefully not another kitten. I'll get it."

No matter what Dawn said, Jazzi knew she loved the kittens too.

Jazzi was hanging the dresses that had been left on the bed when Dawn returned with Erica.

"Did you come by to play with the kittens? They have lots of energy to expend." Jazzi gave Erica a conspiratorial smile.

Erica plopped on the bed and picked up a scarf still flung across it. "I can do that. But that's not the only reason I'm here. I have some news."

"News about what?" Dawn asked.

"The investigation into Brie's murder." Erica's brown eyes were deeply sober and seemed darker brown than usual.

Jazzi's breath caught. "Did they find the killer?"

Erica was quick to shake her head before Jazzi got caught up in the idea. "No, and worse yet the detective seems to be focusing on Delaney, since she found Brie's body."

"Oh, no." Dawn's hand came up over her mouth. "They can't find the right person so they're blaming *her*?"

"Can you tell us who your contact is?" Jazzi asked. It would be good to know who was feeding Erica information that should stay within the police department.

"I shouldn't tell you, but since she's the only patrol officer who's a woman, you'll probably guess. It's Casey Garza. I'm trusting the two of you will keep that quiet."

Jazzi pictured an officer with short, light brown hair who gave an automatic smile when she saw any of the residents on the street. But Jazzi thought that fake smile was a uniform, as much as the tan shirt and trousers she wore.

"Is Delaney the only one they're considering?" Dawn's voice was filled with hope again.

"Casey said Nolan Johnson hasn't been cleared yet, but they're concentrating on Delaney."

"Have they talked with the Covinos?"

"She doesn't think so. It's possible the detective went to their estate but there's no scuttlebutt about that." Jazzi couldn't understand why the detective hadn't spoken to the family.

"Does she have any access to other parts of the investigation?" Dawn seemed to want details. Jazzi didn't feel so bad for pushing too.

"Most everything else is public record. They've subpoenaed Brie's phone records."

Jazzi thought again about those four names she'd glimpsed on Brie's legal pad. Certainly, if the detective would be accessing Brie's phone records, he'd find out who she texted and dated. He could also access her social media exactly as her coworker Lara had done.

"I wonder if the detective has adequate help . . . if he has a tech expert who could scour social media accounts. It takes time to look through comments to investigate if anyone could have been stalking Brie."

"I don't know. Casey didn't mention anything like that," Erica said. "I do know the detective is also getting pressure from the mayor about the robberies in Belltower Landing."

"Pressure won't help him solve either the robberies or Brie's murder." Jazzi scooped up Freya as she scurried between her ankles. Holding her in the crook of her arm, she stroked under Freya's chin. The kitten purred and settled in.

Erica picked up Zander, who easily jumped from her hand to the bed. He rolled over and she rubbed his soft white tummy. "From what I heard, there have been four more—an A-frame on the lake, a cabin at the resort, and two private houses on Forest Road."

"Maybe Detective Milford will call in help," Jazzi suggested, playing her finger around Freya's nose.

"That's possible, but he might not want to admit he needs it. Some men have huge egos."

"Some murders are never solved," Dawn added.

Jazzi couldn't even contemplate the idea that Brie's killer would elude capture . . . or be free to hurt someone else.

As Jazzi parked at Brie's townhouse—she still thought of the home that way—she vividly remembered the last time she'd been here. The idea of her blossoming friendship with Brie still lived in her heart. They could have been good friends.

Estelle's sedan was already parked. Estelle had asked Jazzi to meet her here at eight. But Brie's mom had possibly been here for hours already.

Hurrying up the steps to the door, Jazzi didn't have time to knock. Estelle flung open the door. "I haven't been here long. I was afraid to come and be here alone. You can't imagine how much I appreciate your help."

Jazzi followed Estelle inside. Driving here, she'd thought about the fact that Brie's killer might still be in Belltower Landing. But she didn't believe he'd come back here. Still, she could be wrong.

The townhouse's interior was topsy-turvy. Furniture had been pushed this way and that. The rug that had covered the sitting area was gone.

Estelle took one of the photos from the wall. "I remember when Brie shot this. The wind was in her hair on a sunshiny day. She'd been happy."

Jazzi suddenly realized she hadn't spoken to Estelle yet. "What can I do to help you?"

With a sigh Estelle placed the framed photo on a stack of others on the ottoman. "Can you pack up the kitchen while I go through Brie's desk?"

"Sure." The kitchen would take little thought, just mugs, glasses, and plates, maybe canned and packaged goods.

"We have a neighbor who has pet food delivered. She gave me the boxes. I rented a storage compartment, but I suppose most of this I'll donate to whoever will take it."

"I know it's a lot to handle," Jazzi sympathized. "Just making all the calls takes energy."

"It would be less stressful if Harry helped more, but I've given up on that."

Climbing the steps to the kitchen, Jazzi opened cupboards to see exactly what she'd be packing. Brie's set of dishes with mugs and sandwich plates looked to be in perfect condition. There was another set that she must have used for every day. Picking up the roll of bubble wrap, Jazzi began to pack.

Estelle stood at the small desk in the living room where Brie's laptop had sat the night Jazzi had been invited to dinner. But the laptop was missing.

"It's easy to see the police's forensics team went through Brie's desk," Estelle said. "Her checkbook is missing. I suppose the detective is going to look at each one of her expenditures, but I don't understand why. She was just a single woman trying to make ends meet."

"They're looking for anything unusual, things like regular payments that can't be explained, either deposits or withdrawals."

"You mean . . . like for blackmail?" Estelle pushed the small desk drawer shut.

"Yes, but really anything unusual. They can access bank records, but her personal checkbook might have notes."

"I see."

As Jazzi glanced down the few steps to Estelle, she noticed the wistful look on the woman's face. She didn't have to wonder for long what she was thinking.

Estelle sank heavily onto the straight-backed chair at the desk. "I'm glad I never deleted Brie's emails. I don't do much with my laptop, but I keep all her messages in a folder. Sometimes she'd tell me something and I'd forget the details she expected me to remember. If I kept her emails that way, I could go back to them and look."

"Did you email each other often?"

"Mostly late at night. Harry would be snoring in his recliner, and I'd be watching a movie. Brie would tell me about the kids she worked with that day, and her plans to go paddleboarding. I loved hearing every detail."

Jazzi heard the tremble in Estelle's voice and realized how much Estelle wanted to hear about Brie's day-to-day life. Jazzi realized she should email her own mom more. She'd believed she needed to keep some distance between them to be an adult. Yet . . . they'd been close during her childhood and teen years. Maybe finding her birth mother had interfered with her relationship with her mom, but in other ways it had made it stronger. The whole situation had formed Jazzi into the woman she was now.

What exactly would her mom say if she knew Jazzi was in a

murdered woman's townhouse asking questions about her death?

Jazzi wasn't sure she wanted to open that door between her and her mother.

An hour later Jazzi was finishing in the kitchen. Estelle had used cleaner and polish on all the living room surfaces. She'd climbed the stairs to the kitchen and started wiping down the counter there.

"The landlord will probably clean everything when the furniture's out," Jazzi said.

Estelle kept swiping her cloth over the granite. "I know, but I need to feel useful." She stared down into the living room area. "Will you come back with me to pack up Brie's bedroom? I can only handle so much at a time."

Handling clothes a loved one had worn would be the hardest part of Estelle's emptying the townhouse. "I'll come back with you. Let me take a last look at the drawers to make sure we got everything."

Estelle checked the bottom cupboards while Jazzi pulled out the kitchen drawers. The junk drawer with paper clips, notepads, twist ties, grease pen, and rubber bands had been the last one Jazzi emptied. She noticed now she hadn't removed the drawer liner. Pulling it out she crumbled it and tossed it into the wastebasket. As she did, she noticed a small square of paper had floated to the back of the drawer. It was pale blue, a card from a florist shop. It said—*I hope you find what you're looking for. Gregg*

Gregg Rizzo? Jazzi pictured the brown hair and boyish grin that she'd glimpsed in Brie's social media photos.

"Estelle, did Brie ever email you about a man, Gregg Rizzo?"

Estelle straightened, holding on to the counter for support. Sadness crossed her face when she shook her head. "Brie never talked to me about men. I'm not sure why. Maybe she wanted to keep her dating life private. Not unusual, I suppose."

No, it wasn't unusual. Jazzi hadn't confided her problems with Mark to her family, not until it was over. Even then, not a deep dive into it.

"Why are you asking?" Estelle wanted to know.

Jazzi showed her the card.

Estelle looked thoughtful. "Maybe he sent her good-bye flowers. That sounds like something a gentleman would do."

Was Gregg a "gentleman"? And just what had Brie been looking for? The right man? Perfect husband material? This did sound like a breakup bouquet. Did Gregg resent the breakup? How long had they dated?

Those were questions to ask Gregg Rizzo.

The next few days passed without Jazzi hearing from Estelle. Maybe Brie's mom had decided to take a break before tackling packing up Brie's most personal belongings. Jazzi kept her focus on the Welcome Summer weekend preparations. A day before Emilia's book signing, Jazzi was nervous. The store looked ready for the summer festival, but was *she* ready? How about her team?

Dawn seemed to have a laissez-faire attitude about it. And truthfully that calmed down Jazzi. That's one reason they complemented each other as roommates. But in the back of Jazzi's mind, the idea also played that Dawn didn't have as much to lose as *she* did. Making Tomes & Tea succeed wasn't merely about money. It was about Jazzi's life, the independence that she craved. Dawn could sell her interest in Tomes, but Jazzi . . .

This was her opportunity to make her mark, to fly on her own, to become successful and a savvy businesswoman. Her mother had done it, and Jazzi intended to do it too, right now, at age twenty-five. She'd been given the opportunity and she was going to take advantage of it, not flub it.

She spotted Derek talking to Dawn at the tea bar. She was pouring him a cup of iced tea. Derek drank lots of iced tea.

Jazzi didn't think that was because he enjoyed their daily brew so much but rather because he liked being around Dawn.

Seeing Jazzi was free, Erica rushed over to her. "Have you taken a look at the numbers of our online tea sales?"

"I looked over them last night. Why?"

"They've exploded this morning, and I can show you why." Erica was waving her phone at Jazzi.

Jazzi caught hold of Erica's arm. "Slow down. Let me see."

After Erica shoved her phone in front of Jazzi's face, Jazzi backed up a few inches. Then she watched the video. Emilia Perez was holding a belfry tea box and mentioning Tomes & Tea in Belltower Landing, New York, where she would be signing her new book tomorrow.

"Oh, my gosh!" Jazzi was practically vibrating with excitement as she watched Emilia tell her followers:

> *"I know not all of you can find me at this wonderful bookshop and tea bar tomorrow. But you can order books and tea from the shop online, and I will be signing one hundred copies that you can order at their website. First come, first served. By ordering books and tea, you're not only supporting my new book, but also a brick-and-mortar independent bookstore. You're the best. See you tomorrow."*

"Delaney told me about the hundred books." Jazzi returned Erica's phone to her. "This will assure we sell them all quickly. Are we prepared to send them out?"

"We will be. I have two teen nieces who like to make extra money. I can convince them to come in Sunday if you want."

"I want. This Welcome Summer Festival is going to raise our visibility. If we're a great success this weekend, I'll have Delaney to thank for enlisting Emilia's help."

"And you can thank Theo if Evan Holloway comes through our doors," Erica reminded her.

Jazzi couldn't keep her grin from becoming wider. "Theo texted me last night. Plans are still on for Evan Holloway to stop in around four p.m. on Saturday. We'll have time to reorganize after Emilia's appearance on Friday."

"Have you downloaded his music?" Erica slid her phone into her Tomes & Tea apron pocket.

"I'm streaming it on my music app so I'm familiar with it. Hopefully one of us can make a connection with him."

Erica glanced around the store to see if she was needed anywhere. "He might just want to come in, say hi, and leave again."

Jazzi took a look around the store for about the hundredth time to make sure everything was in its place. "Theo said Evan won't be putting the word out on his social media that he'll be here because the store would get rushed. Better if he mentions Tomes and Tea after the fact. He'll leave signed photos we can hand out with purchases."

"That's smart." Erica spotted a group of four come in who headed to the tea bar. "I'd better help Dawn."

As Erica said that, Jazzi noted a customer heading toward the cookbook section. Casper Kowolski. He looked very different today than when she saw him last at his food truck. At his truck, with his red plaid hairband smashing down his black hair and his white apron sometimes smeared with sauce, he worked hard and looked it.

Today, however, he was dressed like most of the locals who browsed in the store. He wore denim shorts and a heather-colored tee, boat shoes, and he was sockless. She crossed to "help" him and maybe talk to him for a few minutes.

"Hi, Casper. Is there anything I can help you with?"

Turning, he recognized her. After all, she and her friends often patronized his food truck. "Hey, Jazzi. Just looking.

Though maybe . . ." He pointed to a shelf of books. "Are those new?"

She crossed to the shelf. "These are from an estate sale. Many were never used. I think we have good prices on them. Are you looking for something in particular?"

Standing in front of the shelf, he ran his forefinger over the spines. "Maybe something with Thai spices. I need to change up a few dishes I sell. I'm trying for a broader appeal with tourists and all."

"I get it. You want to please old and new customers. The Welcome Summer Festival is a terrific time to do it. I think there are two here you might be interested in. They have great photos too." She pulled out a volume that was almost the size of a coffee table book.

"Wow. That does look brand-new." He leafed through some pages, running his finger down recipes. Jazzi gave him time to consider the book.

He paged through it. "I hear you're having quite a book signing tomorrow." He glanced over his shoulder at the display. "There's buzz about it going around the trucks."

Just like any community within a community, the chefs at the trucks gossiped. "We've been posting about it on social media all week. Emilia Perez did the same thing this morning."

"Wow, no wonder the word is getting out. We should all do well with the festival. I guess the next noteworthy event will be the regatta."

While Casper continued to meander through recipes, they talked about the regatta the following weekend. Jazzi pulled out a second book from the shelf, showed him one section in particular and waited for his thoughts. Instead of giving her his views on the Thai recipes, he closed the book and held it against his chest. "You know, everyone around the marina is talking about Brie Frazier's murder."

The non sequitur surprised Jazzi. "I thought talk might have died down by now."

"No, I think that's because of the festival. Anyone who owns a business is afraid the murder could damage attendance. I heard some tourists shortened their stay at the Stars Above Resort and the Lakeside Condos."

"Not surprising," Jazzi murmured. "Dawn and I put a peephole in our door, and Dawn's dad attached a better dead bolt. I hate the idea of locking ourselves up inside because we don't know if there's someone out there who could hurt us."

She took a longer look at Casper and decided that, while she had him, maybe he'd answer a few questions. But before she could ask one, he said, "It was even all over the marina about Nolan Johnson yelling at you. No wonder you don't feel safe."

Since everyone seemed to know everybody's business, she'd ease into her questions. "I was getting to know Brie before she was killed. I'm helping her mom go through Brie's townhouse. Did you know Brie?"

"I don't know if anyone could really know Brie." His frown indicated he'd been frustrated by something in their relationship.

"I thought she was fairly open, though I have to admit I didn't know her long." If Jazzi played devil's advocate, she could possibly learn more.

Casper gave out a short grunt. "I thought she was open too when we first went out. But we only dated a few weeks before she cut it off. There was something about me that she didn't like, I guess."

Not Brie's type? Not enough income? Not many future prospects? She'd never know.

"When did you date?"

"In the new year. Then I ran into her again at the maypole celebration on the green. I thought maybe we'd reconnect. We had drinks together."

"*Did* you start dating again?"

He shook his head. "No. When I called her to set something up, she seemed on edge, wouldn't talk about it. She just said now wasn't a good time."

"When was *now*?"

"A week before she was killed."

Casper looked sad and seemed like a nice guy. But was he?

Chapter Fourteen

The Welcome Summer Festival was off to a grand start. Stepping outside of Tomes & Tea for a few seconds, Jazzi could see tourists and locals strolling in and out of all the shops along the sundrenched street. She checked her watch—an hour and a half until Emilia arrived. Jazzi could feel excitement buzzing from her bangs to her sandals.

Parker strode up the walk toward the store as Jazzi was turning to step back inside. After a smile and an after-you gesture, he followed her in. "Do you have enough help today?"

The tea bar was crowded with folks waiting for tea and baked goods. Today the Dockside Bakery had provided peach walnut muffins and chocolate mini-tarts. Three customers stood in line at the sales desk. Jazzi moved that way.

Over her shoulder, she said to Parker, "I hope so. But once Emilia arrives, it could get hectic."

"I can always help bag books."

Jazzi turned to face him. "I can't let you do that."

His wide grin was self-deprecating. "Why not? Think I can't put the right books in the right customer's bag?"

"No, of course not. But aren't you going to enjoy the festival? Almost every shop has sales or special events. The marina and the community center boardwalk are decorated for this weekend. Even the food trucks are giving out samples."

"Do I look underfed?" he joked. Then he turned serious. "You do realize, don't you, that I'd rather be out on the lake fishing than participating in the events."

Obviously, Parker enjoyed peace and quiet. That was no secret. "Then why aren't you?"

"Because even the lake traffic is heavy today. Sure, it's a thirty-mile-long lake, but tourists have found us for the summer, and this weekend is especially crowded. I set up a client meeting for later. My office will be the quietest place in town."

"And after the meeting? Will you be hibernating?" She didn't like to see Parker close himself off, but he often said he could only handle so much noise and stimulation.

With a one-shoulder shrug, he gave her a coy smile. "It depends on your definition of hibernating. A friend is joining me for a gaming session."

As he saw *that* look pass over her face—the one that said she worried about him—he waved his hand in front of her face. "I will come out of my lair for evening festivities tomorrow night. I appreciate Shakespeare, though I might use earplugs for the Evan Holloway concert. Always too much bass."

She couldn't keep from laughing. "I won't tell him you said that."

"Do you think you'll actually get chat time with him?"

She slipped behind the sales desk with Erica. "You never know. I'm trying to be flexible this weekend for whatever happens."

"You're so much better at that than I am. Must be because of my childhood," he said, "and being homeschooled."

"Or maybe it's because you have a genius IQ. You like routine. There's nothing wrong with that."

Dawn had confided that fact about Parker's IQ shortly after Jazzi had met him.

Parker's face turned slightly red. "That's an unverified rumor."

Shaking her head, Jazzi went along with his proffer of help. "You're welcome to bag, but I pay in cups of tea."

"Fine with me."

Jazzi kept an eye on her watch as well as activity in Tomes. The shop became more crowded as noon approached. She told herself to breathe . . . breathe . . . breathe. At noon, a sleek gray SUV drew up in front of the store. A hefty man in a black suit opened the SUV's passenger door and Delaney emerged. She was wearing a bronze-colored two-piece suit dress. The man stood at the front passenger door and then Emilia slid out one very long, well-shaped leg. Her heels had to be at least five-inch spikes in the same red as her dress.

On the sidewalk now, Jazzi could see the slim fire-engine-red dress did indeed have wings. Emilia had worn her hair up in an intricately woven design.

As Jazzi took in Emilia Perez's appearance, Delaney beckoned to her and then to Dawn. They both hurried to her. Too quickly for Jazzi to remember exactly what happened, Emilia's bodyguard—Jazzi had assumed the man in the suit was her bodyguard—had directed her and Dawn on either side of the model, in front of Tomes & Tea. Delaney was snapping photos and possibly video with her camera. Passersby were doing the same.

It all took a matter of minutes until Delaney ushered them inside.

Jazzi caught her breath as she and Dawn actually had the chance to say hello to Emilia.

After greetings all around, Emilia took a seat on the desk chair at the table. "This looks wonderful."

Her bodyguard had placed a bottle of water on the table

even though Jazzi had put one there too. "If this chair isn't comfortable, let me know and we'll find another."

Dawn straightened the stack of books. "If you'd like iced tea, say the word."

Customers were already lining up to receive numbers to have their books signed. "I'm good for now. Let's get started."

Jazzi let Emilia shine. Her being there caused business to flow in several ways. Dawn and Jazzi had decided to give out numbers for customers who wanted books signed. The numbers allowed book buffs to browse while they waited for their number to come up. Others had books signed and then stayed to listen to Emilia speak to fans. They also moved around the store, picking up other books that captured their interest.

Jazzi had to admit that she was surprised when Connie Covino came into Tomes & Tea with Andrea. Jazzi couldn't help but notice Connie. She looked like a model herself this afternoon, wearing a red-and-white patterned sundress with red Louboutin sandals. Crystals embellished the straps. Jazzi had often glimpsed shoes like that while window-shopping. They were way out of her budget. It was easy to see that Connie was fit. Had those upper arm muscles developed simply from tennis? Or perhaps she worked out with a personal trainer.

Jazzi watched Connie as she learned she had to take a number and wait until it was called. She huffily moved around the store. Although concentrating on Emilia, making sure her stack of books wasn't diminishing, ensuring each customer could have a minute or two with her, Jazzi still realized what Connie was doing. She was trading numbers with an older woman who was browsing. Apparently, Connie had better things to do than wait for her number to be called.

Entitlement. Connie apparently believed she was entitled to anything she wanted.

Andrea tagged along with her mother and seemed disinterested. She was wearing white designer jeans and a cropped short-sleeved top. The label on the back pocket of the jeans was a giveaway. The two women had their heads together just as Connie's number was called. When Connie stepped up to have her book signed, she easily started a conversation with the model as if they were on equal terms.

As Connie ignored Jazzi, she said to Emilia, "I was once a model too. I know it's not an easy life. That posing . . . that takes a toll on your body even if you're fit. You certainly do look fit."

Emilia gave Connie a tolerant smile. "So, you would like me to sign this book for you?"

"Yes, I would like that. Maybe you could sign it—to a fellow model in a difficult business."

Emilia narrowed her eyes and took another look at Connie. "It might be a difficult business, but it's given me a bright future. This book is only one part of it," she admitted.

"Are you going to go into acting?" Connie asked.

"I've taken some acting courses. My agent is discussing other possibilities."

"Maybe a talk show?" Connie wanted to know.

But Emilia wasn't disclosing her plans, or anything about her personal life. She was too smart for that.

"I couldn't keep up the hours and the traveling," Connie confessed. "That's why I took a job with a cosmetic company."

As Jazzi straightened the stack of books next to Emilia, a question popped out of her mouth. "Is that how you met Joseph Covino?"

Connie gave Jazzi a dark look.

But Emilia turned to Connie as if her curiosity had gotten the better of her too. "Did you meet your husband while you were modeling?"

"Not modeling exactly. I was working for the cosmetics company as their spokeswoman. We met at a charity event my company was sponsoring. It was love at first sight. We had a whirlwind romance."

Andrea, who had been quiet until now as she stood next to her mother, chimed in. "It's a good thing she did. We live in an awesome house now, and I had my first choice at a college. Her romance, as she calls it, made life better for all of us."

Andrea almost sounded like a teenager with no filter. Was she this open with other people? Or was it just that Emilia was a celebrity, and celebrities were worth the mother and daughter's time?

From the day Jazzi had met the Covino family, she'd wondered if Connie and Joseph's relationship had been a love match or if it was something much more practical.

With adept polite persuasion, Emilia managed to say to Connie, "It was so nice to meet you."

Mother and daughter finally moved away from the table toward the sales counter.

After a sigh of relief, Jazzi waved to Giselle Dubois as her friend wandered around the shop, picking up a cup of tea and a number. When it came to her turn with Emilia, she pointed to a group of four men standing near the biography section. "I think you have a fan club," she told Emilia. "But they might be a little afraid to talk to you."

Emilia laughed. "I doubt if they're afraid to talk to me. I'll make it easy on them."

"I wanted to be a model," Giselle told her. "But I'm too short. Five-four isn't modeling material."

Emilia studied her. "You have a beautiful heart-shaped face."

Jazzi didn't think Giselle needed all the eye shadow that she wore. Her hair was short and shaggy, sometimes poufy. She was adorable but always felt as if she had to make up for her short height. "Giselle is one of our women entrepreneurs in Belltower Landing," Jazzi told Emilia.

"Tell me about that," Emilia said after asking Giselle how to spell her name.

"I went to a community college, took a couple of online business courses and accounting courses and decided to open my own business. I figured out what Belltower Landing needed most—a cleaning service. There are so many moms who just don't have time to clean their houses as well as work and take care of kids. I developed reasonable rates, and now I have a staff. I work for some high-end clients too, and there are a lot of them in Belltower Landing."

Emilia leaned forward to Giselle. "I bet you see a lot of family drama."

"Or the aftermath of it," Giselle said with a smile. "I certainly do see a cross section of Belltower Landing and how they live. And you'd be surprised at what people just leave sitting around. I could write a book."

Jazzi said, "Giselle is one of my book club friends, along with Delaney. Delaney could always hook her up with an agent."

All three women laughed, and Giselle realized she should move on and not tie up Emilia any longer.

One by one, the men who were standing over to the side came up to have their books signed. Emilia spent a few minutes with each, easily conversing with them, delving into their life, finding something to talk about besides how to spell their name.

Jazzi recognized one of the men from the pictures she'd seen on Brie's social media that Lara had shown her—Gregg Rizzo. As Jazzi listened to their conversation, she heard Gregg say, "I have an office nearby. I often stop in here to look around." After Gregg and Emilia conversed for a few minutes and he walked away with his book, Emilia said to Jazzi, "I need a break. Ladies' room?"

Jazzi showed her where the ladies' room was located, then

came back to the table. She told those in line that they'd resume the book signing in a few minutes.

Gregg was standing in the check-out line. She crossed to him, wondering if Erica needed help. She went behind the counter and took the opportunity to bag Gregg's book.

"I wonder if Emilia has a date for the concert tomorrow night," he joked.

"I think she has another book signing tomorrow and will be leaving as soon as she's finished here," Jazzi answered.

He gave a self-deprecating chuckle. "That was a wild thought that entered my head. I don't know where it came from."

Jazzi rang up his sale and bagged his book. "Never let an opportunity pass you by. You never know what can happen."

He shook his head. "I might be more successful with Emilia than with my last date. I found her on a dating app."

"Not enough in common?" Jazzi asked innocently, wondering how much he'd say.

"I thought we had a chance, but the woman didn't. I was sort of ready to settle down, but certainly not start a family. And she wanted to do that right away."

Was that Brie's criteria? Whoever she dated not only wanted to get married soon, but start a family too? It was a lot to ask. How could anyone know if they'd be ready for that? But apparently Brie had been.

Erica had made quick work of the customers and only one still stood in front of her.

Jazzi said to Gregg, "Maybe you could both give it another shot."

A look of supreme sadness passed over Gregg's face. "I can't. That woman was Brie Frazier."

Jazzi's gaze met Gregg's directly. "I'm so, so sorry."

"We weren't that close," he said offhandedly. "We only had a few dates. But I really liked her. I can't believe what happened."

Is this something Gregg told many people? Was it easier to discuss Brie with a stranger? That was often the case, whether it was talking about a loved one who passed, adoption, or a murder.

"When I think of Brie, it seems impossible that she's not still here," Gregg added.

It was hard to believe that this man could have had anything to do with Brie's death. Or maybe it was a good act. Maybe he was an actor. Except the next thing he said threw Jazzi off balance.

"I thought I knew Brie. But I guess I didn't." Gregg shook his head.

Before Jazzi could ask any more questions, Emilia came back to the signing table. Jazzi knew she couldn't prolong this conversation. She handed Gregg his bag and went to help Emilia.

Chapter Fifteen

Tomes & Tea closed after probably the busiest day it had ever had. Jazzi was upstairs in her apartment playing with the kittens, simply attempting to wind down from the excitement. She shuffled the kittens' play wand with its flannel tail and let it trail over her bed. When she dragged it into the living room, they chased after it.

After about a half hour of that, both kittens conked out on the sofa. Jazzi thought about what she wanted to do. She could sack out too. But she was still . . . energized. Dawn had gone out to dinner with her parents and their friends. Jazzi felt antsy, not wanting to watch a movie. Maybe she needed a walk. She grabbed a container of yogurt, wolfed it down, grabbed her purse, then locked up the apartment. There was activity on the green tonight, and she felt like she wanted to be part of it.

Jazzi crossed the street, taking her time walking on the sidewalk along the green. Some of the benches were full and some weren't. The acting troupe was setting up for *A Midsummer Night's Dream* the next evening. Fairy lights danced around the bell tower. Since Evan Holloway's concert would be staged here too, there was a platform set up on the lakeshore. Not much else going on there yet, but she knew tomorrow there would be techs all over it to handle lighting, stage set, and the sound system. The powers that be had decided to place the concert here instead of down at the marina because the marina boardwalk would be used for other Welcome Summer activities.

Finding an empty bench, she watched the troupe set up props. She could hear the water lapping against the shore every once in a while. Lifting her chin, she could feel the mist in the air. Good weather was forecasted for tonight and tomorrow, so setting up for both events was suitable. She smiled at the ceramic toadstools being placed here and there for *A Midsummer Night's Dream*. There wasn't a stage per se for the troupe, but there were more lanterns and lights wound over and through the branches of trees in a certain area, which designated where the play would take place. Residents would bring blankets and chairs and set them on the grass. She heard that onlookers could even be pulled in to take part in the performance. It would be interactive. This was a romantic comedy, so to speak, and it would all be great fun.

Suddenly the hairs on the back of Jazzi's neck prickled, and she felt a presence. She soon learned who that presence was. Oliver came around the bench and sat beside her.

As if some explanation was in order, he said, "My manager is closing up for me tonight. It was a record day for restaurateurs. We had a full house all day. How did your store do?"

Did Oliver want to talk business? Or perhaps he was simply making conversation. It didn't matter. A little nervous because she was aware of him beside her, she calmed her questions . . . and feelings. He'd brushed his short, wavy blond hair to the side. He ran his hand over his scruffy stubble as she turned toward him and studied his face.

There were enough lights glowing that she could see the determined set of his jaw as well as the hue of his blue, blue eyes. He was wearing a yellow polo shirt tonight and navy shorts. In spite of her efforts to be cooly detached, she was aware of the woodsy scent of his cologne. It was a recognizable scent and suited him. She wasn't sure why, but she had to take a big breath and swallow before she was ready for a conversation with him.

"It was a record day today, that's for sure. And I can thank Emilia Perez for it. Our social media feed exploded too. A lot of people have now heard of Tomes and Tea."

"Congratulations." He lightly placed his hand over hers, but then removed it.

She felt sorry that he had. That wasn't like her at all. "Are you here to watch the setup?"

"I am. I just wanted to unwind. You the same?"

"Me the same. It was a busy day. I played with the kittens for a while after we closed. You'll have to stop in and see Freya sometime."

"I suppose I will. She was a little minx, and I guess she still is."

"Oh, she is. And she and her brother make trouble. But they're so adorable. It doesn't seem to matter. We've kitten-proofed most of the apartment."

"Pets can be such an important part of growing up." Oliver's tone was a bit wistful.

"Did you have pets? A kangaroo, maybe?"

He laughed, a deep, rich laugh. "No, afraid not. Though I did volunteer on a rescue ranch when I was with my dad. When I was here with my mother, sometimes I volunteered at local shelters. But I never had a pet of my own."

"A rescue ranch?" The idea of that experience sounded fascinating. She didn't know anything about rescue compounds in Australia.

"Yes. We've had a lot of wildfires there in recent years and animals get hurt—kangaroos, koala bears, anything running around that gets caught in the fire. So, I helped."

Jazzi found herself still studying Oliver's face and wanting to know more about him.

He motioned to the troupe setup committee who were handling the toadstools and benches and whatever else they needed for tomorrow night. "Are you a fan of Shakespeare?"

She considered her experience with the Bard. "I like some of his plays. I took a course in college—The Complete Works of Shakespeare."

"*Othello* or *Romeo and Juliet*? Which is your favorite?"

"How about *Twelfth Night*?"

Oliver laughed again. "Where does *A Midsummer Night's Dream* fall on your list?"

"It's fun. I'll enjoy watching it. Are you coming tomorrow night . . . or do you have to work?"

"We'll be serving until ten tomorrow night. It seemed obvious we should stay open. So I'm not sure. It depends if my manager will close up again, or if I'll stay and do it. I'll see how the services go. Did you and Theo ever reconnect about Evan Holloway?"

One thing she was learning about Oliver—he listened. "We did. I was honest with Theo, and I think he forgave me for what I almost did. But, yes, he's going to see if Evan will stop in at the store."

"You're on your way to success, Jazzi. Go for it."

They were staring into each other's eyes, and she was getting chills up and down her arms. Nevertheless, just then a black Mercedes pulled up to the curb along the green. A tall man in a tux crossed the street to meet it. When the driver of the Mercedes climbed out, Jazzi thought she recognized him. He'd parked under a streetlamp, and she could see his long face,

Roman-style nose, dirty-blond hair styled thick and high, shorn short on the sides. Yes, she recognized him from Brie's social media stream. As she watched, Vic Finch took the suited man's credit card, scanned it with his phone, and handed it back. The man slid into the car and closed the door.

Vic walked down the street whistling.

Oliver cocked his head toward the street. "Vic has a great detailing business. Do you know him?"

"I know who he is." She didn't say how. "Detailing? You mean he cleans cars?"

"It's much more than car washing," Oliver explained. "It's an art. His crew are professionals at the fine points. They try to restore a vehicle to a like-new condition, and they have special products to do that for the outside and the inside. Guys that are good at it, and Vic has a reputation for being good, can do well. I don't know if he'd do as well if this wasn't a resort town. There are customers here who will pay for detailing quite often."

"Do you think The Wild Kangaroo could do as well in another type of town?"

Instead of giving a ready answer, Oliver thought about it. "Good food, creative drinks, friendly customers, and a good staff should be welcome in any town."

Jazzi had a feeling Oliver's personality and business skills could make the restaurant work anywhere. Although she'd like to linger here, the troupe setup team was leaving.

Jazzi checked her watch. "I should be getting back."

"The kittens give you a curfew?"

"Something like that." The smile in her voice made him smile too.

"Would you like me to walk you home?" His tone was serious, not the least bit romantic. "You know, there still could be somebody running around out here who shouldn't be."

She wondered if he'd walk home any woman who might have been alone here tonight. "That's a terrible thought, isn't it? But yes, I'd like that."

They both stood and Jazzi wondered what she was doing. She didn't have far to walk. And she did know a bit of self-defense. But she had to admit to herself that having Oliver walk her home felt very different than having Parker walk her home.

If nerves could jangle, Jazzi's were overdoing it. It was Saturday morning and she was expecting Evan Holloway today. That's if Theo came through. Business was brisk in large part due to Emilia Perez's post on social media. They still had books that she'd signed, and customers were snapping those up. She said she could send another box if Delaney let her know. Jazzi would keep her eye on the pile.

At one point Audrey sidled up next to Jazzi and asked, "How long do you think Evan will stay? Long enough for everybody to take a selfie?"

"I have no idea," Jazzi told her. "I just hope he's coming."

They hadn't posted anything about it or even hinted at his appearance because it would be a big disappointment and letdown if he didn't show up.

Even Erica had stars in her eyes. "He looks a little like Luke Bryant, don't you think?" She was looking at his photos on her phone.

If one had to make comparisons, Jazzi thought that was a good one. Evan was tall, slim, and fit with a mop of brown hair that was styled. She imagined the hairdresser who did his hair charged more than Jazzi could pull in at the store in a week. But that could also be an exaggeration.

Because today seemed special, Dawn had primped this morning and spent a huge amount of time messing with her hair. Her makeup was fitting for a night out. Her blouse was orange and terribly cute with a ruffled V-neck and fluttery sleeves. Her apron covered the rest of her. Still, she'd worn platform white sandals with her white slacks today and she never wore those in the shop simply because they all ran around and stood for hours at a time. Comfortable shoes were a must.

At the sales counter, Dawn leaned in close to Jazzi. "I heard he's going to drop a new single tonight at the concert. What do you think?"

Jazzi wasn't sure what she thought. She'd love the concert as much as any other country music fan. And the drop of a new release would be great. But for now she just hoped Evan Holloway had the time to stop in and the inclination to meet and greet fans. Did he enjoy meeting his fans? Did he enjoy signing autographs? She'd set up a special section of books since he liked to read about music history. Whether he bought books or not wasn't the issue. She just hoped she could manage to interest him in staying in the store a few minutes longer.

Jazzi hadn't primped like Dawn this morning. She'd French-braided her hair and used the same amount of makeup she did every morning, maybe with a tiny little bit of extra mascara. And her lip gloss might be just a little bit darker. Okay, she was excited too, and she had to admit it. Meeting a country music star. Who wouldn't be excited?

"Do you think he'll arrive in a limo?" Dawn asked.

"No knowing," Jazzi answered with a shrug. "He has to get around town somehow, unless he lets Theo drive him. But I highly doubt that."

"Do you think he and Theo are friends, like Theo makes him out to be?"

"I didn't really talk to Theo about that. I just knew Evan Holloway was a contact."

"You're too calm," Dawn teased.

If Dawn only knew what was going on inside her body — the

nerves jangling, her heart racing, her stomach turning upside down. Oh sure, she was calm on the outside. It was a trick she'd learned while she was growing up. She hadn't wanted to show her grief over her adopted father's death. She hadn't wanted to show her worry as well as interest in searching for her birth mother. She hadn't wanted her mom to be upset when they'd found Portia and Jazzi had gotten to know her. She'd kept a lot inside, hoping to keep her newly found birth mother interested and her mom from getting upset.

And then there had been Mark. At separate colleges she'd been afraid to show him exactly how much she missed him. She didn't want to bog him down or divert his attention from his studies. When she'd transferred to his college, she'd wanted to show him they could coexist on the same campus, nurture their relationship without tying each other up in knots or absorbing all their free time. Had that been the problem? Hadn't she shown him enough how she'd felt?

Possibly. But what he'd said when he'd broken up with her was that their interests were taking them in different directions and on different life paths. And when she'd moved here on her own, yes, she had depended on Dawn and her family. She'd been afraid to show exactly how much she depended on them. Didn't everyone hide their deepest emotions? Didn't everyone pretend they were calm when they weren't? Maybe she'd gotten too good at it.

Giselle had stopped in, just as she had yesterday when Emilia was there. But today she'd been in and out a couple of times, hoping to get a glimpse of what was going to happen next. She told Jazzi, "I'll text everybody as soon as we know Evan has arrived."

Now she looked disappointed as Jazzi's excitement seemed to be fading away. It was getting late, almost four thirty. "He's a busy guy," Giselle told her. "He has to do a sound check for tonight and all of that. Maybe he just won't have time."

"I understand that. I just wish Theo would give me a heads-up one way or the other."

Then it happened. "It" started with a buzz that seemed to come from outside. Onlookers began gathering as if lining up for a parade. Chatter in the store ceased and started up again as customers gathered to look out the windows.

Someone opened the door and the boulevard seemed to be abuzz with, "Evan Holloway's coming!" No one could know for sure that Evan Holloway was in the stretch limo with its dark windows, but enough residents of the town knew he was going to be playing at a concert tonight and they didn't know who else might be traveling that way.

Jazzi watched, thinking Evan's arrival was sort of like a parade. There was a car in front of the limo and a sedan behind the limo. An escort? Jazzi was surprised the mayor wasn't escorting Evan Holloway himself, but maybe he wasn't aware of Evan's time schedule either.

All three cars double-parked. Two men hopped out of the limo. They definitely looked like bodyguards, not in a suit as Emilia's watcher had been, but rather blue jeans with white T-shirts with EVAN HOLLOWAY printed on the front. They were husky like football players, but not as tall as Evan himself. They practically surrounded Evan as he climbed out and headed for the store.

Jazzi's heart flipflopped like a fish out of water.

Suddenly, Theo appeared inside the store, looking out of breath as if he'd run up the boulevard to make sure he was here when Evan arrived. Maybe he'd had to park a half block away?

Evan Holloway was definitely any country girl's dream. *Any* girl's dream, Jazzi supposed. At six-foot-four, incredibly long-legged in blue jeans, and with wide shoulders filling up his black shirt with a stand-up collar, he wore an incredibly wide smile. His green eyes twinkled as he entered the store and spotted Jazzi.

"Hey, Jazzi. Theo showed me a picture of you."

Jazzi felt herself blush. So many selfies had been taken in the last week, so she wasn't surprised Theo had one.

"Welcome to Tomes and Tea, Mr. Holloway."

He chuckled, "It's Evan, darlin'. I'm sure we'll be friends after today."

"Can I . . . can I get you anything?" Jazzi stammered. "Tea . . . a muffin?"

Evan's eyebrows flew up under his forelock. "No sirree. I only have a few minutes." He leaned over and whispered to her. "I'm a straight caffeine kind of guy."

She whispered back. "You'll have to try black tea sometime."

He looked surprised for a moment, then he laughed. "Theo told me you can be sassy. I guess he was right."

"Over to the signing table, Jazzi," Theo whispered to her, signaling Evan wouldn't be in the store very long.

She felt as if she'd been lost in a daze. "Of course."

Theo, prepared for an autograph session, had a stack of Evan Holloway's photos in his hand. Evan took a seat at the table and customers began lining up, hoping for a signed photo and a selfie.

After Evan had asked for the names of about twenty-five customers, signed photos, and took selfies, he stood. "I'm sorry this meet and greet is so quick, Jazzi, but I'm on a tight schedule. Why don't you take a selfie with me before I leave?"

Immediately, Jazzi got hold of Dawn's arm and pulled her into the photo too. Everyone in the store was snapping cell phone pics, and Jazzi hoped they were also posting them on their social media pages. The whole storm of stirred-up enthusiasm seemed to be over in a sparkling minute.

One bodyguard stood behind Evan and one in front of him. But Evan sidestepped them both and ended up close to Jazzi again. He leaned over and asked, "Do you have any books about country music history and maybe the Grand Ole Opry?"

Ready for this opportunity, she showed him the books she'd ordered in case he asked. He picked up a few and handed them to Theo. "Buy these for me, would you?"

A minute later he was gone with his bodyguards, and she wondered if the whole experience had ever happened.

Beside her once more, Theo asked, "Are you going to check me out?"

Turning to him, she knew her eyes were wide and her smile too big for her face. She grabbed his elbow. "Thank you, thank you, thank you. I can't tell you how grateful I am to you for bringing Evan here."

Theo narrowed his eyes. "Are you grateful enough to have dinner with me?"

"I *am*," she responded quickly.

"I'll text you once the excitement dies down."

Jazzi knew he would. He'd kept his word about Evan Holloway. He would keep his word about this too.

That evening, Jazzi dressed in her sundress with all the swirly colors and the sparkling shrug that Dawn had wanted her to wear. Dawn had dressed up fancy too. Her outfit was more country with sequins and embroidery. They couldn't help but be pumped up as they set up their camp chairs where they could view the stage. They'd gotten there early enough that they'd enjoyed the troupe's performance of *A Midsummer Night's Dream*. They'd watched Puck run around causing mischief, and the lovers finally joining together. But now there was an excitement in the crowd that hadn't been on the green before, and Jazzi was taken up with it too.

A lesser-known country band played for about twenty minutes to warm up the crowd, but they didn't need to be warmed up. After Evan Holloway stepped out onto the stage, big black hat, black shirt with bolo tie and black jeans, everyone on the green went wild. The applause and whoops had to reach the next town.

Delaney, Addison, and Giselle were seated with Dawn and Jazzi, huge smiles on their faces, clapping and hooting as loud as everyone else. Evan had been performing for about a half hour when commotion to the right of the crowd caught Jazzi's attention. Near one of the barricades set up to keep the crowd somewhat organized, she spied Damon and Andrea Covino . . . arguing.

It was obvious they were angry from the expressions on their faces. Damon's face was red, his blond hair wild. His lips were twisted into a furious expression. Andrea, dressed in jeans and an embroidered country-western shirt, seemed to be ready to take on anything he had to give. She pointed her finger into his chest, shook her head, and seemed to yell something at him that Jazzi couldn't hear.

A brother and sister fighting. Was it normal for them? Did it happen often?

Suddenly Damon pushed Andrea into the fence. She sank against it and slid down to the ground, not seeming to have any more fight left in her. As Damon stalked away into the crowd, Andrea dropped her head into her hands. It didn't seem anybody else had noticed, not with all the attention focused on the stage.

Jazzi patted Dawn's hand and leaned close to her so her friend could hear.

"I'll be right back."

Dawn nodded absently, engrossed with Evan's song about a broken heart.

Hurrying to Andrea, Jazzi dropped down beside her, unmindful of her sundress. "Are you okay?"

Andrea didn't look at her but just held her head in her hands. "My brother is such a bully. He always has been."

The words had spurted out. But once they had, Andrea looked at Jazzi. The expression on her face said she realized she had said too much.

Climbing to her feet, Andrea turned her face away from Jazzi and brushed off the backside of her jeans. "I'm fine. I'm always fine."

As she walked away, Jazzi stood and watched her go. Yet she wondered just how often Damon's anger steamed out of control.

Chapter Sixteen

On Sunday morning, Jazzi hopped on her bike, took it out onto the bike path on the boulevard, and rode toward the marina. There wasn't that much traffic this early. The wind pushed against her helmet and blew her hair away from her neck. She'd caught it in a low ponytail.

The sky was already a fabulous shade of blue with not many clouds, and the trees along the sidewalk were lush with leaves. She took in the end-of-June colors, from the baskets hanging on the streetlights filled with petunias and marigolds to the bright colored awnings on some of the shops. Not far from the marina, she could smell the aromas from the food trucks—bacon and fried potatoes, tacos and waffles, grilled onions and peppers, and even marinara sauce being prepared for later in the day.

The trucks were preparing for another day of tourist trade from anyone who went boating and paddleboarding to those simply meandering around the marina and heading toward the stores. The boulevard ended at the marina, changing into a two-lane road that circled around that area and led to the developments along the shore of the lake. Jazzi often rode her bike here for the solitude and the scenery. This morning, however, she headed for a development known as High Point. It veered to the east, away from the lake.

The houses were located about an acre apart, some with trees separating the properties, others with privet hedges. Tall fences surrounded a few of the backyards for privacy. All of them boasted green manicured lawns, annuals dancing around the corners in flower beds, and trees like Kwanzan cherry, sweet gum, and gnarled redbuds dotting the lawns, their color traded for greenery, with summer starting. Jazzi branched off onto Dewdrop Circle, which surrounded the entire development. Her legs pumped up the hill and she decided to turn right and venture into the development itself. She'd just turned onto Hemlock Road when she saw flashing lights at the end of the street. As she drew closer, she spotted two police vehicles in front of one of the properties. She slowed, wondering if the police would chase her away. It depended on what was happening.

As she pedaled slower and then stopped, she recognized the one officer who was about her age. He often patrolled the marina. She knew the patrol cops were shifted from one area of town to another. The officer, she knew his name was George, was leaning against the vehicle and peering down at his phone. He often came into the bookstore and browsed while his wife sipped tea and searched for a new mystery title to read.

Looking up, recognition sparked in his eyes as Jazzi removed her helmet.

"Hi, George. What's going on? Another robbery?"

"Yep. Milford's going to be tearing his hair out. He doesn't need this."

"No suspects for the robberies?" she prompted.

Immediately, he directed a steady-eyed glare at her, which she imagined he'd practiced. "I can't talk about the investigation."

Looking as apologetic as she could, she grimaced at her blunder. "I understand. I often take this route when I'm bike riding. I guess I just wanted to know if it's safe."

At that moment the other patrol car pulled away, and George stared at the house. "I don't know what to tell you, Jazzi. This house is vacant right now. Its owners are away. I'm trying to get in touch with them but not having any luck. A neighbor called this in. I can tell you, having two investigations going at the same time has everybody stretched thin."

He wasn't answering her question and she understood that he couldn't. "Last night would have been ideal for a robbery, with everyone's attention on the concert."

He nodded to the adjacent house. "The neighbor came over this morning to feed the property owner's two cats. She has a spare key and knows the alarm code."

"Was the place ransacked?"

He thought about answering, then warned her, "You didn't hear it from me, but just the bedroom was tossed."

Prodding a bit more, she decided, was only natural. "No electronics gone?"

"Nope."

Only the bedroom ransacked and the electronics untouched. "So that probably means that if the owner had any jewelry, that could have been taken."

"You could be right. I can't affirm or deny."

Like a trail of crumbs, that info led to other basic questions. "If there's an alarm—I saw a green light on the doorbell—how did the crooks get in?"

"I can't tell you any more, Jazzi. I've already told you too much."

She took a guess. "Through the back somehow? Maybe they only have one of those front doorbell video alarms?"

George narrowed his eyes. "Do you ride around out here often?"

"Probably twice a week. I don't always come this way."

Obviously trying to change the subject, he pointed toward the lake. "Do you like to ride along the lake?"

"I do, and at this time of the morning, there's not much traffic. Even less back here in the development."

George's phone dinged. He must have been waiting for the text. "You'd better be on your way. I have follow-up to do here. I'm going to do some of the report in my car rather than back at the station."

The situation didn't take a seasoned investigator to figure out. George wasn't about to answer any more of her questions.

Tossing her helmet back on her head, she fastened the strap. She hopped on her bike but before she took off, she said, "Take care of yourself, George. I'll see you around."

He waved as she pedaled away.

Jazzi pedaled hard, not exactly sure why. Maybe it was because the robberies and a murder led her to think about Brie once more.

Pedaling strenuously, she hardly registered the miles that slipped by. Before she realized time passing, she returned to the food truck area. Checking her watch, she thought about stopping for breakfast.

Slowing, she spotted Oliver. He waved at her. At first glance, she recognized exactly what he was carrying—strawberry breakfast waffles.

With a grin he pointed to a nearby table and mouthed, *Do you want to share?*

After riding over to him, she stopped and hopped off her bike. "I don't know. You might need all that for a day at the Kangaroo."

He shook his head. "Too much for one bloke to eat."

She doubted that but she liked the idea of sharing the confection with him. After he'd walked her home on Friday evening, she'd often found her thoughts circling around to their conversation. Or maybe it had been her feelings of anticipation yet safety as he'd walked beside her.

Oliver headed for the food truck and grabbed another plate and fork from the shelf on the truck. She met him at the picnic table and they climbed onto the bench beside each other. His elbow brushed hers as he divided up the strawberries and the waffle.

Jazzi's mind veered somewhere other than the waffle as she caught the scent of his piney woodsy aftershave. She took notice of the blond hair on his well-muscled forearms and wondered why she was having this reaction to him. They didn't even know each other.

Oliver could be called rugged, but in a way he was refined too. And that accent . . .

He handed her a fork and she immediately cut off a piece of her waffle to busy her hands. The whipped cream on the top of the strawberries made this a dessert. But it looked scrumptious for breakfast too. It would give her energy for the day. At least that's what she told herself.

"Do you always go riding this early?" he asked.

"It's the best time. Very little traffic, and just me and the sunrise. It sets me up for my day. Do you know what I mean?"

"I know exactly what you mean. I had a late night with customers stopping in after the concert. The Welcome Summer Festival did us all a favor, didn't it?"

She watched his large tanned hands as he cut a piece from his waffle. Keeping her mind on the conversation, she answered him. "It did."

He pushed a few strawberries onto his section of waffle. "Sometimes I sleep late after a night like that, but this morning I just wanted to get out in the air before all the tourists clump around us again. Sometimes it's a right mess all day, and I just wanted to get away from it."

"You like winter better?" she teased.

"In some ways I do. I ski, and in the winter season I can get away more. But now my getaway time is early mornings and late at night."

For some reason, not exactly sure what it was, she shared, "I rode up to the High Point development today."

"I often do that too," he said. "More and more developments that are being built are gated. I'm glad that one isn't yet."

"I wonder if there are any robberies in the gated communities?"

"I don't know, but the police might not be releasing all the information on all the locations. Why are you thinking about that?" He took a large bite of his waffle, chewed, and swallowed.

She poked her fork into a strawberry. "I ran into two patrol cars up there."

"Really? Do you know why they were there?"

"Yes. There was another robbery. Do you know George Engle?"

"The patrol officer who often patrols the boulevard?"

"Yes, he's the one. I saw him at one of the cars. A neighbor who was taking care of the owners' cats went over this morning. The bedroom had been vandalized."

Oliver stopped eating and held her gaze. "George told you this?"

"He did. I'm not sure why. Maybe because the police department doesn't know what to make of it all. I asked him about suspects and he said he couldn't talk about it."

"But he told you the rest," Oliver scoffed. "That's not solid police work. I would think none of the detail should be let loose."

"I get the feeling they're all inexperienced with real crime. Maybe Belltower Landing has never experienced it before."

Forking a section of waffle with a strawberry, Oliver nodded. "That's true. The PD mostly handles neighborhood disputes and domestic calls. Those are very different from what they're dealing with now."

She said in a low voice something she thought often. "I still can't believe Brie was murdered."

Oliver laid down his fork and turned toward her, his blue eyes sympathetic. "How are you dealing with it?"

"I play with the kittens a lot." She managed a small smile.

"I imagine they're good company."

"They are. They help distract me. But Brie's mom has been counting on me too, and I don't know if I'm supporting her in the right way."

"How are you supporting her?"

"She asked me to go through Brie's things with her at the townhouse, and I said I would. We did the kitchen and the living room over a week ago. But tonight, I think we're going to go through Brie's clothes and her more personal possessions. She has to have it done in the next few days."

Oliver's expression was concerned and kind. "Not just anybody would do that for her. What about her husband?"

"He's in mourning, and he's pretty much checked out. I'd want someone to help me in the same situation." It was time to change the subject before she teared up. She didn't want that to happen in front of Oliver. "Does Damon Covino come into The Wild Kangaroo often?"

"He comes in enough. He's there for happy hour . . . tries to pick up women. Sometimes it works. Sometimes it doesn't. Why?"

"Have you ever seen Damon be aggressive with women at The Wild Kangaroo or anywhere else?"

Oliver gave her a perplexed look. "I imagine you're asking for a reason. What is it?"

"At the concert, I saw him and Andrea having an argument. He pushed her against that temporary fence. And then he just walked away as if she didn't matter at all. He didn't even know if he'd hurt her."

"Had he?"

"Not physically. But she did say that he's a bully. That's why I wondered if he's been aggressive with anyone he tried to pick up."

Oliver's expression became hard. "He's been pushy, but I've never seen him become aggressive. If he had been, I would have shown him the door. I won't tolerate that in my pub. I suppose you're thinking he had something to do with Brie's murder?"

"It's possible if he valued his inheritance more than he valued Brie's life."

After that conclusion, they both finished their breakfast in silence.

Jazzi was changing into something cool, for her evening packing up Brie's apartment with Estelle. She'd chosen lime-green shorts and a simple white short-sleeved blouse. She was ready to step into her sandals when Dawn called to her from the living room.

"Come here, Jazzi. You're going to want to see this."

It was possible Freya and Zander were doing something cute, but Dawn's voice was too serious for that possibility.

Slipping on her sandals and adjusting the strap, she saw Freya scamper into her bedroom. Okay, not the kittens then.

Hurrying to the living room, she spotted Dawn at the counter, studying her phone. She handed it to Jazzi. "Read this."

Taking Dawn's phone in hand, Jazzi studied the screen. She scanned the heading. Dawn had been reading the latest issue of *The Landing*. "What is it?"

"The police chief and his team won't be happy. Scroll down to the last article on the page—'No Progress on the Frazier Murder'"

Jazzi was disgusted that Brie's murder had already been relegated to the bottom of the page.

With frustration, she skimmed the article. "I wouldn't want to be Detective Milford." She read aloud the last sentences.

> The detective on the case, Detective Sergeant Paul Milford, must have been enjoying the town's Welcome Summer celebration because he and his team for the past five weeks have been collecting their paychecks but not turning up any leads. Maybe the mayor should put someone else in charge of the Frazier case. Are the police incompetent, or is the killer wily enough to avoid detection?

"That's brutal."

"Do you think the mayor will step in?" Dawn looked as worried as Jazzi felt.

"Mayor Harding should do his job and let Detective Milford's team do theirs." Jazzi knew solving a murder was *not* as easy as rounding up suspects and questioning them. A lot more went on behind the scenes. Subpoenas and warrants for financial and phone records, lab work, and dozens of phone calls to ferret out more information. All of it took time.

"This article could cause an uproar," Dawn said. "Certainly comments and emails to the editor."

The reporter was Charmaine Conner, who Jazzi supposed was trying to make a name for herself. "They have to build a solid case that will stand up in court."

"You're pro–Detective Milford then?"

"I'm pro anyone who finds Brie's killer. Adding more pressure to the team trying to solve the case will only slow it down."

Jazzi felt Freya resting on her foot. With a smile that mostly wiped the press from her immediate focus, she said, "I have to go. Estelle is probably already at Brie's."

At that comment Dawn's eyes filled with tears. "Tell Estelle I'm thinking about her." She took a deep breath. "The munchkins and I will solve the world's problems while you're gone."

Jazzi surely hoped they could.

Estelle had turned on the porch light at Brie's townhouse. Apparently she was feeling more comfortable here again. While they'd been packing last week, she'd told Jazzi she'd often stopped in at Brie's to have coffee and something sweet she had brought with her. Those were the memories Estelle needed to concentrate on right now.

Jazzi went up to the door, saw that it was open, and knocked.

Estelle called from inside. "Come on in, Jazzi." She must have seen Jazzi's car coming up the drive.

"It's hot in here," Estelle claimed. "Brie's landlord turned off the air. He doesn't want to pay the electricity if someone's not living here, even though he's going to turn it back on in a week. I have the windows open. It's not too bad. Harry has agreed to pick up everything tomorrow."

The inside of Brie's townhouse was hot, but not stifling. Jazzi followed Estelle to Brie's bedroom, not sure if she was any more ready to do this than Estelle was.

"How are you tonight?" Estelle asked.

"I'm good. The store has been busy. How about you? How are *you* doing?"

Estelle brushed her hair away from her brow. "I'm geared up for this. I'm detached. I'm not going to get sucked into grief while we're here."

Jazzi knew from experience that wasn't the way grief worked, but if Estelle thought she could handle it that way, more power to her.

"How's Harry?" Jazzi asked.

"I'm really not sure. Sometimes he just sits in his chair and stares into space, and other times he's out and about like nothing has happened to our lives. I know he's doing the best he can," Estelle said. "But I want him back—the old Harry—the one who used to joke with Brie and go fishing with her. You know what I mean?"

"I know."

"Let's tackle the closet first," Estelle directed. "Then we can box up the rest."

Jazzi had noticed the cartons in the living room. Estelle pointed to a large box of garbage bags. "I thought we'd put the clothes in those. They're easier to lug."

With a modicum of worry, Jazzi predicted Estelle's bravado would only go so far. Dumping her daughter's clothes into black garbage bags had to have sad and melancholy significance.

There was a breeze floating in the bedroom window but Jazzi realized the day's high temperature had remained within the townhouse's walls. She was already sweating. She took a clip from her purse and pinned her ponytail on top of her head. That would keep her hair off her neck.

Estelle smiled at her. "You girls and your long hair. I know it's the style now, but short hair is so much easier to take care of."

"In some ways," Jazzi agreed. "Though I don't have to do much with mine except let it dry after I wash it. And I like to braid it."

"No curling iron?" Estelle asked in a motherly way.

"Sometimes a flatiron."

Jazzi knew Estelle was making conversation to keep her mind away from what she was doing. They started on the left side of Brie's closet.

"She was organized, I'll give her that," Estelle murmured.

Yes, Brie was. Tank tops and blouses hung on the left and

they led into skirts, shorts, and dresses. Estelle began with the tanks and didn't seem attached to any. Once in a while she took one off the hanger and lifted it to her nose. "She must have washed all of these. I can't even smell her perfume."

From her own experiences, Jazzi knew smells awakened memories, and Estelle was hoping for those.

Jazzi folded while Estelle sorted and laid the clothes on the bed. She let Estelle stow them in the garbage bags.

Suddenly Estelle froze when she pulled out a plaid skirt. Pleated, it was short and sassy. The spell of memories apparently awakened, Estelle waved it back and forth. "Brie wore this on her last birthday. We threw a little party for her. Harry had given her tickets to a concert she wanted to see in New York City. He was up-to-date on her music. I wasn't. She and Delaney went and had a glorious time from what I understand. On the other hand, I'm sure they didn't tell me all the details."

"When was her birthday?" Jazzi asked.

"November. She seemed excited that night. She said she had plans for her future. I wasn't exactly sure what that meant."

Jazzi suspected what Brie had said meant that she was going to start using dating apps, and she believed she'd soon have a family. Or maybe that was when she'd made the decision to search for her birth father.

Estelle confirmed that idea. "It was around Christmastime that she told me she was going to search for her birth dad. I guess that was all part of her plan. Sometimes I wonder if she'd still be alive if she had just let fate take its course instead of searching and going after something she thought she wanted."

"Brie didn't strike me as a passive sort of person." Jazzi admired women who would go out and fight for what they wanted. She was trying to be that kind of person. She couldn't fault Brie for doing that.

The plaid skirt went on a separate pile on the bed, and Jazzi knew Estelle would be taking it home with her. Sorting through the dresses took a little more time than the rest. Estelle expressed her happiness or sadness over the memories that each held—an emerald-green dress that Brie had worn for Christmas, a camel-colored power suit she apparently used for meetings at the organization she worked for, a designer sundress that Brie had shown Estelle and said she was going to wear to a few parties.

"She wore this one on Valentine's Day when she was going out," Estelle said. "She looked beautiful in it. Now I wonder who she met. If a man who asked her on a date could have killed her. Isn't that awful?"

It was. All of Estelle's memories were marred by Brie's murder. The pile of the clothes Estelle would be taking along was growing larger.

Studying the pile for a moment, Estelle sighed. "I'll hang these in my closet and Harry better not say anything about it."

There was that bravado again, mixed with fear that she'd lose remembrances of her daughter.

Next, they emptied dresser drawers. Most of those items went into the big black trash bags. Estelle pulled out one creamy cashmere sweater and held it to her nose. "This smells like her perfume," she said as if she'd found a treasure.

Jazzi discovered a small box that Estelle could use to pack up the clothes she wanted to take along. Soon they'd emptied all the drawers. While Estelle went through Brie's jewelry box, Jazzi put odds and ends into an open carton to gather what was left on Brie's nightstand—a photograph of her parents, a book she had been reading, a jar of vanilla-scented hand cream.

Jazzi reached for a pink cartoon-like pig—obviously a bank—sitting by the bedside lamp. She shook it when she put it into the box and then she studied it. A clinking sound alerted her that there might be something other than coins inside.

Turning it upside down she found an opening that was

stopped with a rubber plug. She showed the pig to Estelle. "Do you recognize this?"

"No, I don't. I imagine she kept it to drop in loose change."

Jazzi shook it. "There's loose change in it, but I think there's something else in it too."

Estelle's eyes opened wide. "What do you think could be in there?"

"I think we should find out," Jazzi said.

Estelle removed the black rubber plug and shook the piggy on top of the dresser. Coins fell out, but something else was still lodged in the bank. Estelle handed the bank to Jazzi. "See if you can get it out."

Turning the pig sideways then straight up and down, Jazzi finally positioned the object directly over the hole. It fell out with a clunk onto the dresser top. It was a flash drive. The silver rectangle was only about an inch long.

"What is that?" Estelle asked.

"It's a thumb drive or a flash drive. If I load it into my computer, I can find out what's on it. What do you think?"

"I think you have to. If she hid it, it must be important."

The whole time Jazzi and Estelle finished tidying up Brie's townhouse, the thumb drive burned in Jazzi's pocket. She couldn't wait to get to her apartment to see what was on it. It might be nothing and she kept telling herself that, but, on the other hand, if Brie had taken the time to hide it, chances were good something important was on it.

The kittens came to greet Jazzi after the bells stopped jingling when she opened the door. They were still afraid of the noise, and that was good because that noise would keep them safe.

She scooped up both of them. "Let's go to my room and see what's on this thumb drive. You can play in there, okay?"

Dawn had left a note: *Went to my parents' house to talk*

about next weekend's regatta. Jazzi could see there were scraps of food left in the kittens' dishes. Obviously, Dawn had fed them.

Jazzi set the cats on the floor and they came scampering after her as she went into the bedroom, pulled her laptop from her desk and settled on the bed. Propping her pillows behind her, she sat cross-legged with the laptop on her knees. Both kittens climbed up the side of the spread. Zander jumped over his sister to reach Jazzi first. When she opened the laptop, he nosed the keyboard.

She picked him up and looked him in the eyes. "If you want to stay here with me, you have to be a good boy."

His golden-green eyes said that he understood—at least that's what it looked like to her. She kept cat toys on her nightstand. She picked up one shaped like a mouse and tossed it to the bottom of her bed. Both kittens raced after it, then took it to the floor and tumbled over it. In the meantime, her laptop booted up and she inserted the thumb drive. Several files loaded.

With the first file, Jazzi understood what kind of documents she was reading. This was a diary of sorts. Keeping it on a thumb drive and hiding it away made sure it was private. First Jazzi read through the diary from two years ago. It was filled with thoughts and feelings about Brie's work, about her mom and dad, about possibly searching for her birth dad someday. She hadn't been ready then and she wrote about the risk involved—possible rejection. That could be worse than not having her questions answered. The same thread wove through many of her postings over the next year and a half. Each file related Brie's thoughts and activities for about six months at a time. Jazzi quickly scanned them and then settled on the last file.

Looking over the side of the bed, Jazzi could see the kittens were still playing with the mouse, getting caught in the folds of the bedspread that fell onto the floor. But they were having fun and they were busy. So was she.

She reached January of this year. She saw that Brie had started writing differently. There was one section about her urge to date, to marry a good man, to have a family. But after that . . .

She wrote about Vic Finch. She'd apparently swiped right on the dating app. Her thoughts wandered around her own personality after she met him. She wondered if she was stuck-up. Had he said something to make her think that?

Brie thought of Vic as rough around the edges, needing to climb any ladder fast. He'd wanted to have sex on the first date. Maybe he was the kind of man who believed the woman owed him for buying her dinner. Brie made some notes about his car, his apartment, his love of anything shiny and new. That was why he detailed cars.

Jazzi skimmed day-to-day activities until she reached another name she recognized—Gregg Rizzo.

Handsome. Could be a possibility. Seems like a gentleman. Is he? He has a romantic streak. If we keep dating, he'll probably send me flowers and buy me pretty cards. He's tame and a little set in his ways.

Brie's notes on Casper Kowolski followed.

Friendly with boyish charm. His food truck is his life. He lives to cook, but he doesn't aspire to be a famous chef. He has no ambition. Could the food truck eventually fund a family?

The next entry paragraph concerned Nolan Johnson.

Nolan's red hair is a sign of his hot temper. He doesn't show it much, but I glimpsed it. A waiter brought us the wrong meal. Nolan was mean to him. He likes nice things. He wants to own a Lamborghini someday. He isn't family man material. Too much golf talk.

Underneath that she'd written:

Will I ever find the right guy?

Then Jazzi came to the last entry. Damon Covino.

He's condescending with a tongue that could lash through a woman. I heard it. Connie is just as bad. I heard her talking to Damon about Andrea. Connie runs the family, not Joseph. Even though Joseph holds the purse strings.

Brie also wrote:

Connie doesn't have a heart. She only cares about Gucci purses and Jimmy Choo shoes and the best bottle of Dom Pérignon champagne that money can buy.
Andrea Covino. Can I ever break through Andrea's walls? She protects herself or thinks she is by being sarcastic, short, her language filled with quips, not real sentiment. She's still the younger version of herself who can't play tennis anymore, not professionally anyway. Does she want a life of simply coaching? Really designing pontoon boats? Or maybe she wants to work for Joseph like her brother does. Is she jealous of him? I didn't talk to her long enough to decide. I'd like to get closer to her, I really would, but I don't think she'll let me.

Brie's thoughts returned to Damon again.

Damon Covino thinks I'm a bother. He obviously doesn't understand love between parents and children. He takes whatever his mother will give him, but does he love her?

Does he even respect Joseph? Maybe he sticks it out with his stepfather because he wants to run the company someday. He has a sharp edge that I don't want to see. As long as I stay in my lane, he might let me alone. If I step out of it, I hate to imagine what will happen.

A chill ran up Jazzi's back. Brie was explicitly direct at pointing out character flaws. She seemed intuitive to all of these personalities. Did that make her a threat to any of them?

The last comments that she'd ever written were about Joseph Covino.

Joseph is a dear, and I'd be glad to call him my father. My adoptive father might have a problem with that. He'd feel as if they were competing, but they don't have to compete. I can love them both. Just how can I convince them of that?

Jazzi deeply felt Brie's words. As Jazzi had gotten to know her birth mom, she felt she could love her mom and her biological mom. But balancing relationships wasn't easy. Taking a deep breath, Jazzi knew what she had to do about the flash drive. She picked up her phone and called Detective Milford.

Chapter Seventeen

Jazzi peered through her apartment door's peephole and wasn't surprised by who she saw. Detective Milford stood there in a rumpled, light linen, gray sports jacket, his tie a bit askew. After she'd called him, he said he'd be over in fifteen minutes. It was fifteen minutes to the dot.

The sleigh bells on the door jingled as she opened it. He gave her a questioning look as she motioned him inside. The kittens, who had been sleeping on the sofa, stood and were looking her way.

She gestured to them. "The bells keep the cats away from the door."

"I see," he said, but she wasn't sure he did. Non-cat people didn't understand some cat moms' quirks. "Can I get you a glass of iced tea?"

He swiped his hand over his brow, studied her for a minute, and then acquiesced. "Sure. Do you have that thumb drive handy?"

It was obvious that he'd come to confiscate it. She pointed to it on the table.

"Did you copy it?" His question was stern.

"No, I didn't copy it. But I do hope that you're going to give it to Estelle once you're finished with it. That's Brie's personal diary. If she wasn't dead, we wouldn't be reading it."

He nodded as Jazzi went to the refrigerator to pour them both a glass of iced tea.

"Did you read the whole thing?"

She'd summed up what was on it when she'd phoned him. "I read through the beginning pages to see what she'd written. And then I went to the end because I knew that was probably the most important." She brought the two glasses of iced tea to the table and they both sat.

Milford stared at the thumb drive and then spun it around with his forefinger. "You said nothing incriminating was on here."

"Not in what I read. All the men she talks about are suspects, I suppose, as well as the Covinos. That isn't anything new."

After he took a few swallows of iced tea, he set down his glass. "Are you *looking* for something new?"

She made sure she was meeting his eyes directly. "Detective, I do *not* want to do your job. From what the newspaper printed today, everyone is making this hard enough on you and your team." *The Landing*'s article opining on how little the police knew about Brie's murder wasn't news reporting.

Detective Milford practically scowled. "And you're sympathetic to my plight."

"I don't know if *sympathetic* is the right word. But I know how difficult an investigation can be. It takes time to follow every lead, and I assume that's what you're doing."

"And why do you assume that, when so many other people don't?" His scowl had abated and he looked genuinely curious.

She ran her fingers up and down over the sweating iced tea glass as she put her thoughts in order. "Because I think you want the best for this town and its residents. You don't want Brie's murder to go unsolved, or the robberies. You wouldn't be in this job if you did."

"Maybe I just plan to stay in a small town and sail through until my retirement. My wife would certainly prefer that. My former position was giving her anxiety attacks."

It surprised Jazzi that he'd shared that with her. But maybe he was just frustrated, fatigued, and needed a good night's sleep.

"My mom married a former detective who left a big-city police department after he was injured. I think he'd had enough of crime and mayhem."

"You're old for your age."

The detective's comment was low under his breath. It didn't sound like a compliment when he said it.

"Does your definition of *old* mean I'm wise?" She took a stab at a little levity.

"No, it means you see too much, hear too much, and are perceptive enough to know what to do with all that information. My son is twenty and still can't remember where he puts his keys."

After they were both quiet for a few beats, the detective asked, "How did you become so involved in this?"

"Brie came to me for advice, I told you that. She wanted to know what it was like to meet biological parents. She wanted to know what questions she should ask, and how she should act."

"I suppose finding out where you came from could be life-altering. Besides discovering why they'd abandoned you."

"Exactly. And then after Brie was killed, her mom needed someone to lean on. Her adoptive dad isn't coping with his grief very well. I understand grief. My adopted dad died when I was eleven, and then I found out in college that my bio dad had died."

The detective eyed her bangs, her braid, the expression on

her face. "You've established an emotional connection to Brie's mother, haven't you?"

This detective wasn't all cut-and-dried. Dealing with motives, various personalities, his team, and all the residents of a town or a city had made him perceptive rather than stone hard.

"I do," Jazzi admitted. "Maybe I simply miss my mom and the rest of my family. I don't admit that to many people."

He seemed genuinely surprised. "Whyever not?"

"I guess I don't want to seem . . . too young, too immature, too needy. I'm a woman on my own and that's what I want everyone to think of me."

His eyes narrowed. "Including your family."

"Yes, including my family. They took good care of me through my childhood, my teen years, through my college life. And now I want them to see that they did a good job."

"You're definitely more mature than that reporter who wrote that article in *The Landing*."

It was obvious that story was nagging at him. "I Googled her."

A smile spread across his face. "And what did you find out?"

"She's fresh out of college with a journalism and a communications degree. She's trying to make a name for herself, but I don't believe she has to tear you down to do it."

"Do you think her question was legitimate?"

The reporter had ended the article with the question—*Are the police incompetent, or is the killer wily enough to avoid detection?*

Jazzi took hold of her glass as if she needed the ballast of it. "I don't think incompetence has anything to do with this investigation. But I do think this killer might be wily."

The detective actually smiled. "Do you want to become a profiler now?"

"Absolutely not. I merely want you to catch this person, whoever it is, and bring them to justice. He or she can't avoid detection forever."

When the detective frowned, she didn't know whether he agreed with her or not.

The following morning, Jazzi poured boiling water over orange pekoe tea. She was involved in her thoughts, mostly about Detective Milford and his visit, when Erica came up beside her. "Why don't you come for dinner tomorrow night before book club? I'll ask Dawn too. I haven't seen much of you girls outside of the shop for a while. Audrey might even join us."

"Are you sure you want to go to that much trouble? That's a lot of us with your family."

"I have an easy chicken fajita casserole I can make. It's no more extra work than when I cook for them."

"In that case, I'd love to come."

"The kittens won't get too lonely, will they?"

"I'm glad they have each other," Jazzi said with a small laugh. "I'll make sure I play with them before I leave and after I get back. They'll sleep with me or Dawn."

"You're a good cat mom."

"I'll appreciate a home-cooked meal. I haven't cooked much lately," Jazzi admitted. "Too much on the go."

"Dawn told me you had a visit from the detective last night. Do you think that thumb drive will help solve the murder?"

"It's probably better if nobody knows Estelle and I found it," Jazzi said. "If that got out, the murderer could get really antsy."

"You know it will get out. Dawn told *me*. Have you talked with Estelle about keeping quiet?"

"No, I haven't, and maybe I should. There really wasn't anything on it that was incriminating. But the killer won't know that."

As Erica moved away, Jazzi realized they'd had a nice stream of customers this morning, both at the tea bar and in the store.

When she saw Parker step up to the baked goods case, she went that way. "What can I get you this morning?"

"How about one of those vanilla cupcakes with peanut butter icing? But I want something else, too."

She stopped reaching toward the inside of the case and asked, "What?"

"Your reassurance that you're not getting more involved in this murder investigation."

"Why would you think I am?"

He leaned closer to her over the case. "I heard about the thumb drive."

Jazzi froze, and then words sputtered out as she waved the tongs for the cupcake in front of him. "How did you hear about that? No one is supposed to know."

"Oh, Jazzi. I'm in the tech business. This was a thumb drive. Of course, the word spread."

"I'm sure Detective Milford didn't spread it," she mumbled.

"Are you and he becoming friends?"

"I don't know about friends, maybe a healthy respect. That's awful that the word is out."

"You're not responsible."

"I just told Erica . . . or rather Dawn just told Erica. One person tells somebody else, and the whole town will know soon."

"The killer could be on his best behavior because of that."

"Or grow more reckless. I don't like this, Parker, I don't like it at all."

"I understand. The word of the thumb drive is circulating, but I don't know that anyone has heard you're the one who found it. I know you were with Estelle yesterday so it makes sense that one of you found it."

Jazzi reached for the cupcake again with the tongs and set it on a dish. "That's something, I guess. Did you just come in to see if I was safe, or do you want a cup of tea with that cup-cake?"

"Tea with the cupcake would be good. I just picked up my car from having it detailed with Vic Finch."

Her ears actually perked up at that name. "Did he do a good job? I was just talking about his service with someone the other night."

"He did an excellent job. But I must say detailing cars must be a better business than I ever thought it was."

Jazzi slid the plate with the cupcake across the glass case, then she went toward the other end of the bar to pour him a cup of tea. He followed her. "Vic bought himself a shiny new sportscar. You should see it—all leather, every tech gadget imaginable, and the door opens upwards instead of across."

"Wow. Did he give you a ride?"

Parker winked at her. "Not yet."

She laughed. "I'm sure you'll convince him to give you a ride."

Erica crossed over to the tea bar. "I need two hot teas for the table in the back. I heard you mention Vic Finch."

"Do you know him?"

Erica wasn't a gossip, but she'd grown up in Belltower Landing, and she knew a lot of people here. She was talkative, sociable, and friendly. People gravitated to her because of that.

"I don't know Vic per se," Erica said with a shrug. "But I do know his dad. He used to complain long and hard about Vic. He was a troublemaker in high school. He was suspended for stealing money out of somebody's locker, and he was truant a lot. But that was years ago. It's good to see he turned his life around and is making a success of his business. He has a good reputation now."

Jazzi remembered what Brie had written about Vic Finch. Jazzi had gotten the idea that he was brash and maybe a bit of a peacock. But that didn't mean he was a murder suspect, did it?

*   *   *

What Jazzi liked most about summer was the daylight stretching to eight or eight thirty, sometimes even nine o'clock. After playing with the kittens, she decided to skip supper and take a long bike ride. Brie's murder, the Welcome Summer Festival, the Covinos, and Estelle played in her mind like a playlist that wouldn't quit. She'd distracted herself for a while with the kittens, but Dawn said she was staying in tonight, so Jazzi knew they'd have good company.

Something else she needed to think about was the bookstore getting prepared for the upcoming regatta weekend. Summer was one event after the other, and she had to figure out how to make the event more profitable for her store. The book club would be meeting tomorrow night, and she suspected they'd have titles for books about sailing that she could order in for the weekend.

As she biked down the boulevard, she noticed Oliver standing outside of The Wild Kangaroo. She was surprised to see him. Wasn't he usually inside his restaurant in the middle of dinner service?

She pulled up close to the curb. "Are you taking a break?" she asked curiously.

"My manager is taking over closing tonight. Would you like a bike riding partner? I need to clear my head."

"Sure, you can ride along. I'm going to ride up into the Sycamore Hill development."

"Brilliant," he said. "My bike's right next to the restaurant."

A narrow walkway snaked in between The Wild Kangaroo and the next store, a leather shop. When he emerged from the walkway again, he was wheeling a silver bike, a black helmet hanging from the handlebars. Just from everything she knew about Oliver so far, she suspected he was a no-frills kind of guy. She wondered what was going on that he needed a break.

Maybe he'd tell her during or after the ride. She wasn't going to pry.

Riding on the bike path, Jazzi was aware of the few cars passing her. Oliver rode behind her, past the marina and the food trucks. As they rode along the lake, grasslike sedges and bullrushes populated the area. The rushes, with their cylindrical stems, grew in bunches. Patches of algae, bright green, floated here and there.

Oliver drew up beside her, eyes straight ahead. "I was going to go for a run but this is just as good."

"I've never run," Jazzi said. "Except for field hockey in college, and I really didn't like that."

He glanced over at her and she could see his smile along his chin band. "I'm working out employee issues. I think someone is skimming the till, but I'm not sure who. I can't confide in anyone because I might be confiding in the wrong person."

"You don't have any guesses who it could be?"

"A few. I had background checks done on all my employees, but that doesn't tell me much, just whether they have a criminal record."

"I guess the next thing to look at is who might need the money and is desperate enough to do that."

He slowed his bike a little and so did she. "You ask the right questions."

She didn't know what to say to that, so she pedaled faster again. Sycamore Hills was a private development . . . private in the sense that the developer had laid out the plots carefully. They were each about half an acre. The houses were all nestled among trees.

Jazzi signaled that she was turning onto the road to the right that led uphill. She had heard all about this development from Erica and Audrey and Dawn. They considered it the premier place to live without being in a gated community. Some of the houses were more private than others. At the end of June, there was a lot of color in the yards from trees and shrubs like hydrangeas. Knock Out roses added color to the landscaping.

Suddenly Oliver asked, "Do you aspire to live in a house like this someday?"

"By *this*, do you mean a house that someone in the middle class probably couldn't afford?"

"I suppose." He looked straight ahead again. "Many blokes dream of it, just wondered if *you* do."

"I haven't thought that far ahead. But my first inclination is to say no. I just want to be happy wherever I live, whether it's a shack at the beach or my apartment where I am now. How about you?"

"My apartment now is fine. I'd like to own a house eventually, but I don't know if it would be one of these. I kind of like smaller neighborhoods, community chats, that kind of thing."

"That sounds nice. That's what I think I'd want if I had a family."

"I know a couple of people who live up here," he said. "One friend has two kids, a wife who's a flight attendant, and he's in the resort business."

"Are they happy?"

"Not sure about that. I don't know how much husband and wife actually see each other."

"Not what I want." Jazzi was sure about that, as she tightened her hands around her bike handles.

"No?" The question in Oliver's voice made her look his way. He looked at her, but they still kept pedaling and eventually stared straight ahead again.

"No, not what I want. I want to be around the house with my husband a lot, and definitely with my kids. I'd take off a few years to stay home with them if I could, but that's so much in the future. I don't even think about it."

While they were riding, a dusky gray had settled over the

trees and houses. They had pedaled far out of town, and night would be falling soon. Normally Jazzi would have turned back at this point. Instead she kept pedaling, feeling a kind of peace rising as she rode beside Oliver. They'd reached a corner lot when Oliver slowed. She noticed he was studying the house's backyard.

"Do you see that?" His voice was low and husky, as if he didn't want it to carry in the silence.

She peered toward the back of the house and guessed she was seeing what he'd caught sight of. A light bobbed in the screened-in back porch.

"What's on your mind?" Jazzi slowed to a stop, staring at the bobbing light.

"I know the family who lives here—the flight attendant and her husband. That's why I came this way. They're away this week. Stay here. I'm going to get closer." He jumped from his bike and laid it on the ground, expecting her to do what he said.

She didn't. She climbed from her bike and laid it on the ground near his.

Oliver had hunched down and crab-walked near a large spirea.

Staying low, Jazzi did the same.

A gunshot rang out.

Jazzi didn't know if it had been aimed into the sky, or towards them. But she took out her phone and called 911. Lights from their bikes had probably been easy to spot.

Oliver tilted his head to hear her describe to the dispatcher what had happened. She and Oliver were hunched up back-to-back. She could feel the heat of his shoulders against hers. Sweat broke out under her bangs, and her stomach did a flip-flop. This scenario scared her, and her fight-or-flight adrenaline had been kicked up. Part of her wanted to jump on her bike and pedal away from here. The other part of her wanted to see what was happening around that spirea bush.

She did neither. She stayed put. It was only a matter of minutes until they heard a siren blaring, and a patrol car rolled up at the front of the house. The bar lights flashed on the front lawn as two policemen climbed out of their vehicle.

Jazzi tapped her phone light on, and officers came toward them crouching low. Jazzi was glad to see George.

"Hey, George." Her voice was shaky.

Oliver explained what had happened again in a low voice.

Both officers produced guns from their holsters. George ordered, "Stay here."

"Belltower Landing really isn't safe anymore," Jazzi whispered to Oliver.

"Safety is an illusion," Oliver said acerbically. "You have to make your own safety wherever you can find it. Stay there. I'm going to—"

She grabbed his arm. "Let's make our own kind of safety. Stay here until the officers come back."

The night had grown darker, and Jazzi couldn't quite make out the expression on Oliver's face.

"Are you trying to save my hide?"

"Something like that. Why didn't a house alarm sound?" she wanted to know. "There *is* a sign outside the front walk advertising a security system."

Oliver turned to look that way then settled behind her again. "My guess is the screened-in porch didn't have a sensor. To get into the house, the intruder would have had to have the code. But he might have spotted us before he tried to break in."

"If you think about the other robberies, most of those expensive properties would have alarms." Jazzi thought about the areas where houses had been burglarized. "I believe the cabins in the resort have cameras but not alarms. Someone with know-how could get around those cameras."

The officers apparently had called for backup. A patrol SUV came up the road and parked in front of the house.

Jazzi's mind was speeding into ideas about what would happen next. The burglar probably ran off at the wail of the siren.

Apparently Oliver was thinking ahead too. "We're going to have to stick around to give statements. If you want to ride back with the officers, I'll figure out a way to get our bikes back."

Hearing the sound of voices, Jazzi saw two officers talking as they approached the spot where she and Oliver were sitting.

She was shaky but she had to get over that. She was a woman pretty much living on her own. She had to take responsibility for her own safety and her own life.

"After our statements, I'll ride back with you." Her voice was sure.

With their arms touching, Oliver nudged her. "Are you okay?"

"I'm as okay as you are."

He nudged her again. "You have grit."

Jazzi almost smiled. "I learned it from my mom."

Chapter Eighteen

For about the tenth time, Jazzi turned her head and caught a look at Delaney's face. Her friend was upset tonight and quiet. Jazzi could tell from the way Delaney tried to smile but couldn't . . . from the way her eyes expressed sadness rather than interest. Book club discussion had been going on for about an hour. They'd even had new members from the tourist stream join them. Still Jazzi wondered what was going on with Delaney.

At refreshment time after their discussions were over, Jazzi watched Delaney wander over toward the self-help area in the store. She pulled out a volume on overcoming grief.

Jazzi went to her and laid her hand on her friend's shoulder. Delaney jumped, startled by the touch. She swung around, book in hand, looking surprised to see Jazzi.

"I didn't mean to scare you."

"Scare is the right word." Delaney's shoulders drooped, her expression becoming less frantic. "Can you sleep at night? Do you check that your door is locked five times before you go to bed? Do you hear a noise and grab a cast-iron frying pan you've left on your nightstand in case an intruder barges in?"

Jazzi thought about all the days since Brie's death. No, she hadn't slept well at first, but that was because her thoughts had been going a mile a minute, not because she was scared.

"Since I live with Dawn, two against one helps. So, no, I haven't felt like that. And with the kittens, I'm hearing noises all the time. I think I've become immune to that. I do check the locks on the door more than usual. We had a sturdier dead bolt installed. But *I* didn't find the body, Delaney, *you* did. That makes a difference."

"Yeah. Detective Milford must think there's a difference too because he had me in there again." Delaney's face showed every bit of her dejection.

"Why, this time?"

"He wanted access to my phone so he didn't have to subpoena my records."

"It's faster that way. Did you let him have it?"

Delaney made a face as her eyelashes fluttered. "Yes. I don't have anything to hide. Though another friend of mine says I should hire a lawyer, keep my mouth closed, and not show them anything."

"That could send them the message that you *do* have something to hide." Jazzi found she had faith in Detective Milford, that he knew what he was doing.

"That's what I think."

"Was there anything in the texts that could help them find out something about Brie?" Jazzi asked, considering why she hadn't wondered about Brie's messaging with others rather than the men she'd dated.

"They were interested in all of our conversations about who she was dating. They got access to her social media somehow. And I understand you gave them a thumb drive that you found."

"I did, but I don't think it told them much. Would you mind if I look at the texts?"

Delaney shrugged and reached for her phone on a nearby table. She unlocked it and handed it to Jazzi. Jazzi scrolled back through the texts and there were many. Finally, she arrived at February. The texts about Brie's dates in between the other chatter gave a picture into especially her evening hours. Many guys like Casper had drinks with her two or three times. Brie herself mentioned that these dates were like speed dating—trying to find the right man who would make good husband material. Sometimes she didn't mention the men by name.

When Jazzi reached the week before Brie was killed, she spotted Nolan's name. At first Brie had liked him, but then she complained to Delaney that all he wanted to talk about was golf and developing his own golf course someday. She couldn't see years ahead with him. There was a text or two about meeting Joseph. She'd been hesitant and nervous beforehand, but then she'd admitted to Delaney that she liked him. He was kind to her and seemed to want to get to know her.

"I can see why the police have interviewed you so often. You had a deep connection with Brie, and she texted you often about her life."

"Wait until you get to Damon," Delaney muttered.

Jazzi turned her attention back to the text messages on Delaney's phone. Brie had texted that Damon looked at her in an odd way. She believed if looks could kill, she'd be dead. The sentiment had been similar in her diary.

"I wonder if the police have brought Damon in yet," Jazzi said.

"I don't know. They didn't tell me anything. They just wanted information from me again. But Brie definitely didn't like Connie."

That was true. Jazzi saw it as she turned her gaze back to the phone. Brie had texted about Connie's coldness. She'd also asked the question—**How could Joseph, a decent man, live with a woman like that . . . a woman so shallow that all she cared about was shopping in New York City?**

"Maybe Connie has good qualities that Brie couldn't see."

Though as she said it, Jazzi realized she had gotten the same impression of the woman.

All of a sudden a text caught Jazzi's eye. Brie mentioned a man who could be her soulmate.

"Did Brie tell you about her mystery man, the one who could be her soulmate?"

"No, she simply mentioned that she was connecting with someone new. They had drinks. I don't think she saw him often, but when Nolan didn't pan out, I think she was looking at this new guy more seriously."

"Her diary didn't mention anyone after Nolan," Jazzi said.

"Maybe she simply didn't have time to write down her thoughts about him," Delaney offered. "I'm not sure she wrote in that diary every day."

"No, it wasn't that kind of diary. There were clumps of thoughts as if she might have done it once a week."

"That sounds like Brie," Delaney said. "Why take the time to use her laptop and write it up every day when she could be more efficient and do it once a week?"

That was possibly true. But Jazzi wished with all her heart that Brie had written more about her mystery man.

Detective Milford's text was specific and clear. **Come to the police station at ten a.m.**

Erica and Dawn agreed to open Tomes & Tea that morning. Jazzi hoped she wouldn't be gone long, but that depended on the detective and how many questions he had about her statement concerning the shooting. She wondered if he was calling Oliver in too.

She'd worn aqua-colored capris, a flowered aqua-and-white blouse, and white sandals today. She'd fastened her hair in a low ponytail. The receptionist knew her now and gave her a tentative smile as Jazzi checked in. She didn't even have time to sit on one of the chairs in the lobby before the detective opened that door in the back and beckoned her in.

"I have questions about the statement you gave the officers."

"I thought you might," she said, as she slipped past him into the hallway.

"I got busy and couldn't follow up right away."

"I know you have a lot to handle right now."

Her statement seemed to take some of the stress from his face. A few of the lines smoothed out. "You might be the only person in Belltower Landing who understands that."

"I'm sure that isn't true."

Jazzi had learned that tact was her best resource for dealing with the police department.

He opened the door to the same room as before, and they sat at the table looking at each other. "I need to ask you why you were biking where you were biking."

"I vary my route each time I go out, just to make it interesting. That development is pleasant and quiet . . . usually."

"Why were you biking with Oliver Patel?"

"He was taking the night off after the crazy weekend. I was biking past The Wild Kangaroo and he saw me. He asked if he could go along. I said sure, company is always nice on a bike ride."

"It wasn't any more than that?"

Her gaze narrowed. "I'm not sure what you're getting at, Detective."

"Are you and Patel seeing each other?"

"That's not any of your business."

"Because of what you experienced with him, it is. Can you just answer the question?"

Should she, or shouldn't she?

"Oliver and I are just friends, if even that. We don't know each other very well. I stop in at The Wild Kangaroo and sometimes we talk. That night, all that was on my mind was biking, letting the air blow clouds out of my head from the busy week-end. We both had had a hectic few days with lots of customers. It made sense."

The detective's shoulders hunched up again. There was no evidence of a smile on his face as he looked at her as if he didn't believe her. Goodness, what did he think? That she and Oliver were going to rob the houses along there?

"If you ask me what you really want to know, Detective, I'll be glad to cooperate."

"Had you and Patel ridden together before?"

"No. I just told you, we don't know each other very well."

"Do you eat often at The Wild Kangaroo?"

"Maybe once a week. I've gotten to know Oliver a little more since he brought me a kitten that he found at the back of The Wild Kangaroo."

The word *kitten* seemed to totally confuse the detective. "A kitten? What does that have to do with this?"

"I've gotten to know Oliver better because of the kitten." She briefly explained how she'd found one kitten and then Oliver had brought them another.

The detective leaned against his chair back. "Miss Swanson . . ." Jazzi waited.

He shook his head. "The unexpected always comes out of your mouth."

What was she supposed to say to that?

He sat up straight again, took his notebook out of his pocket and brought out a pen. He clicked it a few times, then he looked her in the eyes. "Back to your bike ride. What made you stop?"

"You mean in the development?"

"Yes, that's exactly what I mean."

"I told the officers all about it. There was a bobbing light in the screened-in porch at that house. Oliver knew the people who lived there and he also knew they were away."

"So you decided to chase the bobbing light?"

"Not exactly. Oliver wanted me to stay with the bikes—we had put them down on the ground—while he went behind the bush to get closer to the house."

"Did you stay with the bikes?"

"No, I followed him."

The detective closed his eyes for a moment and his brows furrowed as if he was trying to keep his patience intact. "Of course, you did."

"Once we heard the shots, we stayed behind the bush."

"At least that showed some sense."

He was treating her like his daughter. "I wouldn't put myself in danger on purpose."

"What did you and Patel think would happen if you went after the bobbing light?"

"We acted on instinct, I guess. Oliver and I didn't talk about it. Things just happened. I guess we might have thought that if we showed ourselves and the person in the screened-in porch knew somebody else was there, they'd run off and leave the house alone."

"Did you and Patel talk about this incident?"

"Not exactly. We were both shaken up. We were mostly quiet when we biked home."

After a few moments' pause, Detective Milford asked, "Do you have anything to add about that night that you didn't tell the officers, maybe something you remembered after the fact?"

"No."

"Maybe you should think about your answer first." It was a warning.

"I don't have to think about it. I laid awake all that night thinking about it, going over what happened. We were shot at, Detective. Having that happen made me pause for a while till it sank in. I decided the good part of it was, whoever shot at us didn't know who they were shooting at. There was nothing personal about it. We were in the wrong place at the wrong time."

"That's one way of looking at it," he agreed.

"Do you have any suspects? Do you have any idea of who was at that house?"

"We have a few clues. We found a shell casing. Whoever fired wasn't aiming right at you. I think it was a warning shot. You and Patel were lucky."

The detective closed his little notebook and put the pen away in his pocket.

Jazzi decided to take advantage of this meeting. "Do you have any clues as to who killed Brie?"

"We're narrowing it down, not everybody has an alibi."

"There will be crowds in Belltower Landing for the regatta this weekend."

"And you're worried Brie's killer will kill again?"

"We don't know, do we?"

"Miss Swanson, I suspect that the killer murdered Brie in a moment of extreme rage. I agree that that doesn't mean he or she won't kill again. We're bringing in reinforcements from a nearby town to patrol during the regatta, but we can't be everywhere at once. We're hoping that seeing extra patrol officers will make a difference in anybody's attitude toward doing something wrong."

Could extra police presence make Belltower Landing safe? Only if criminals were afraid of the consequences or had a conscience.

It was evening and the lake itself was calm, except for a few outboards coming and going. The water sparkled with leftover sunshine as dusk began to overtake it with long shadows. The Belltower Landing marina was well lit as many boats buzzed with activity and their owners decorated them for the upcoming regatta weekend.

Jazzi had joined Dawn to help Dawn's parents ready their boat. They were using red, blue, and white ribbons and fairy lights to wind around the Bimini top. LED lights were embedded in it, but more lights could make the boat stand out. There would be prizes for the best-decorated pontoon boats. First prize was a nice-sized gift certificate from the marina shop. Second prize was dinner at the Silver Wave Eatery. The third prize was a Belltower Landing marina cap and T-shirt. The pontoon parade wouldn't be about the prizes, however; it would be about the fun of having the boats on the lake and enjoying the day. Pontoon boats were a chance for families to escape the everyday bustle and leave shore for the blue water. The sailboat race was a crowd-drawing event but the pontoon boat parade wasn't far behind.

"There's more blue ribbon under the first lounge seat," Dawn's mom, Gail, called to Jazzi.

Jazzi could see that some of the pontoon boats were being decorated for an overall theme. One was decked out like a gondola, another like a pirate ship. Jazzi particularly liked the pontoon boat that was decorated like an ice cream truck. Dawn and her brother had worked on a five-foot-tall seagull head to put in the middle of this boat. The outside perimeter of the boat would be decorated with red, white, and blue swags.

There were sixteen slips that extended from this particular dock. The next dock over had the same number of slips. As Jazzi had been working, she noticed Oliver helping a friend of his on a nearby boat. She didn't think he'd caught sight of her. She vividly remembered what had happened to them the other night, especially when they were sitting behind the bush, arms brushing, hearts racing.

A few minutes later, Jazzi handed Gail a swag of blue material for the side of the boat. Gail took it, but then eyed Jazzi with a mother's eye. "You look contemplative tonight."

"Not really. It's just nice to enjoy the quiet out here."

"Quiet?" Gail said with a little laugh. "Do you see how many people are on these boats?"

Jazzi gave a shrug. "It's different from being in the store and having customers buying books and asking questions. I like being out in the fresh air."

"One of the reasons you moved here." Gail said it as if she were confirming something in her own mind.

"Yes. That, but Dawn too."

"You two make a good pair. I just hope it lasts."

"Our friendship?" Jazzi wanted to know.

"Yes. You're professionally and emotionally connected. That isn't always a good combination. But you do seem to work together well."

Jazzi kept silent because she figured that Gail had something more to say, and it didn't have anything to do with her friendship with Dawn.

"I'm glad Dawn wasn't with you the other night."

Jazzi didn't have to ask what night Gail meant. "Dawn doesn't like to bike."

The comment wasn't meant to be flippant, simply true.

"You know what I mean, Jazzi. You and Dawn are sometimes attached at the hip. I'm just glad she wasn't with you. What made you take a bike ride in the dark?"

"The evening wasn't dark when I started out. I've taken many bike rides like that and nothing disturbing has ever happened to me before."

"Belltower Landing isn't the same as it was before. And Dawn said you were with Oliver Patel."

"I was. He likes biking too."

Her eyes went to the pier where Oliver was helping his friend. At that moment he looked up and their gazes connected. He raised his hand in a wave and Jazzi waved back.

Since the other night, Oliver seemed to be more to her than a handsome guy with a wonderful accent. He was *real*, though she couldn't explain it any better than that.

When Jazzi turned back to Gail, she saw that the woman had caught the exchange. "Just how well do you know Oliver Patel?"

"I don't know him well at all."

"I eat often at The Wild Kangaroo myself." Gail's brow wrinkled as if she was talking about something more serious than eating out. "People talk. No one knows him very well and that's a problem."

Jazzi didn't appreciate where this conversation was headed. "Why is that a problem? Maybe Oliver just likes to keep his life private."

"Maybe. But you need to be careful about the company you keep. After all, look what happened to Brie."

Gail's words sent a chill through Jazzi. Yes, Brie's killer was still out there . . . and she wasn't about to forget it.

Chapter Nineteen

The regatta weekend started with a bang. Friday was all about drawing tourists into the shops and revving them up for the celebration that weekend by expanding on the events and encouraging everyone to participate. Jazzi handed out sailor caps to any of the children who came in with their parents. The chamber of commerce had spent a bunch to give the caps to all the stores. The thinking was, if the children wanted to come in and have a good time, the parents would too.

At the end of June, the day was hot and sticky outside and cool within the store's air conditioning. Even though Jazzi had brewed a double batch of iced tea, they ran out and had to brew more. Audrey was handling the tea and baked goods while Jazzi, Dawn, and Erica migrated through the shop to help anyone who needed it. The computer hummed with sales. Jazzi was particularly proud of their sailboat section with books on historic sailboats and modern-day ones too. She had one cubicle designated just for pontoon boats. *Moby Dick* and *Treasure Island* were on special, and the kids and their parents gravitated towards those books.

At the sales desk, Erica nudged Jazzi's elbow. "We might have to hire extra help if this keeps up."

"We'll have to see if the crowds last past the regatta weekend. But we can be hopeful about that, can't we?"

Erica was a hopeful person. She put her hands together as if in prayer and looked heavenward. Jazzi would take all the help she could get.

At one point, Dawn floated by her. "Do you know what you're wearing tonight for the community party?"

Jazzi was looking forward to the party at the marina that evening. It was in preparation for the parade and the race the following day. It was a chance for everyone to mingle. From what she heard, Theo would be deejaying and there would even be dancing. It was going to be a fun time. The mayor and his staff planned community bashes like this to bring in even more tourism. Belltower Landing was a resort town after all, but it was so much more.

When Jazzi gazed around the store, she recognized regular customers. She noticed her friends and she was happy that they were here. Her mom often asked her if she was happy, and Jazzi unabashedly always answered that she was. Friends, books, and paddleboarding. What more could she need . . . or want?

Two tow-headed little boys who must have been around eight, and maybe brothers, ran toward the children's section as if they knew exactly where it was.

They almost bumped into Jazzi and she steadied one of them. "Whoa. Do you know what you're looking for?"

"*When You Trap a Tiger,*" the little boy answered.

Jazzi went toward the section where he was headed and pulled the book. It was the winner of a Newbery Medal, also a winner of the Asian/Pacific American Award for children's literature.

A man who looked a bit harried, probably in his forties,

came running after the boys. "Hey, you guys, wait up. I'm the one who has to pay for the book."

Jazzi had to laugh as the man sat down on the floor with the boys and opened the book to show them about the resilience of family.

Jazzi was backing away to give the dad and his boys some privacy when Audrey rushed up to her. "Two men are having an argument outside. Somebody has to do something, Jazzi. They already bumped against our windows once."

"You mean it's physical?"

"Oh, yeah. Somebody just might get a fist in his jaw."

As Jazzi opened the door and hurried outside, she spotted a skinny man in jeans and a ragged T-shirt running down the opposite side of the street. Vic Finch, however, was standing about ten feet from the store looking in that direction. His face was red, his mouth was grim, his brow was furrowed, and he looked angry, angry enough to boil over. Audrey must have seen him arguing with the other man. This probably wasn't the best time to talk to Vic about Brie, but maybe she could find out what had been going on. After all, it could affect her store.

"Hey, Mr. Finch," Jazzi said, keeping her tone respectful.

"It's Vic," he grumbled, still looking across the street.

"Is there something wrong? One of my staff came in and said there was a problem out here."

Vic turned to look at her. "Everybody sticks their nose where it doesn't belong."

She held up her hands as if in surrender. "I'm sorry. I didn't mean to bother you."

"No, I don't mean you. Jazzi, isn't it?"

Lots of people knew her name, so that wasn't a total surprise.

"You're probably worried about something chasing your customers away. I get that. I know what a bad review does for me."

"Is that what happened?" she asked innocently.

"Not exactly. I just have a loyalty problem."

"With employees?"

"I imagine running a bookstore, you know what that's like. Everybody thinks they know how to run your business better than you do. That guy . . . he went off on his own . . ."

Vic seemed like the type who wouldn't mind having his ego stroked. "I've heard you have a quite successful detailing business."

"Who'd you hear that from?"

She didn't want to throw anybody under the proverbial bus, so instead of naming names, she just said, "I heard it at The Wild Kangaroo."

He gave a low chuckle. "Yeah, I am in there a lot. Good food, friendly too." Vic seemed to have simmered down. Should she take this opportunity to ask him a question about Brie . . . or shouldn't she?

She knew what her friends' advice would be, *Let it go.* But she also knew Estelle would probably want her to jump on this moment and ask questions. "Belltower Landing is essentially a small town." She'd see what Vic would do with that.

"That's true. Word of mouth gets around. That's how I get lots of my clients. That and the fact there's nobody else in town who details the same way I do."

"I've heard that. I've also heard . . ." She hesitated now for a moment. "This is a bit personal . . ."

His eyes narrowed, and his lids came down, shuttering his expression. "Yeah. How so?"

"I was becoming friends with Brie Frazier. She was adopted and so was I, so we were sharing some."

His arms crossed over his chest, and his shoulders became more hunched. Protective mode?

"Yeah?"

At least he wasn't running off. "I heard that you dated Brie.

I wondered if the police have interrogated you like they've interrogated me. They seem to want to know every little detail."

"Again, people can't keep their mouths shut," he said with a grimace. "I did date her... briefly. We didn't click. I don't know how the police knew that I dated her, but they did." Vic seemed totally put out by that idea.

"Probably social media," Jazzi pointed out.

He closed one eye as if considering that, thinking hard. "Yeah, I never thought of that. They didn't give anything away when I went in there, but Brie and I did take a selfie together. Do you think she posted it?"

Jazzi shrugged. She didn't want Vic to think she knew more than she did. She didn't want Vic to think she knew as much as she did. "That's certainly possible. People taking selfies at our store has helped our business climb. It's almost automatic to take a selfie and then post it."

"I don't chat much. I'm not signed up for Facebook or Instagram. But I'll have someone check it out for me." He took one last long look across the street, then he shoved his hands into his jeans pockets. "I have to get going. Sorry if I caused any kind of ruckus at your store."

"No need to apologize. The sidewalk's a public place. I just wanted to make sure anybody involved was okay."

Vic swept his long hair back from his forehead and gave her an overall man-to-woman look—up, down, across, and over again. She felt terrifically uncomfortable.

"Yeah, thanks. You have a good day. I'll see you around."

Like Brie, Jazzi didn't like the vibes that Vic gave off. Was he capable of hurting anyone? Hard to tell. But she'd certainly keep him in mind.

That night the marina looked festive enough for the whole town to be drawn to it. Lights had been strung everywhere they could be. The boardwalk itself was surrounded with torch lights, flameless candles that were run by batteries. The mayor and his staff were aware of safety regulations. There were rows of red, green, blue, and yellow party balls hanging about.

Jazzi stared at the night sky. It was ablaze with stars that even the marina lights couldn't dim. A moon on just the other side of full cast silver light over the lake. She felt naturally drawn to the lake rather than to the party. But Dawn was waving at her from one of the high round cocktail tables that had been set around the edge of the marina. No alcoholic beverages were being served tonight, but that didn't keep residents from bringing their own. Silver Wave had set up a bar with every kind of smoothie along with lemonade and soda. Drinks were not free. There had been an article in *The Landing* about how the mayor expected to bring in enough money to cover some of the decorating costs with those drinks. Jazzi had just purchased lemonade when she went to one of the high tables to meet Dawn, Derek, and Addison.

"What do you think?" she asked.

Derek grinned. "It's a fine party, don't you think?"

Dawn leaned close to Jazzi. "Theo set up his system. We'll soon have music flooding the whole marina."

Jazzi glanced to where Theo was set up near the food trucks. Andrea Covino had joined him on the platform. As Jazzi watched their interaction, smiles seemed to flit back and forth between them. Andrea laid her hand on Theo's arm and Theo was gazing into her eyes.

"Do you think something's going on between them?" Dawn asked, always aware of flirtations and interactions between couples.

"I don't know, but it really doesn't concern me, does it?"

"I thought you said you and Theo were going to go out for a drink or dinner."

"Maybe. We'll see if that materializes. We've both been busy."

Dawn noted, "Having Evan Holloway stop by Tomes and Tea was a big ask, and Theo came through. I get why you agreed to go out with him. But you really should put your attention on a relationship that could take off."

"Like you and Derek?" Jazzi whispered. Dawn's face flushed and she glanced over at Derek across the table from them.

"You never know what's around the corner, do you? Doesn't it make you a little nervous to think that Brie's killer could be in this crowd?"

"I thought we were talking about Derek." Jazzi wanted to keep the conversation light tonight, cheerful, away from any dark tones.

Dawn was wearing a floral smocked jumpsuit and looked adorable with her swinging cluster of shell earrings. They swayed whenever she did, whenever she moved her hands to talk, or tipped her head to laugh. Even now, Jazzi had caught Derek glancing at Dawn.

Jazzi had dressed in a banana-leaf print with a cold shoulder top that stopped just at the waist and a midi-length skirt with a ruffle around the bottom. She'd pulled her hair up on top of her head and wound it in a braided bun. Even though it was almost nine o'clock, the temperature still hung around eighty degrees. Her sandals were comfortable on the boards. No way would she wear heels and take the chance of one of them getting stuck in between boardwalk gaps.

Parker suddenly appeared beside Jazzi.

"You came." She was delighted he decided to party with them.

"I did. I told you I would join in some of the festivities. It looks like this party is gearing up to last for a while."

The music had started now, and Jazzi tapped her foot along to the beat.

Parker addressed Dawn. "Do you think your family's boat is going to win tomorrow?"

"If it was a race, we might. Dad has that engine souped up as far as it can go. But I don't think we'll win the award for best decorated boat."

"I don't know, that seagull is pretty impressive," Jazzi teased.

Dawn laughed. "My brother is inventive, isn't he? He still might be putting finishing touches on it. I haven't seen him around."

"I spotted your parents when I first came in," Jazzi said.

"Since Dad helped put the parade together, he's in manager mode. He's probably making sure everyone who's here knows their place in the lineup."

Jazzi understood that Dawn's dad was an organizer. She appreciated that, maybe more than Dawn did.

Parker gave Jazzi's elbow a nudge. "Is that Theo and Andrea up there on that platform?"

"Yes, it is. They look friendly, don't they?"

"Are you disappointed?" Parker wanted to know, his expression telling her he might be overly interested in her answer.

"Not really. Theo will be gone at the end of the summer."

For a few moments they all watched the couples who were dancing to the music. The scuffle of shoes on the boardwalk, the balmy night, and the beat convinced Jazzi that she was glad she had come.

All at once, Parker turned to her. "Would you like to dance?"

Nothing could have surprised her more. "You dance?" came out of her mouth before she could stop it. Then she realized what a gaffe she'd made and she covered her mouth with her hand.

Parker just chuckled. "I *do* dance. Remember, I said I was homeschooled? Because of that, my mom put me in every socializing class she could think of, including a dance class. It was torture, but I learned basic dances. Come on." He grabbed her hand.

Jazzi glanced at their joined hands and decided she shouldn't make too much of this. "Let's dance."

As Parker put his arm around her, she caught the scent of his soap. It was nice. He looked handsome tonight. Instead of his usual T-shirt, he wore a button-down blue striped oxford, its tails hanging out over navy shorts. Their steps were a bit awkward at first, but then they both leaned into the rhythm of the song.

"Do I even know what kind of music you like?" She tipped her chin up to his so she could meet his gaze.

"Classical mostly, but that's while I'm working. Otherwise, I listen to podcasts instead of music."

"I haven't listened to many podcasts."

"You can find one on every subject on this earth and maybe beyond."

As Jazzi laughed, she heard a commotion over her shoulder. She glanced that way and saw two men overly jovial. One had an open bottle of wine in his hand. The other was pouring from a bottle into a glass on the table. The two men were yukking it up, slapping each other on the shoulders, not watching what they were doing. The table turned over and they jumped away, more worried about the wine on their clothes than anyone standing around the table who could have gotten hurt.

The police's presence tonight was evident if you looked hard enough. A patrol officer came to the table in a minute, taking hold of the two men, moving them to a corner where they could talk. To Jazzi's amazement, Connie Covino, who was standing nearby, righted the heavy table in one swift motion. Connie was wearing a dark green sundress, her arms bare. Under the hanging lights, Jazzi could see Connie's arms were well-muscled. Did those muscles come from playing tennis . . . lifting weights?

One thought overtook any other musings in Jazzi's head.

That table was heavy. Connie might have enough strength to have overpowered Brie and strangled her.

Last night's revelry slipped into the following day. The crowd gathered at the marina for the pontoon boat parade. It seemed to consist of shopkeepers as well as residents and tourists. The chamber of commerce had advocated for all the stores to close for two hours that afternoon. There had been a lot of grumbling but even Jazzi knew everyone would be gathered at the marina for the pontoon parade and sailboat race. There would be little traffic along the boulevard. After the race, all the stores would be buzzing again.

Jazzi had worn white capri pants today, and a coral and white pinstriped tank top. She'd made sure to slather on plenty of sunscreen. At the boat slip, she and Dawn waved good-bye to Dawn's parents as they motored the pontoon boat into the lineup for the parade.

Jazzi and Dawn walked down the dock to get a better vantage point for the parade, and to decide which pontoon boat was decorated the best. The grand marshal, the mayor, would be awarding the winners their prizes. He and his nephew were set up on the shore of the lake not far from the marina, and the crowd had gathered all around him. The docks were covered with people too, who faced the lake and the parade of pontoon boats.

Beside Jazzi, Dawn said, "I think the boat decorated like an ice cream truck is going to win. Don't you think?"

"I don't know. I kind of like the circus boat too. It all depends on how the mayor feels about it today."

"There should be a committee deciding," Dawn muttered.

"Maybe. But it would probably take longer to pick a winner, committee decision and all that."

Dawn laughed. "Probably so. We couldn't have a more beautiful day for this. Look at that sky."

The sky was the brightest cornflower blue and clouds were puffy and huge, floating airily by. Jazzi's attention was drawn to the water. It was a mirror of the sky, the same beautiful blue, only marred by the wakes of the boats. As more tourists crowded around them to seek a better view, Jazzi sensed a presence at her side.

"Are you enjoying yourself?" Detective Milford asked.

"I am. How about you?"

"I think you're the only person here today who cares whether I'm enjoying myself."

"Is this work or pleasure?"

"A little of both. I have patrol guys interspersed in the crowd. I'm hanging around, seeing what I can see."

"And what's that?"

He didn't answer her question but proposed another. "Are you staying out of trouble?"

Jazzi had worn a mesh ball cap with a wide bill. She could feel the heat all around her, as well as the expectation of what the detective wanted her to say.

"I'm just living my life."

"Good. That's how it should be. Leave the questions and answers to the professionals."

"Haven't I done that?"

The detective was wearing Ray-Ban sunglasses, but he put his hand to his forehead to block the sun so he could see over the lake. "For the most part. But somehow you got twisted up in the middle of this."

"By *this*, do you mean the investigation? Or by *this*, do you mean caring about what happened to Brie and Brie's mom?"

"You got me there," he said in a low grumble. "Who do you want to win first prize?"

"Who I want to win the prize and who's *going* to win the prize are two different things."

"All right then. Who do you *want* to win the prize?"

"Dawn's parents, of course. That's the boat with the seagull."

"I see what you mean. I don't think they have much of a chance. My bet's on the boat decorated like the *Titanic*."

Jazzi let out a laugh. "You *would* think that."

"I've got to go. One of my guys is beckoning to me. You have a good day."

"You too, Detective."

The pontoon boats had made a huge circle around buoys and were headed back toward the marina area where the judging would take place.

Dawn leaned into Jazzi. "So has the detective become friendlier?"

"I guess you could say that. I'm staying out of his way."

Rows of onlookers were pressing against Jazzi and Dawn now as they peered between the slips to the open lake. The pontoons had slowed their journey around the lake in order for the mayor to get a good look at them. The tail end of the line of boats was rounding the review stand and loud applause was spreading through the crowd. Clapping became louder and louder and cheers went up along with whistles rending the air.

At one moment, Jazzi was standing at the edge of the dock, peering across the lake. The next second—she was in the water, sputtering . . . gasping for breath . . . taking in water because she hadn't been prepared. What many people she interacted with didn't know was that she'd grown up in Florida before her mom had moved them to Willow Creek, Pennsylvania. She was a swimmer and had done well on the swim team and had loved the ocean.

The lake water was cold, but it took her less than the time a thought could float through her head that she had to gather her wits and not suck in water. The cold water had been a shock. Now she kicked with her feet and easily bobbed to the surface.

Dawn called Jazzi's name as her ball cap floated farther out on the lake.

In two strokes, Jazzi was at the edge of the dock, wrapping her hands around the boards. Dawn reached a hand down to her and helped pull her up over the edge. Tourists she didn't know were asking her if she was all right . . . if she needed help . . . if they should call the EMTs.

Jazzi waved them all away. "I was standing too close to the edge," she managed with some aplomb.

Yet she didn't feel at all calm about what had happened. She *had* been standing close to the edge. But she knew one certain fact. Somebody had *pushed* her in.

Chapter Twenty

Jazzi sat on the green on Sunday afternoon for her lunch break, looking down over the lake. Tourists who had come in for the weekend were taking a last walk along the shoreline, dipping their toes in the water or removing their boats from the slips and taking a final glide out on the lake.

Jazzi took a bite of her blockbuster sandwich—Canadian bacon, lettuce, tomato, and mayo—and, while she ate, thought about what had happened yesterday. True, there had been a crowd pressing around her. Dawn had been close to her on one side, but not close enough that she was affected by that push. Yes, Jazzi had been close to the edge of the dock. But if someone *had* pushed her, wouldn't one of the other people around her have noticed?

Jazzi hadn't been jostled. She was sure of that. The nudge, if she could call it that, had come from the middle of her back, right at the center of her body. Someone knew a good push would send her frontward. There had been no room on the dock to stumble. She'd just gone straight into the water.

Afterward, she'd asked Dawn as subtly as she could who had

been around her as she'd stood there. Dawn had been wide-eyed and hadn't known why she was asking the question. Jazzi hadn't let on that the answer was very important. Like Jazzi, Dawn had been looking forward toward the pontoon boats, not around the crowd to see who was gathered.

If Jazzi pursued it further, she could sound paranoid. Did it matter? Not particularly, unless she *was* becoming paranoid. She couldn't put a notice in *The Landing* asking who had been around her on the pier. So she was left with her thoughts and her suspicions.

She suddenly heard the sound of pounding footsteps behind her. She turned quickly to see Theo jogging toward her. He was wearing red shorts, a white polo shirt, and a broad smile. He anchored himself by grabbing onto the back of her bench. He said, "I was hoping I could catch you here. Erica told me you were probably on the green eating lunch."

She lifted the half of the sandwich she hadn't eaten and laid it on the paper in her lap. "You found me. I'm just watching the weekenders take their last look at the lake and gather their gear."

"It was a great weekend," Theo said. "That party on the boardwalk had everybody up and dancing, you included. I saw you with Olsen."

That dance with Parker had been nice, gentle, friendly as they'd danced together for a ballad. They'd really let loose along with Derek and Addison and Delaney for a few up-tempo songs. Jazzi had been glad to see that Delaney had had a smile on her face.

"I saw *you* with Andrea," Jazzi reminded him. "You looked cozy."

"Jealous?" Theo raised a brow and looked mischievous.

"Considering we haven't even had a date, I doubt if jealousy is appropriate."

"Appropriate or not, I'd feel honored if you were jealous."

Throughout the weekend that had seemed like a vacation from the grief, she decided she needed to have more fun, not just go out on the lake with Dawn or by herself. Tomes & Tea was all-important to her, as was her friendship with Dawn and the other book club participants . . . and the kittens. But she needed . . . she needed to socialize. Hadn't she told Parker the same thing? He had to get out of his office, away from his games, and see other people? In person social contact meant so much more than her communities on social media. Social media was what she showed the world. But spending time with her friends was her real life. And her real life needed a little red-pepper activity to spice it up.

Theo had sat down on the bench beside her, and he was opening his phone. Had he sat down beside her to take time to scroll on his phone?

She looked over his arm and saw that he'd pulled up his calendar. It was full of so many dates and meetings, she couldn't even process it. It only took her a moment to see, however, that some of the engagements were in green, some were in blue, and some were in red. The red ones, which stood out to her, were mostly in the evenings and two on Sunday afternoons. She imagined those were his deejaying gigs.

"Checking what you're doing next?" she teased.

He looked up, straight into her eyes. "That's what you think I'm doing? Seeing where I'm going next?"

"I don't know what you're doing. Tell me."

"I'm trying to find a spot so we can have dinner."

She felt foolish, embarrassed, yet pleased all at the same time. "That calendar looks pretty full. Am I going to be green, red, or blue?"

He laughed. When he did, crinkle lines came up around his eyes, and she couldn't help but keep her gaze on them.

"You're definitely green. Green are my important personal engagements."

This time she had to laugh. "Does that mean there's an important girl that you're going on a date with at each of those green spots?"

"You caught me," he said nonchalantly. Then he said, "No. Some of the green ones are personal appointments that have nothing to do with dating."

"And the blue?"

"The blue is definitely business. Now, let's get back to the green. How about Thursday around seven thirty?"

"Thursday is good." She was glad her memory was usually solid, and she didn't have anything planned for evenings this week.

Delaney came up along the other side of the bench and spotted Jazzi. She stopped but looked hesitant. "Am I interrupting?"

"Not at all," Jazzi told her, then wondered if Theo minded she said that. He didn't look bothered as his phone dinged and he scanned the screen.

Delaney moved close to the bench. "I just wanted to check if we're still on for breakfast tomorrow morning at the waffle truck."

Delaney knew the waffle truck was her favorite. They often made plans for breakfast while Dawn slept in. "We sure are."

"I've got to go," Theo said with a smile. "I'll text you the deets for Thursday night, okay?"

"Sounds good to me," Jazzi answered.

"Thursday night, huh?" Delaney gibed as Theo walked away. "Are you two finally going out on a date?"

Something else had started dancing around Jazzi's mind. Then she realized Delaney had spoken to her. "Yes, I guess we are."

"Are you going to be enthusiastic about it and let Dawn dress you?"

"If I let Dawn dress me, I'd be ready for a night in New York City at a club."

"Would that be so bad?"

"I'm not sure. I don't know how I feel about Theo." That was absolutely the truth because she needed to get to her laptop and look up something. But now she was late getting back to the store, and that had to come first.

Jazzi asked, "Were you looking for me, or did you just spot me by accident?"

"I was looking for you," Delaney responded. "I need to know if you need more of Emilia's books. She texted me this morning and said she can sign another fifty."

"Another fifty would be great. I'm sure they'll sell within the next month or so as long as we have tourists." Jazzi popped the remainder of her sandwich into the bag and took it to the nearest trash container. "I've got to get back to the store. Want to walk with me?"

"Sure. I need to pick up a copy of Emilia's book for one of my clients. She couldn't make it to the store the day of the signing."

Jazzi felt emotions tighten her throat. "Thank you for everything you've done."

Delaney simply replied, "That's what friends are for."

Jazzi had believed that once the regatta was over, business would slow. However, it didn't. When she returned to Tomes & Tea for the afternoon, she didn't have a minute to slow down and search for what she wanted to check on her laptop. She was afraid of what she was going to find. Maybe she was suspicious for no reason. The thing was . . . she couldn't figure out what was connected and what wasn't.

Still . . . she hadn't imagined being pushed off the dock. She'd spoken to all the men Brie had dated. Had one of them told her a clue she hadn't picked up on? And now one of them felt threatened? Lots of people had seen her speaking with Detective Milford on the green and at the regatta. *Was* she being targeted? Or was she paranoid?

It was her night to close Tomes & Tea. Dawn had already headed up to the apartment. Finally finished for the day, Jazzi used the back stairs from the storeroom to go up to her room. She was careful to look for the kittens when she entered her bedroom. A string of bells on her doorknob announced her entrance.

Dawn called from the kitchen. "Zander and Freya are in here. I'm serving their supper. What are *we* having?"

Jazzi grabbed her laptop from her desk as well as a legal pad and pen. As she entered the kitchen, she could see that Dawn had scooped wet canned kitten food into Zander and Freya's dishes and set them on a silicone mat on the floor.

Setting her laptop and legal pad on the counter, she quickly jotted down notes on the pad. Freya was making little kitty noises as she ate, and it sounded like a low purr. Zander just gobbled his food and was usually finished before his sister.

To answer Dawn's question, Jazzi looked up. "We still have salad greens left from yesterday. How about grilled cheese sandwiches to go with a salad?"

"Sounds good. I only had yogurt with strawberries for lunch."

"Can you wait a few minutes until I check something on my laptop?"

"I can survive a few more minutes. What are you looking for?" Dawn had already gone to the refrigerator and pulled out a salad bowl filled with greens.

Sitting on the sofa, Jazzi opened her laptop. "I'm looking for an article in *The Landing*. Parker told me about it after the shooting. It listed the dates and locations of the robberies."

"Why do you want *that*?" Dawn pulled a cucumber and baby carrots from the crisper.

"Just a hunch."

Dawn stopped what she was doing and stared at Jazzi. "Let me think about it. *The Landing* always prints more news on the weekend, especially on Friday with the regatta. It was pages longer with ads. I was thinking maybe we should have taken an ad. There was a human interest piece about one of the sailboat races. The racer had broken his arm and his leg in an accident and had recovered to enter the race."

"Friday," Jazzi repeated, as Zander used his claws to climb over the arm of the sofa. He clambered over to her and she picked him up, cuddled him, and returned her attention to her laptop. When he aimed to crawl on top of the keyboard, she picked up a fuzzy ball on the sofa cushion and tossed it across the room. He leapt after it and Freya joined in the fun of pushing it around.

After Jazzi brought up the paper's website, she scrolled through the pages. Although she had an online subscription, she didn't often peruse the paper. Gossip in the store kept news flowing and relevant.

Hearing a clatter on the stove, Jazzi saw that Dawn had placed the griddle on the burner. In the next moment, she was opening the loaf of multigrain bread. Jazzi scrolled faster. The column of locations and dates of the robberies caught her attention as much as the headline—"Belltower Landing's Burglaries Multiply."

She checked her notes on the legal pad. Then she scanned the list, and her heart lurched. This couldn't be a coincidence, could it? Maybe her memory wasn't as reliable as she'd considered it.

She must have let out a small gasp because Dawn asked, "What'd you find?"

"Something I didn't want to find," she muttered.

Should she call Detective Milford? What did she really have? A hunch and no proof.

Coincidences *did* happen. There were so many variables. So many people who could be involved. Yet the center fixture that everything revolved around about the robberies unsettling their town was . . . Theo. She had to be wrong.

* * *

At the marina the next morning to meet Delaney for breakfast, Jazzi saw many of the food trucks were closed. They probably had to regroup and restock supplies after the busy weekend. The waffle truck was open, though, as well as the burger truck that also sold breakfast sandwiches. She could order two coffees; she knew Delaney liked mocha lattes best. She did that at Casper's truck, then chose a picnic table away from the trucks near a parking lot. The table was located under a tall silver maple in the shade. Even at 7:30 a.m., the day was heating up into the eighties.

Jazzi spotted a humongous silver SUV parked about fifty yards away on the grassy lane that led away from the parking lot to a back road that aimed toward the shore docks on the east side of the marina.

She was pulling her pink hat with the wide visor from her crossover bag when the hair on the back of her neck prickled and her hand stilled.

A crawling sensation alerted her to—

The feeling didn't coalesce into a thought because someone tall and strong and bulky clasped a hand over her mouth. Her hat slipped from her fingers and fell to the ground. Before she could manipulate her feet under her body, her assailant yanked her from the bench with the backs of her legs scraping against it. She couldn't see who was dragging her. Small stones from the pebbled area infiltrated her sandals.

As her assailant pulled her, Jazzi dug the heels of her sandals into the dirt and pebbles. She had a sense of rounding the food trucks, and she snagged her foot on a paddleboard rack. They were often set up here for tourists to rent for the day.

She managed to knock over a green paddleboard on the end of the rack, but didn't deter the guy from yanking her farther away. Her senses had been frozen for a few startled and panicked minutes but now she caught a whiff of his cologne. She knew that scent. Musk and patchouli. That scent belonged to Theo.

Her suspicion of him had materialized into this . . . this . . . what? Kidnapping? She remembered the silver SUV parked off the beaten path.

Her mother had drilled safety rules into her when Jazzi had begun dating. "If you want to end a date because you don't like the vibes you're getting from a man, never . . . never . . . ever get into a vehicle with that man. NEVER."

Her mom's rule didn't quite apply to this, but the sentiment would be the same. Somehow she had to prevent Theo from taking her anywhere.

Gearing herself up for something foreign to her nature, she bit into his hand. He yelped and changed tactics. Switching his position, he clamped his good hand over her mouth harder this time and wrapped his free arm around her waist. He was at least a foot taller than she was, but that didn't mean she had to submit to whatever he had planned for her.

Not caring if she ended up on the ground, she kicked out over and over again. His hand was clamped so hard over her mouth and nose, she was having trouble finding air to breathe. He was out of breath too. The more she kicked, the more out of breath he became as he attempted to secure his hold on her. Struggling became her chosen method to attempt to free herself and get away. Or at least free enough to scream.

"Stop it," Theo growled. "You're just like Brie."

For a moment, frozen from his revelation, she did stop struggling. Robbery was one crime, but murder was another!

He must have seen her eyes go wide or feel her mouth slacken because he huffed into her neck, "A text from Vic when Brie and I were having dinner alerted her to our robbery spree. Vic isn't too smart. He asked about the next heist. Brie saw the text. I couldn't explain it away. As soon as you glimpsed my calendar—you're too smart. Now let's get you into the car so I can take care of you too."

No way. No how. Her stepfather had taught her self-defense moves, and she had taken a course in college so long ago. But she remembered one main tenet of the course. Go for the eyes, the throat, the groin, and the knees.

While Theo had been relaying his threat practically in her ear, she'd managed to slide her feet into a more grounded stance that gave her leverage. Because she was shorter than Theo, he was slightly stooped over.

All at once she made her body limp as if she'd fainted. The sudden slack surprised him, and his hand over her mouth loosened so he could catch her. She took full advantage of the release.

She yelled "Help!" and pushed at him. His clutch loosened, and she kicked at him, hoping something landed in the right place. He couldn't fend off her wild attempts to jab at him and he released her. As soon as he let go of her, she screamed again and aimed her sandaled foot at his knee. She made contact.

When he yelped and dropped to his knees, she took off sprinting as if her life depended on it. It did.

Breathing hard, he snarled, "I'm going to hurt you. Vic and I had something good going until nosy—"

Her heart was pounding so fast she didn't hear what he yelled. If she could just make it to the front of the food trucks. Glancing over her shoulder, she saw Theo was hobbling but coming after her faster than she ever would have expected.

Maybe she could reach Casper. Maybe. Maybe Delaney had seen her hat and their coffee and called for help. Maybe.

Better to make a stand and not count on someone else to save her.

Panic crushing her chest, fear in every stride, she remembered what she'd passed by before for tourists to rent. She also remembered how she loved everything about her life—family, friends . . . and the kittens.

The paddleboard stand was in sight. Would she have enough time to grab a board and use it for defense? She had to have enough time. She had to grab it and make it work for her, just like a heroine in one of Parker's virtual reality fantasy games.

Nearing the boards, she started screaming like a banshee . . . or a woman who was almost about to be murdered. Certainly the chefs in the food trucks could hear her, couldn't they? Lifting the thirty-pound board, her fingers slipped and she almost dropped it. Her hands were sweaty from fear.

Grabbing it with a better grip this time, she wheeled around just as Theo reached her. Hesitating only a second, she swung the board with all her might. It hit him squarely in the face. She didn't stop to consider damages or consequences. She sprinted toward the trucks again, yelling for all she was worth.

To her astonishment, Oliver was jogging toward her, phone in hand. She careened into him and he held her by the shoulders. She finally took the time to turn around toward Theo. He sat on the ground holding his jaw, his nose pulsing blood.

Her breath was coming too fast to let her release many words. "Theo . . . killed Brie."

A siren blared. Patrol officers ran toward Jazzi and Oliver.

Oliver pointed to Theo, who was climbing to his feet, scrambling in the other direction.

"He tried to kidnap Jazzi. He killed Brie Frazier." With that explanation the officers drew their guns and ran after Theo.

Oliver told her, "I called 911 when I heard you scream. Delaney's at the table. She found your hat and bag and flagged me down."

Suddenly Jazzi's legs wouldn't hold her. She sank to the ground.

Oliver peered down at her. "Do you need the EMTs? Can you breathe okay? Should I carry you anywhere?"

Taking a few gulps of fresh air, she protested, "I don't need to be carried anywhere. And I can breathe just fine."

Oliver's hand gently clasped her shoulder.

She heard Oliver say, "I've got to say one thing about you again, Jazzi Swanson. You've got grit."

Delaney rushed to Jazzi, dropped down beside her and wrapped her arm around Jazzi's shoulders. As she did, Oliver moved away. Jazzi felt bereft he hadn't stayed close.

"You're in good hands now," he said. "I'll follow the officers and make sure Theo doesn't get too far."

"His SUV is parked back there," she somehow managed to say with a lump closing her throat because of the realization of everything that could have happened.

"Good to know." Oliver gave her a wave as he jogged toward the officers.

Jazzi watched him as he ran toward danger, all the adrenaline in her body flooding from her head down to her feet . . . and dwindling out.

She let Delaney keep her arm wrapped around her as her friend explained, "Casper saw Theo stalk you right before I found your hat and bag. He called 9-1-1 too. Your face is bruising." Delaney gingerly touched the area around Jazzi's mouth.

"Theo had his hand clamped hard over my mouth. Thank goodness for you . . . and Casper . . . and Oliver." She felt tears and a shivering reaction setting in.

"Miss Swanson." The voice belonged to Detective Milford. He was peering down at her. "I just heard on my mobile that we got him. Theo Carstead is in custody."

Epilogue

A week later when Parker entered Tomes & Tea, Jazzi was still reeling from all that had happened. The day Theo had tried to kidnap her, Delaney had found a beach towel somewhere and wrapped it around Jazzi to stop her shivering. Detective Milford had actually sat on the ground with her to record a preliminary statement on his digital recorder.

After Jazzi related that she'd been pushed off the dock on Saturday, he'd frowned, his brows puckering. He'd said, "You should have called me," but let it go to record the rest of her statement.

Oliver too had returned to sit on the ground with her until her legs no longer felt like jelly. She'd insisted on walking back to her apartment rather than letting the detective drive her. Oliver and Delaney had walked her home, one on either side of her. Once there, they'd explained to Dawn what had happened so Jazzi didn't have to. After Dawn headed down to the bookstore at Jazzi's urging, Oliver had left. Delaney had stayed with Jazzi and the kittens, sharing a pot of tea until Jazzi stated she was going to work. Delaney didn't argue.

Since then, rumors had circled around town about what really had happened that day. But Jazzi's friends knew the truth. Her mother did too.

Now Parker nodded to her and pointed to an empty table and chairs. She'd been working all morning. She nodded back to him, thankful to spend a few minutes with a friend who knew what had happened and wouldn't ply her with questions. She'd been patient all week with customers who had.

Parker had brought two cups of tea, one with milk and honey as she liked it, and two peach muffins. He pushed one toward her. "You look as if you need something sweet."

She accepted his offering with a crooked smile. "Erica brought us pineapple upside-down cake she made herself. Dawn brought me chocolate turtles and Delaney napoleons from the Dockside Bakery. Giselle dropped off a blueberry lemon loaf, and my mother overnighted snickerdoodles. I'm so sweet I'm going to have syrup running in my veins."

Parker laughed, took a good look at her face and sobered. "You just have a yellow tint around your mouth."

She rubbed over the area that had turned miserable shades of blue and purple the day after Theo had tried to kidnap her. "I forgot to plaster it with a coat of foundation this morning. No wonder customers have been staring at me."

"So your mother sent cookies? Does that mean you had a lengthy chat with her?"

"I did, with her and my stepfather. They were upset, of course, but they hid it well. Mom understood I just sort of fell into the investigation."

"Will you have to testify at Theo's trial?"

"I don't think there will be a trial. I met with Detective Milford yesterday. The crime lab had returned the DNA results. Theo's DNA was on the paddleboard leash he used to strangle Brie. One of his biggest mistakes was not taking it with him."

"Criminals aren't known for their brain power. The impulse to flee probably took over and that's why Theo left evidence."

Parker's tone was acerbic . . . and he was correct.

Jazzi said, "Apparently Detective Milford had been closing in on him and Vic for the buglaries. He made the connection I did with the dates. Theo deejayed at rich clients' homes and the robberies took place a day or two after. The timing was too obvious to be a coincidence. Apparently one of Vic's guys had gone off on his own the night someone shot at me and Oliver. The detective also talked to a server at Vibes who had seen Theo with Bric the week she died and become suspicious of him for Brie's murder too. After Theo was arrested, he heard Vic was spilling everything to the detective who had brought him in for questioning about the robberies. He was under suspicion because the PD kept tabs on the known fence he used."

"How was Vic mixed up in this?"

"He had brought the scheme to Theo, saying Theo could keep his hands clean. He just had to give them a way into the houses, the security codes, to share in the profits. Vic and one of his employees stole the jewelry and fenced it."

"So they definitely have a solid murder case against Theo?" Parker looked hopeful.

"All of Theo's text messages to Brie are in the detective's hands," Jazzi explained. "They'd traced his phone to Brie's townhouse the night of the murder. The last important evidence they needed for the case was Brie's laptop. After my kidnapping, they found it where Theo was staying. They think he might have tossed her phone and tablet into the lake or somewhere remote."

"So what part *did* Vic have to play in all this?"

"When Theo deejayed somewhere, he'd get security code information or scout a way into the house that wasn't monitored. A few days later, that place would be robbed by Vic and his friend. Resort residents are often out of their homes to enjoy